# *The* INITIATION

## FILTYH RICH AMERICANS | BOOK ONE

*WIN AT ALL COSTS!*

## NIKKI SLOANE

*Nikki Sloane*

Demeter Edition

ISBN 978-1-9494090-3-1

*For Nick,*
*who has all the best ideas.*

# ONE

RAIN STREAKED ACROSS THE WINDOW, BLURRING THE VIEW OF the landscape out the back seat of the car as it hurried my sister Emily and me past the front gate. The drive leading up to the Hale estate was long, straight, and lined with tall, manicured hedges. It was a tunnel of green. The only escape was the impressive fountain at the end where the driveway circled, and the historic stone mansion loomed beyond.

I clutched the book in my lap tighter, my fingers tensing on the edges of the hardcover, making the dust jacket crinkle against the skirt of my dress. The sound drew my sister's attention, and she shot me one of her famous disapproving looks. It was the same one my father had wilted under earlier this evening when he'd suggested Emily find something more appropriate to wear.

Her cocktail dress was as black as the limo we were traveling in. The fabric plunged deep down her chest, flaunting her impressive cleavage. The flouncy skirt was cut short in the front, teasing well above her knees, and hemmed longer in the back. It showed off her legs and the precariously tall heels she wore. Her lips were stained a vivid red. She had blue undertones in her pale skin, so it looked terrific on her.

In theory, that same lip color would work on me. My sister was only fifteen months older than I was, and although we weren't twins, people often asked if we were. Except we were easier to tell apart these days. On a whim, I'd dyed my hair an unnatural shade of deep green during spring break. It had faded since the last time I'd had it colored, but the hue was still there.

As I'd discovered with the hair color, I could pull off bold colors like Emily. We had the same sable hair and crystal blue eyes, but in stark contrast to her, tonight I wore a white dress with lace cap sleeves. It was fitting. I was the weird, virginal loner, and she was the confident, sexy bombshell.

We looked nothing alike on the inside.

She was friendly, quick-witted, and a pleaser. She had a knack for putting people at ease.

I had the ability to make everyone uncomfortable with my awkward bluntness but had learned not to care what others thought. My sister was the darling of the social scene, and she was destined to be the queen of Cape Hill—one of the wealthiest villages in Massachusetts. It had bay views, sprawling estates, and private golf courses, and each year the housing market climbed closer to matching the Hamptons.

My destiny, however, was to be left alone. I could do whatever I wanted, which suited me just fine. I'd never have to fulfill obligations or handle the family duties. I'd been given my mother's maiden name as my first name to appease my rich grandparents. That was the only responsibility I had to carry.

"Marist." Emily placed her hand on my wrist and eyed the new Greek mythology book in my lap. "If that doesn't fit in your purse, don't take it inside. You can't show up to a party with a book to read—and definitely not to *Royce's* party."

Because Royce Hale was a modern-day Gatsby. He'd thrown ragers nearly every weekend when he'd been in high school. I was several years behind him, but they'd still talked about it at our elite prep school, long after he'd gone off to Harvard.

I stared at Emily as the car promenaded around the fountain. When it pulled to a stop, my sister's dangling earrings swayed and glinted in the fading sunlight.

"It fits in my purse," I said softly. "Don't worry."

Even though I didn't give a shit what people thought of me, this was a huge night for my sister. I wasn't about to screw it up for her. I was fiercely protective of her, and she was my best friend.

The door on Emily's side opened and a man stood at the ready, an oversized black umbrella in one hand, and his other extended to help her out. "Good evening," he said.

As she took his hand, I shoved the book into my bag. I watched the pair of them as he ushered her up the stone steps, sheltered under the umbrella so her hair and makeup wouldn't be ruined by the drizzle.

I was out of the car before she'd gone inside, and when the man turned and saw me walking toward the house in the rain, he sprinted in a panic, rushing to get me safely under his protection. It was ridiculous. Besides the fact it was basically misting, no one really cared how I looked—most of all me. I was only here for my sister's benefit. The invitation had been for both Northcott sisters, and it would have been rude for me to decline.

Besides, part of me was curious. I'd been to the Hale's house many times over the years, but never for one of Royce's parties.

The usher's voice boomed when I stepped through the front door. "Miss Marist Northcott."

It stunned me motionless. Had he legitimately announced me? Like this was some social ball from the 1800s? I waited for a chaperone to appear and pair me up for a stilted dance with a suitor, but thankfully no one came.

There were a few people milling about in the foyer, but no one I recognized. Conversations and laughter buzzed from the next room over, echoing in the large entrance. I faced the grand staircase that split halfway up, running away from the enormous painting of the Hale family centered over the landing. I stifled the urge to slink up the staircase and away from the horror of having to mingle.

Emily was just inside the front sitting room. She snatched two glasses of a bubbly drink from a waiter's tray as he passed by and then held one out without even turning to glance over her shoulder at me. I took the glass and slipped by her side.

I was only twenty, but no one cared whether it was legal. We'd all been drinking since high school.

"Christ, I think half the company's kids are here," she

muttered beneath her glass the moment before she took a sip.

I surveyed the crowd and came to the same conclusion.

Hale Banking and Holding Company had started out as a simple bank, but over the last one hundred and fifty years had grown into so much more. Now the eighth largest bank in the world, they had financial and wealth management, commercial banking, and were pressing deeper into the global markets.

At the helm of HBHC sat Macalister Hale.

He controlled an enormous empire and was barely fifty years old.

I'd only spoken directly to him once. He was tall, broad-shouldered, and handsome, but also the kind of man who made you feel like a nuisance. Like you had no business being near him and using up any of the air in the room to breathe because that was his air. It, along with everything else, belonged to him.

Mr. Hale didn't appear to be around. It was unlikely, anyway. This was Royce's party to celebrate his graduation from Harvard Business School. His father had better things to do than hang out with college kids on a rainy Saturday night.

Conversations bounced off the dark paneled walls, high ceilings, and hardwood floor; the sound was too loud to be soaked up by the Persian rugs and expensive couches. I lingered at Emily's side as a shadow while she mingled. She made effortless small talk with a dozen people I recognized from school or our father's job.

We believed Charles Northcott, our father, was on the cusp of making the board of directors at HBHC now that Mr.

Steinway had retired. Twenty percent of our sleepy Cape Hill town was a company employee.

I didn't miss the way my sister's gaze subtly darted around the room, searching for—but not finding—the man of the hour. Royce would emerge later when all pretenses of this civilized soiree were dropped. Eventually, people would indulge in the hard liquor and the best drugs their overpriced dealer could procure for them. Then the party would *officially* start, and Royce would make his appearance.

Emily latched a hand on my elbow and pulled me close, bringing her lips right by my ear. "Where the fuck is he? I'm dying here."

"You want me to go look for him?" *Oh, God, please say no.*

"No," she sighed.

Relief swept through me. I made other people uncomfortable, and yet Royce Hale? He seemed to be the only one able to do it to me. His piercing blue eyes were always hungry and relentless. Like his father, he dominated all the air in the room.

I didn't envy Emily's situation. Our mother had been best friends with Mrs. Hale, and before she had passed away, they'd always joked that their children would marry. Even after her death, our parents had remained friends—if you could call it that—with the Hale family.

Arranged marriages didn't typically exist in our tightly woven circle, but there was an unspoken understanding between our families. Perhaps it was to honor his late wife's wish, but Macalister Hale had decided long ago it would be advantageous for Royce and Emily to partner. They were a good match in every area. Wealth, intelligence, looks. Together, Royce and Emily would be the unstoppable power couple, and now that he'd finished school, it was time for him to make his move.

It should be easy. Royce had essentially been granted first right of refusal over my sister.

The situation was sort of fucked up, but Emily didn't protest. In fact, she didn't seem to mind at all. She liked the idea of dating him.

The thought made me uneasy. Like an itch that wouldn't go away no matter how much you scratched.

I hovered beside my sister for an eternity, wearing a perpetually amused expression on my face to mask that I was dying of boredom on the inside. I didn't care Rachel Sanderson was going to do a semester abroad in Spain, or Eric Hineman had a venture capitalist interested in investing in his dumb start-up idea. I did my time beside Emily until she finally gave a slight nod. It was her signal I was about to be released.

She dug out her tube of red lipstick and held it up. She'd pestered me the whole car ride tonight to put it on, but I'd refused. I'd won the battle, but I was about to lose the war.

"Bitch," I groaned under my smile and snatched the tube from her.

She laughed. "It'll look amazing on you."

Once I'd smeared on the red lipstick and returned it, I stole away through the kitchen. Up an empty back staircase I went, seeking out a quiet room where I could read until Emily would text me it was time to go. No one would miss the weird Northcott sister with oddly green tinged hair and bright red lips.

The first room I came to was dark. The door was open, just a sliver, but enough for me to see it was occupied. A girl was perched on the edge of a bed, her dress pulled down around her waist and her pale breasts undulating with her shuddering breaths. A man, his back to me, was on his knees before her, his head buried between her spread thighs. She threaded a hand in his hair and clenched it tight as she gasped in contentment.

I hurried past the open door with my cheeks burning, and a rope of desire tightened inside me. Was it envy, or curiosity, or both? I wanted to know what that felt like. The sensation of someone besides myself giving me pleasure.

I was so fucking curious about sex.

But I wasn't going to find out tonight, here on the mostly empty second floor of the Hale estate.

My footsteps were quieted by the plush carpeting as I wandered down the corridor. The walls were covered in more intricate paneling. The whole enormous house felt masculine and cold, and I couldn't imagine growing up here. Not that I pictured Royce, or his younger brother Vance, as the poor little rich boys. They were quite the opposite. The Hale men were cunning, ruthless predators.

But all this space wasn't so much secluded as it was *isolated*. Did they ever get lonely? Macalister and their stepmother were workaholics and never around. In fact, Alice Hale was currently at a spa for "an intensive cleanse," but there were whispers. Rumors that Macalister had put her in rehab.

I tried several doors until I found one that didn't lead to

a bedroom, but a library. Or maybe it was a home office. A warm toned writing desk was placed across from a marble fireplace.

I didn't turn on the six-armed chandelier overhead. Instead, I flicked on the desk lamp, which cast soft amber light up onto the shelves of books. The gold embossed titles on the spines glinted back at me. The bookcases spanned every inch of the room except for the curtain-draped window at the back, where bronze velvet fabric pooled on the floor.

It smelled like books in here. Like leather, and logs that had been burned during the winter, and . . .

Power.

I fell in love with the library in one slow, wonderous blink. There was a brown arm chair with a matching ottoman back-lit by the window, and I was drawn to the spot like a magnet.

I curled up there, tucking my legs beneath the scratchy crinoline of my white dress, and pulled my mythology book from my oversized purse.

Outside, the sun set and darkened the room, but time halted as I read. My obsession with mythology had begun a long time ago. I liked how twisted the stories were. Murder, and betrayal, and jealous wrath . . . all the worst traits were displayed in the Gods' behavior, and they were unapologetic about it.

It was fascinating.

The book was so engrossing, I didn't hear the door open, or click shut, or the footsteps that approached. It was only the unnerving sense I was being watched that caught my attention. I glanced up from my book to find a pair of hungry eyes staring at me.

# TWO

MY LUNGS SEIZED WITH AN AWFUL, CUT-OFF SOUND.

Royce Hale's thick, wavy brown hair was swept back over his high-arched eyebrows and hypnotic eyes. He was tall and trim with broad shoulders and stood with his hands hooked in his black suit pants pockets, his thumbs peeking out. His posture was causal, yet it wasn't a word I'd use to describe him. Perhaps oppressive, or invasive, or . . .

*Sexy.*

I narrowed my eyes. No, he was only sexy if I found arrogant pricks appealing, and I'd decided long ago I didn't. Besides, he was Emily's. Over the years, the only attention he'd given me was when he wanted to be mean. It was entirely possible he didn't remember my name.

"Marist Northcott," he said, his tone like sweet liquor with a sharp, bitter aftertaste.

The jerk remembered me. I lowered the book in my lap. "My sister was looking for you."

The corner of his mouth tugged upward. It wasn't exactly

a smile, but he was amused. "I bet she was."

I gave him a slow, plain blink, letting him know I wasn't going to engage. Lots of women fell all over him, but I wasn't one of them.

He took a step deeper into the room. The tie around his neck was the same green as his daddy's money and the knot at his collar was askew. Had he loosened it recently, or not quite finished getting dressed? Perhaps he'd been the man on his knees in the other room, making the woman moan. His suit was the same shade of black, but his hair wasn't rumpled.

"Did you find Emily?" I asked.

He sobered. Something ghosted through his eyes, but it was gone too fast for me to recognize the emotion. "Yeah."

The single word carried an unmistakable finality to it. This was something he didn't want to discuss. Instead, all he did was trap me with the gravity of his gaze.

This was what I remembered most about him, how he'd stare intensely. He didn't break eye contact, didn't flinch. He peered at you as if it were only a matter of time before he discovered all your secrets. Everything you tried to hide or were ashamed of, he'd find it. His scrutiny always forced me to look away first. I had to run before he learned just how exposed I felt around him. He'd take it as an advantage and somehow exploit it.

He was so fucking comfortable holding my gaze too long, staring into the depths of me. Like me, he typically said whatever he was thinking. Honesty was a great trait, until it wasn't. Too much of it and it cut painfully deep. As acute as his stare was, I tried not to wither.

"Congrats on your MBA," I said flatly.

He waved my insincere pleasantry away like it was an annoying fly. "It must be some book to have you hiding up here."

"I don't like parties."

It came out before I thought better of it, but Royce didn't seem offended. "Yeah, me either."

What was he talking about? "Do you know how many times my sister snuck home after curfew from one of your parties? If you don't like them, why'd you throw so many?"

He considered my question. "The bigger the party, the more freedom I had." He grinned. "Fuck, half the time I wasn't even here."

He'd revealed it like a secret, and an unwanted thrill shot through me. If this wasn't widely known, why would he share it? Everything in Cape Hill was about being elite and exclusive. Money was easy to come by, but power was harder, and knowledge was its own form of currency.

"What are you reading?" His question was simple, but a demand, nonetheless. His father was the king of Cape Hill, which made Royce a prince, and I was merely a subject in his castle. So, I was forced to hold the book up for him to see. His eyes sharpened on the gold and white artwork on the cover. He sounded dubious. "Mythology?"

I nodded then dropped my gaze to the pages, striving to look indifferent. I couldn't read as he stood over me, but I'd act like I was. I could pretend I didn't smell his cologne or was wondering if he'd just finished fucking the girl down the hall and was prowling for his next meal.

"Is that for a summer class or something?" he asked.

"No."

As I tried to focus on the page, his confusion was distracting. "Why are you reading it?"

"Because I want to?"

My tone was a bit more pointed than I meant for it to be, and the silence that hung in its aftermath was taut. I glanced up to find Royce's eyebrow arched halfway up his forehead. He didn't like my sass.

Or . . .

*Did he?*

Something thickened in his eyes, hot and heavy.

"And this is more riveting than my party?" He placed his palm on his chest, covering his heart, feigning I'd wounded him. "I'm deeply offended."

"I'm sure," I said dryly then refocused on the printed page. I scanned the words and absorbed none of them. It didn't matter. Seconds later the book was yanked from my hands. I scrambled up out of the chair, chasing after it. "*Hey.*"

Royce held the book out of my reach and wore an evil grin.

"Oh, my God, are you five?" I said. "Give it back."

Instead, he clamped one of his large hands down on my shoulder, keeping me an arm's length away as he skimmed the passage I was reading. My heart skipped as his fingers tensed against my skin, the heat of his palm soaking through the lace cap sleeve. I didn't like the way his touch buzzed through my body. He'd probably touched a hundred women who'd melted from it. I wasn't going to add my name to that list.

"Is that why your hair looks like that?" he asked. He kept

the book high and far away, and it was easy for him to hold me in place, no matter how I struggled. "I get it. Medusa was always my favorite too."

I choked on a breath and jerked to a stop. "What?"

"I assume you're a fan. With that green hair and those red lips, you sort of look like her."

My heart banged in my chest, a side effect of the anger bubbling in my bloodstream. Had he just called me ugly? "Actually," I snapped, "in most versions of the story, Medusa was beautiful."

"I know that." He looked at me strangely. "Do you . . . *not* think you're beautiful?"

*Wait, what?*

He didn't think I was ugly, but beautiful? The floor beneath my feet softened, and I struggled to stand on this newly uneven ground. I could handle Royce treating me a variety of ways. He could be indifferent, or annoying, or even cruel, but he'd never been *nice* before.

It was unsettling.

He'd sounded sincere, but I refused to believe it. He was working some angle, and I just hadn't figured it out yet. I had to regroup.

"What I meant," I said, "is that in the original versions, she was gorgeous. But once she became a symbol for feminist rage, men retold the story and made her ugly. I assumed that was the version you'd know."

His hand slipped from my shoulder, and I was cold in the absence of his touch. His eyebrows tugged together. "Feminist rage?"

I was vaguely aware this was a ridiculous conversation to be having, but my mouth ran away with itself. "Yeah. She was raped by Poseidon, and after that she could turn any man who looked at her into stone." I reached for the book. "Not women," I clarified. "She only used her power on men."

I tugged the book gently, but Royce wouldn't release it. "Interesting." He cocked his head to the side, and his icy eyes sharpened. "So, you *are* Medusa." A smile tilted on his lips. "It was temporary, but you turned me to stone just now."

My mind went blank. "What?"

"Do you have any idea how long I was standing there, watching you?"

And with that, he let go of the book. The sudden lack of resistance, or perhaps it was the seriousness in his expression, left me stumbling backward. This version of Royce was lethal. He'd sold it well enough for me to believe him.

But only for a single breath.

The idea of my beauty turning this man into stone, the one who could have nearly any woman he wanted, fluttered in my belly. And then it soured and crashed to my toes. He wasn't really a man, but an entitled brat, and it was just a line. I knew better. His favorite toys growing up were the ones that lived and breathed and had feelings that could be manipulated.

I wasn't going to be his plaything tonight.

"Did you forget which Northcott sister you're talking to?" I tightened my grip on the edges of my book. "Save your attempts at being charming for Emily."

It was like I'd unexpectedly punched the hollow laugh

from him. "I'm not attempting to be charming. And, Jesus, what happened to you? I don't remember you being so prickly before."

"Really? I'm amazed you remember anything at all about a *nobody* like me."

The half-smile on his lips froze and his shoulders stiffened. His reaction was probably as close to embarrassment as he got.

"You remember saying that, I guess," I said.

He let out a long sigh.

Back when I'd been a sophomore in high school, I'd begged Emily to let me tag along to some crappy dive bar on the outskirts of town. It had been a school night in the middle of the week. The bar agreed not to serve liquor until after ten to allow the group of kids from Cape Hill Prep, who had formed a shitty band, to perform for an underage crowd. Emily had been dating the drummer—who had zero fucking rhythm—and we'd stood in the crowd sipping sodas as her friends fumbled their way through a pathetic set of five songs.

I still remembered standing on the sticky floor in the dark, in a place I wasn't usually allowed to go. The too-loud guitars and muddled music vibrated in my chest as the band covered songs and butchered them, and I thought up to that point it was the coolest moment of my life. All the popular kids were there, swaying to the haphazard beat, and I'd been included. For the first time, I felt like part of something.

Later that night, we'd wound up at an all-night diner.

Royce hadn't seen Emily and me come in. He'd been drinking coffee at a table on one side and his back was turned, and we'd arrived just in time for him to recap his night. He'd announced he thought the evening was cool . . . up until the moment he'd "seen a nobody like Marist Northcott was there." My presence, according to him, had made the whole experience lame.

Sophia Alby was sitting across the table from him and lifted her surprised gaze to me, and it was enough to grab his attention. He turned over his shoulder, just enough to give me a view of his side profile. I saw him, and he saw me, and he had to know his comment had registered, given my shocked expression. He didn't care how his words had landed or stripped me down. He just shrugged, turned back around, and rolled right on into his conversation.

I was worthless. He was the prince of Cape Hill, and he had declared me a *nobody*, which meant it was now law.

His offhanded comment decided my whole fate at Cape Hill Prep and the social circles I would never be allowed into. He'd labeled me a leper. It wasn't like I couldn't survive, but he'd made the last five years so much harder. Not to mention lonely.

I didn't like how he'd had that kind of power over me. If there was a specific moment in my life when I'd decided I didn't give a fuck what other people thought, I'd point a finger to that moment.

It gave me satisfaction to know if things went well between Royce and Emily as his family wanted, this *nobody* would become his sister-in-law. Royce's blue eyes clouded over, but the tension in my body firmed up as the memory drifted through my brain. I wouldn't show any emotion.

I wasn't going to let him know his offhanded comment had affected me or shaped me in any way.

"That was a long time ago." His voice was hollow.

"Hmm." Funny. The lingering sting was still sharp enough it felt brand new.

When his gaze slid down the length of my body, his voice went as smooth as buttery leather. "I was wrong, though. You're not a nobody."

Unwanted heat sparked inside me. It was impossible to look at him and not think about sex. His cheekbones were cut high and elegant, and his mouth could twist into a devastating smirk. Life had cast Royce as a playboy, and he looked every bit the part.

"Again, save it for Emily." I'd strived for an annoyed tone but faltered, and it came out breathy. Like I was begging, rather than chiding.

He took my reaction as a small victory, and it flashed in his eyes. "But I'm not interested in your sister."

His meaning was perfectly clear when he drew in a deep breath, his broad chest expanding and filling the space between us. The library was suddenly cramped and tiny. The shelves closed in, the curtains strangled, and there was no escape.

An insidious voice whispered inside me, telling me I didn't want to escape, anyway.

A war waged between my body and my mind. Physically, I wanted him. I was starved for attention when it came to boys, and on the surface, there wasn't one more appealing than Royce Hale. But he was also the very reason I had such a hard time finding someone to date during my cloistered life. The crop of eligible men in Cape Hill was small, and I was awkward, and Royce's comment had been the nail in the coffin.

He was fucking with me. There couldn't be any other explanation. What was his end goal? Did he want me flustered and falling all over him like the other girls did? Was he going to pretend to seduce me and then spur me off, humiliating me at the last second? Run to my sister and tell her how pathetic I was?

"Oh, yeah?" I blinked innocently. "What exactly are you interested in?"

He matched my harmless attitude, threading his tie through two fingers and slid them down the length. "Avoiding people and staying here in the library with you."

It was a rare misstep for him. He'd overcompensated, and this was a bluff. I was excited to have the power to call him on it. I swallowed in a preparing breath, shifted the book into my left hand, and set the palm of my right on the center of his tie, my fingertips resting on his dress shirt. The silk was cool and soft, contrasting against the warmth seeping through the fabric covering his hard chest.

I wasn't practiced at seduction, but I threw everything I had at it. "What should we do?"

His eyes widened. *Oh, my God.* There wasn't anything more exciting than seeing the prince caught off guard. It lasted only long enough for me to recognize it before his large hand came down on mine, trapping my fingers in his and pressing my palm flatter against his chest.

"I have some ideas," he said.

With my hand pressed to him, Royce's heartbeat was a slow, steady drum. If the roles had been reversed, he would have felt mine hammering in my chest. His thumb moved, brushing slowly over the back of my hand, and tension coiled in my body. I thought he'd back down, but instead he'd returned the challenge, upping the ante. How far was he willing to take this? And . . . how far was *I* willing to let it escalate?

Each tiny stroke of the pad of his thumb made me want to push further. Every quiet breath we took with our stares locked on each other gave me the courage to keep playing the game.

"Was the girl down the hall not enough for you?" I asked.

"Girl down the—" Confusion darted through him, only to be replaced with a slow smile. "Vance was fucking some blonde when I walked by the guest bedroom. You thought that was me?" When I didn't answer, his voice dipped lower. "My brother probably left the door open because he wanted an audience. Did you watch them?"

"Maybe." I dropped my book, and it thudded onto the leather of the ottoman. I graduated from pressing my hand to him to my whole body. The crinoline beneath the skirt of my dress crushed softly between our thighs. Pleasure washed through his expression and simmered into something else.

Something darker and hotter.

His hand was gone, only so he could slip it behind me and lock me in place to him. My white dress was demure in the front but backless, and a shiver glanced down my spine as his fingertips settled on my bare skin. I tilted my chin up, wanting to look strong as his unwavering eyes threatened to undo me completely.

"I like this dress," he said, trailing his fingers up my back, dragging them along each ridge of my vertebrae like he was counting stacks of money. "But would Medusa wear white? She wasn't a virgin, after all."

There was so much sex laced in his voice, I was going to combust and spoke without thinking. "Well, I'm not Medusa."

The corner of his mouth lifted like it was on a hook. "Is that so?"

Was I supposed to feel shame I hadn't fucked anyone when I was twenty years old? Like there was something wrong with me? Or was I supposed to feel pride I was a good girl and had kept myself pure?

Because I felt neither. "So what if I'm a virgin? Who fucking cares?"

Royce did, and I disliked the way he looked at me now, like I was a prize. I hated how society, even today, placed so much value on something entirely worthless. Yes, I hadn't done it yet, but I was sure sleeping with someone wasn't going to change me.

"How is that possible?" His hand continued to stroke lazily up and down my back, perhaps hoping to elicit another shiver. "No boyfriend while you were off at Etonsons?" A smile dripped off his lips. "Oh, that's right. It's an all-girls college."

It was a strange feeling how my body liked being in his arms and yet the rest of me detested it.

Etonsons was one of the most prestigious schools in the

country. They only accepted four percent of the women who applied there, and the private tuition was outrageous. Emily and I both attended, although her acceptance had been more on the strength of our mother's legacy, whereas mine was my grades.

"What's the reason you haven't fucked anyone?" He studied me critically, searching for the answer.

"Economics keeps me busy," I said casually. "I just haven't found the time."

"Bullshit."

"Maybe I'm not into guys."

He leaned down so his face was a scant inch from mine. "*Try again*. Your pupils are dilated. You're out of breath, and I can see your pulse pounding in your neck. I'm sure if I put my hand up your skirt right now, my fingers would come away wet."

"They wouldn't," I lied.

It was like he knew. "I bet you're soaked."

"Fine. Go ahead and do it," I challenged, "and let's see who's right."

I was glad I'd been gutsy enough to say it, and a thrill ghosted down my legs. He couldn't accept my challenge. He'd have to cede ground. Everyone knew which Northcott sister he was supposed to end up with, and I wasn't her. If he put his hand up my skirt, there'd be hell to pay.

But rather than act disappointed, satisfaction flooded the handsome face looming over me. "Oh, don't you worry. I plan to."

Breath stuttered and broke down in my lungs, sapping

my confidence. He was older and had been playing this game a lot longer. What if I was in over my head? It had seemed like a bluff at first, but now I was less convinced. I lifted my arms and set my hands on his shoulders, drawing us toward the edge of danger.

He brushed the long sweep of my seaweed colored hair back over my shoulder, making room for his warm breath to fill the space and remind me just how close his lips were to my skin.

"You're doing it again," he said.

"What?" I whispered.

"Turning me into stone."

My knees trembled but I locked them in place. "I don't have that ability. And if I did, it wouldn't matter. You'd have to actually see me for it to work."

"I see you."

"Come on," I said with irritation. "No, you don't. I'm a faceless girl to you, Royce. A *nobody*."

Fire scorched his eyes. "You have no idea what you're talking about. I fucking *see* you, Marist."

And as if it would prove his point, he slammed his lips down on mine, crushing everything I believed into a million pieces.

# THREE

Royce's kiss wasn't a three-hundred-dollar bottle of champagne you could sip, it was a shot of the cheapest whiskey you could get your hands on and had to take as quickly as possible. He invaded my senses. His taste stormed past my lips, seared against my tongue, and burned all the way down my throat.

Was he the prince of fire?

His kiss ravaged and consumed.

I cried out against it, a mournful sound escaping my chest as my eyes slammed shut. The idea this wasn't real sliced deep and left me gasping from hurt. This thing between us, it couldn't be pretend. It was too powerful, too desperate to be a lie.

His lips moved against mine, demanding I meet his level and match his urgency. His hand on the small of my back drove me deeper against him while his other grabbed a fistful of my hair, tangling my strands in his rough fingers.

Kissing me was forbidden, and I wondered if it was

gasoline on the flame between us.

Not to be outdone, I curled my fingers in the hair at the nape of his neck and pulled. He made me mad. Not angry— but crazy. Out of my mind. Reality sifted through my grasp. I could claim surprise at first, but letting him continue to kiss me was a bad idea, and there were major consequences for actively participating in it.

In some versions, Medusa didn't start as a gorgon. She'd been a beautiful mortal who worshipped Athena and had the terrible misfortune to catch Poseidon's eye. He followed her into a temple and raped her. Outraged at the desecration of her temple, Athena engaged in the ultimate victim-blaming— she cursed Medusa to become a gorgon with snake hair and banished her to live out her days on a secluded island. There were different versions of the myth, but the ending was always the same. Perseus came along, cut her head off, and was hailed a hero.

Would it be the same for me? Macalister decreed Royce and Emily should be together, and I'd seen what he did to people who created obstacles when he wanted something. Nothing as nefarious as death, but just as bad, really. A single negative word from him meant the offender would be shunned. Their status would evaporate overnight, and soon after, their money. It was what Royce had done to me in high school, but on a much grander scale, and one that involved the whole family.

It was a different kind of murder.

And Macalister wouldn't blame his golden son for anything. No, the blame for this dangerous and potentially destructive kiss would fall solely on my head, regardless of who had started it or whether I wanted it or not.

*You do want it. You want more.*

Heat sizzled across my skin, a mixture of desire and anger. I was upset Royce had put me in this position and pissed at how good it felt as his tongue slicked over mine. I didn't like him, but my body didn't care. I tugged harder on his hair, not to pull him off me or break the kiss, but to create a manifestation of the discomfort he'd caused.

He grunted so softly it was barely audible, but satisfaction warmed in my center. It died as quickly as it had arrived, because he tore his lips from mine, jammed his face in my neck, and sank his teeth into my flesh.

"*Fuck*," I gasped, more surprise than pain, although he'd bitten hard enough it was likely there'd be a mark. The sharp edge of his teeth was replaced by the damp velvet of his tongue, and the shiver that flitted through my shoulders was unstoppable.

"I see you," he murmured. "And now I've tasted you."

*Oh, God.*

In addition to Macalister's threat, my sister's face flashed through my mind. "No one can know."

"Who the fuck would we tell? You don't have any friends." His mouth latched onto the spot where my neck met my body.

I tried to shove him away but put no effort behind it. His kisses sucked all my strength. "I have friends."

He straightened and gave me a hard look. Then I was turned roughly in his hands until I was facing the bookshelf and his chest was a wall at my back. "Fictional friends do not count."

I had to move forward to try to turn and protest, but he just used it as an opportunity to advance on me. We shuffled two small steps until I was trapped and all I could see were the different colored spines of books. And then his lips were on the curve of my neck again, and his fingers traced a line down my bare back.

I peered at the titles before me and slipped deeper into his seduction.

I wished for a lot of things at that moment. To know if my sister had legitimate feelings for the man at my back, whose erection was poking against me. I wanted the door to this library to have a lock on it, and for Royce to use it. And I needed to know, since everything was going to hell anyway, when he was going to make good on his threat of sliding his hand up my dress and discovering how badly he'd turned me on.

I didn't have feelings for him. At least, not in the way a normal girl would. He used people, and I was eager to do the same to him. He could satisfy my curiosity about sex, and hopefully be very satisfying while doing it.

His hot, hungry mouth roved over me, like he needed to press his lips to every inch of my defenseless flesh he could find. I put my hands out and grasped the dusty shelf before me. Once again, he pushed my hair over my shoulder and out of his way, exposing my back, and I tilted my chin down to my chest.

"This is my favorite part of a woman." He drew a line across my shoulder blades with his tongue. Goosebumps pebbled on my skin. Of course, this was his favorite spot. Not the breasts, or the ass, or the legs . . . but the place that controlled all of a woman's physical power.

The place where she was most vulnerable.

If someone walked in right now, they'd have to think the scene was beyond strange. A girl with green hair in a virginal cocktail dress, clutching the bookcase for dear life as the man in the suit behind her worshiped her back with both his hands and his mouth. It was relatively benign what we were doing, but it was the most erotic moment of my life.

Pleasure radiated from his kisses, and the warmth spread deep between my legs. It got worse as he gripped my hips and ground himself against me. I wasn't sure which was more shocking, the sensation of his hard length, or that he found kissing me arousing.

Royce's words twisted with lust. "I want to fuck you under this white dress."

He kept one hand tight on my hip but slid the other up the curve of my body. All the way until it was cased around my throat, forcing my head back onto his shoulder. His fingers flexed, constricting just enough to make me feel his dominance but not outright fear.

He growled roughly in my ear. "I want to see your red lipstick smeared all over my dick."

I exhaled a sharp breath.

His voice was abruptly so low and smooth, it sounded like he was inside my head. "Would you like that?"

Would I? The image of me on my knees, his belt and pants undone flickered through my mind. It was undeniably hot, but what about Emily? What about the door that anyone could walk through and catch us?

He sensed my hesitation not by my lack of answer, but by the tension in my body.

"No?" His question was rhetorical. The hand on my hip snaked down to the center of my skirt where he pressed his thick fingers between my legs. The dress had many layers of fabric, but as he rubbed me, the sensation was pleasurable enough to make my heart stop.

When a moan drifted past my lips, a satisfied chuckle rattled in his chest. My legs shook as he deliberately worked the layers of the skirt up, and I jolted when his palm found my inner thigh. What we were doing was bad.

But—God—it would be worse if he stopped.

I couldn't control my breathing as his hand inched upward and brushed the damp crotch of my panties. His tone was pure evil. "What's this?"

I didn't defend myself. I just stood there, waiting patiently for him to cross the line. His phone chimed in his pocket, but he ignored it. He was more interested in teasing and balancing me on the knife's edge of desire.

Royce finally stroked his hand between my thighs, touching me through the thin satin. He wasn't gentle about it either, and I was glad. It made it easier to remember I didn't like him. Plus, the heat between us was searing and urgent, and I'd rather have his touch now than wait for him to be careful.

"I want this," he said. "Give it to me."

He couldn't have sounded more like the spoiled rich brat he was if he'd tried.

But a shudder wracked my body. This was a demand from the prince and one I would have to obey, but I'd do it gladly, even when I didn't understand exactly what I was surrendering. My body? My virginity? More?

It was poetic justice that the man who'd caused the delay in my sexual journey would be the same one who'd start me on it. And he fucking owed me.

"All right," I whispered.

My agreement was a release. It was a signed contract, a done deal, and tension poured from my muscles. It made me malleable in his steady and no doubt experienced hand.

He dug his fingers inside my underwear, and I tightened my grip on the bookshelf, clamping my teeth together to hold back a breathy moan. His touch was so different than my own. Rougher. Confident. Greedy.

It was so much better.

Could he feel my pulse roaring in my neck? His hand still collared me, but there wasn't aggression there. He saved all of that for the hand strumming between my legs, stirring my clit. I was going to melt. Drip down his fingers, pool onto the floor, and seep into the fibers of the Persian rug.

His phone chimed again.

Its mechanical noise didn't belong here. The only sounds I wanted ringing in my ears were my whimpers of pleasure and his hurried breaths. But the second text alert was a trigger. It felt like a bomb had been armed and we only had so much time left before it blew up in our faces. Someone was eventually going to come looking for him.

Royce's tie swayed against my back as he moved his arm,

working me over. Then he slid a finger inside, and I wanted to curl up onto my toes.

"Oh, fuck," I groaned. I tilted my head forward, letting it thud onto the bookshelf with a soft bang. It wasn't that his intrusion felt particularly good, but the *idea* of it? That, I enjoyed very much. I liked his possession.

His tongue was at the shell of my ear, and although he wasn't saying anything with words, his hot breath whispered dark thoughts directly into my mind. I spread my legs wider, increasing my stance, and rocked on the finger pulsing inside me.

"You sure you're a virgin?" He nipped at my earlobe, and his tone was teasing. "Because you're fucking my hand like you're not."

"Shut up," I gasped.

He laughed and tightened his hold on my neck, wordlessly telling me I'd better watch it. I didn't get to tell him what to do. His firm hand was a reminder of who was in control right now.

His long, fat finger withdrew, only to rub lazy circles on my swollen, sensitive clit. It was overwhelming, everything that was happening. He returned to kissing my neck, his lips working just under the hand he pressed to my pulse point. I jolted and stretched at the fingers twitching inside my panties, writhing like a mindless animal.

Royce boiled the thoughts in my head down to single words. *Want. Need. Come.*

"This is mine now," he said.

I couldn't see his face, but I pictured his expression.

It was the same one he'd wear someday in the boardroom during a hostile takeover. Absolute.

He said I was his. I tried to understand what he meant, but I was fracturing. He increased the intensity, and pleasure spilled from my center, running down my legs. I was coming apart.

"You wait for me. You understand?"

*Wait for him?* My confusion made the orgasm brewing in my system hesitate.

It was less of an order from him, and more like a plea. "I get to be first, Marist. No one else touches you."

I tried to step away, but his strong arms crushed me back against him, trapping me. And as I settled into my new prison, he rewarded me. His hand fluttered until it became too much. I cried out, my voice soft but soaked with bliss as I came.

It was violent.

I flinched and contracted under the weight of the pleasure, its intensity so strong for a moment it felt like dying.

I hadn't finished recovering when Royce turned my head toward his and captured my mouth in a brutal kiss.

"You'll wait," he demanded. "Say you'll do it."

Nothing made sense right now, but I was under his influence and would agree to nearly anything. His magnetic voice was a siren's call, luring me in.

"Yes," I breathed.

Something oddly like relief filled his eyes and then vanished. "Good."

He let go of me and stepped back so suddenly, I had

to use the bookcase to keep myself upright, nearly toppling it and crushing us both. I got strength back in my legs and whirled around to face him, only to see his broad back heading quickly for the exit.

"Royce." I said it the same way I'd tell him to stop.

But he didn't. He opened the door and disappeared into the hallway, never once looking back at me.

# FOUR

## One Year Later

I WAS STILL A VIRGIN ON MY TWENTY-FIRST BIRTHDAY.

It wasn't done out of loyalty to Royce, I continually reassured myself. I hadn't seen him since his graduation party a year ago and did my best not to think about him at all these days. It had been hard at first. I'd spent an unhealthy amount of time obsessing over our night in the library and wondering what the hell had happened. Had I done something wrong? Or had the whole thing just been one massive mindfuck?

It was going to be tough to get through today without thinking about him. He, along with his father, was due at the house within the hour.

I sat on the tile floor of Emily's bathroom, gazing at my purple toenail polish. She was beside me, and I stroked a hand over her hair as she bent over the toilet and spit the lingering stomach acid from her mouth. I tore off a strip of toilet paper and passed it to her as she leaned back, and I stayed quiet as she wiped the corners of her mouth.

Her eyes were bloodshot. She'd thrown up so many times today, it'd burst blood vessels.

"Feeling better?" I asked.

"A little. God, please tell me it's finally out of my system." Her skin was ashen and waxy. "Shit," she groaned, collapsed back against the wall and put a hand on her forehead. "What the hell am I going to do?"

"People get sick," I offered. "Everyone understands that."

Her red-rimmed eyes popped open and stared at me like I was nuts. "Macalister won't."

She was right, so I wasn't going to argue with her. Humans got sick, but Macalister Hale wasn't human, so he wouldn't be able to relate. Our father had tried to cancel the luncheon, but his boss refused. There were important things that needed to be discussed. Plus, he told my father there was "plenty of time for Emily to get herself together" before they arrived.

Macalister probably thought it was just a hangover and not actual food poisoning as my father had explained.

"Maybe a shower will help," I said, glancing at the screen of my phone. The meeting was unavoidable, and she needed to get her ass in gear if she was going to attempt to look presentable.

"Okay," she said weakly. I helped her up off the floor and plodded over to the shower, turning on the water.

After she finished, there was a knock at the bathroom door, but it swung open without waiting for a response, and our mother floated in. Her dark chocolate colored hair didn't show a speck of gray because she paid a great deal of money for it not to. She wore a red and navy striped dress with a pleated skirt, and although lunch wouldn't be served for another hour, she was all polished and ready to give Martha Stewart a run for her money.

She watched Emily climb feebly out of the shower, and worry streaked across her face. "Did anyone else get sick?"

I shook my head. "Em is the only one who ordered the salmon."

My mother scowled, creating a crease in her forehead. "Don't call her that today, all right?"

My sister's nickname had never been an issue before. Any other time, I'd have been irritated at the idea of changing my behavior to please someone else, but today I would go with it. "Okay."

The Hale family held sway over everything, and my parents would have less stress over the President of the United States visiting. They were supposed to be friends, but every moment with the Hales was rigid and formal. A visit with Macalister was a job interview that never ended. Every answer and action you made was evaluated and catalogued in his brain, and one wrong move would be disastrous.

"I should call the restaurant and let them know," my mother said. "A lot of times it doesn't get reported and—"

She froze as she stared at her daughter's bloodshot eyes. It was obvious the thoughts running through her mind. First was concern over how sick Emily was, but the second thought was given almost as much priority. She was worried what Macalister's reaction would be.

"I think I've got some Visine," I whispered.

My mother's attention swung toward me and, as she blinked, it was like she was seeing me for the very first time. Her critical gaze took in my deep emerald hair, scoured downward over my tank top and shorts, and landed on my flip-flops.

"Marist, please. Get dressed. I'm getting nervous sweats just looking at you."

Emily lurched toward the toilet again. There wasn't much left to throw up, and my mother and I stood helplessly by as she dry-heaved. If there was a way I could have transferred the sickness to myself, I gladly would have done it. It was so hard to watch my sister feeling miserable.

And she'd said the salmon wasn't even that good. We'd gone out last night with her friends to celebrate her graduation from Etonsons. It had been a small gathering. The garden party my parents were planning would happen over Memorial Day weekend when the weather was better.

My mother locked eyes with me as Emily coughed and moaned. "Wear something nice. You might have to represent both my daughters today."

After much arguing, I wore the pomegranate dress Emily had intended to wear. With my green hair, I was modern Christmas colors in May. The V neck party dress wasn't my style, but it fit me and satisfied my frazzled mother.

After getting dressed and putting on the makeup my sister insisted I wear, I lingered upstairs as long as I could when the Hale men arrived. I waited until my father had to call for me to join them. It had been a small miracle I'd gone this long without running into Royce since I'd returned from college, but I couldn't avoid him any longer. I teetered down the staircase on Emily's heels, which were a half-size too big and made me clutch tight to the banister.

The polite conversation ceased at my entrance, and for a moment I became Medusa, turning everyone into statues. My father was the first to break form and gave a surprised smile, happy to see me. There was safety in numbers around the Hales, after all.

The patriarch of the visiting family took longer to recover and look mostly human again.

At fifty-two, Macalister's hair didn't contain a single thread of silver. It was swept perfectly over to one side, not a strand out of place, and I wondered if he simply decreed it in the morning and his hair fell into line. His nose was long, his cheekbones were high, and he was in perfect shape.

And just like his sons, Macalister was ruthlessly attractive.

But there was an unsettling edge in his eyes. As if he'd seen the entire world, down to every crevice, and found all of it so very disappointing.

His top lip curled as his gaze evaluated me top to bottom. Oh, he fucking *hated* my unnatural hair color, and it was so bad, he wasn't even going to acknowledge me. I didn't deserve a sliver more of his attention.

Royce, on the other hand, was frozen and focused only on me. His wide eyes didn't blink for an abnormally long moment, and with the surprised expression fixed on his face, he looked . . . strange. Like he couldn't believe what he was seeing. Otherwise, he appeared the same as last time. Still irritatingly sexy, wearing a cobalt blue suit with no tie, and shoulders set with confidence.

Had he not expected to see me? I guessed that made sense. His younger brother Vance hadn't come, and when Macalister had requested the lunch, he'd only asked Emily attend.

The anxiety of it hadn't helped my sister with the nausea.

Macalister cleared his throat, jolting his son from his stupor, then narrowed his exacting gaze on my father. "Where's your other daughter?"

My father stiffened. "She's still not feeling well."

Macalister was only a few inches taller than my father, but he seemed to loom over everyone, and his displeasure drifted down, permeating the room. "Then she can join us after lunch."

My mother's shoulders sagged, but she nodded and gestured to the dining room, ushering us toward the table our housekeeper Delphine had set with our fine china.

Since my father sat at the head of the table, I ended up across from Royce, and I spent the majority of the meal staring at the gold filigree in my plate, rather than endure his stare that drilled down into me.

The conversation was stilted pleasantries like it always was. Macalister's only hobby was being an asshole, so it made him difficult to talk to. He'd changed so much over the years. I barely remembered how he used to be, or if he had ever genuinely smiled.

As soon as Delphine cleared the plates from the main course and disappeared through the door to the kitchen, my father's boss laced his fingers together and set them on the table. The air shifted in the room. It was time to discuss business.

"Royce will be joining the board of directors," Macalister said.

*Holy shit.*

He dropped his plain statement on the table, but it fell like an anvil and crushed through the floor, threatening to pull us all down with it. It was no secret my father wanted the coveted seat on the board. Royce was a Hale, so it was natural he'd be offered one eventually but, Jesus, he'd only been working at the company for a year.

And he was twenty-five.

Splotches of red crawled up my father's neck and peeked out over the starched collar of his dress shirt. No doubt he was thinking how he'd been working for Hale Banking and Holding from before Royce was born. Charles Northcott was supposed to be next in line.

My gaze snapped to Royce, but he simply stared back, devoid of any emotion. He'd become a statue once again.

"How wonderful," my mother choked out.

"Yes," my father lied.

Macalister gave a subtle nod. "As you know, this is a huge honor." His tone was cursory. "We have a tradition that goes along with it."

A thousand tiny spiders crawled along my back.

The last time someone had joined the board, I'd been

eight. No one explained to me what the process was, and not that anyone could. The tradition went back several generations in the company, and only the board members were privy to it. There was an initiation, or a ceremony, or some weird rite of passage, and then an enormous party afterward to celebrate. Like the private and elusive societies at an Ivy League school, I found the whole secret thing pretentious. Men making a big deal and pretending to be more important than they were.

"Now that Emily has finished school," Macalister continued, "it makes sense that she joins Royce. Once he takes his seat, we will announce their engagement at the celebration afterward."

It was surprising when my jaw fell open, it didn't thump audibly onto the table.

In the past year, Emily and Royce had been on exactly one date, and she'd said it had been horrible. They had little in common and zero chemistry, according to her. I'd found that a little surprising. He was an asshole for sure . . . but no chemistry? I certainly hadn't experienced that issue with him.

His kiss had burned for weeks after.

A part of me was secretly thrilled it hadn't worked out between them.

*Wait for me,* his voice echoed through my mind.

Beneath the table, I pinched my knees together. It was hard to handle the memory while he was seated right in front of me.

But he didn't protest the suggestion of marrying my sister. He didn't say a goddamn thing about what his father had just announced, and irrational jealousy knifed through me. And even if you put the lack of chemistry thing to the side, *Emily wasn't even in the fucking room.*

It shouldn't have been so shocking. This marriage proposal wasn't about love, it was a business merger. Macalister didn't think my sister needed to be included in the negotiations of it, apparently.

My family's confusion came out in a single word from my mother. "What?"

He looked irritated he had to spell it out. "Royce would like to ask for Emily's hand in marriage."

An incredulous laugh burst from my mouth. Was he seriously letting his *daddy* do this? "Maybe we should get Emily in here," I said, my tone sarcastic. "She might have some thoughts about it."

When Macalister's icy gaze turned on me, I shivered. I wanted to fold up inside myself until there was nothing left.

"Then perhaps you should go and fetch her," he decreed.

I stole away from the table, happy to be gone. I stepped out of my heels, depositing them at the base of the steps, and raced up the front staircase, my dress swishing as I went. I burst breathlessly into Emily's room without knocking and discovered her sitting on the side of her unmade bed, her arms folded across her stomach. She looked like she was holding herself together.

"Em," I said. "You need to get downstairs now."

I darted into her walk-in closet and rifled through the dresses hanging there. There was a peach floral dress that was a bit too summery, but it would do. I snatched it off the hanger and stormed back into her room, holding it out urgently.

"Macalister just asked if Royce could have your hand in marriage."

I'd expected laughter. Disbelief. Shock.

Instead, she cast her glassy, red-rimmed eyes down at her damask bedspread. Somehow, she knew this was coming.

A void opened in my chest. My sister was my best friend, and we told each other everything.

*No, you don't.*

I hadn't told her about my night in the library with Royce. I'd had a good reason not to before they attempted a relationship, and after it was clear nothing was going to happen, it seemed pointless to tell her.

I pushed my questions and sting of betrayal to the side. We'd deal with it later. Right now, we needed to handle the situation. I loved my father with all my heart, but he wasn't as strong as he needed to be. He was susceptible. He folded and gave in too quickly, especially when it was something he wanted, like another cigar or glass of whiskey.

What if Macalister offered a seat on the board in exchange for Emily? It was absolutely something the shrewd businessman would do, and it was possible our father would be foolish enough to accept. Not that my sister would ever go along with it, but just the insane negotiation could be disastrous.

"Get dressed," I ordered.

She did as I told her, moving like she was trying to delay the hangman's noose.

Her hair was washed, but not styled, and there wasn't a speck of makeup on her face when I led her downstairs, but it was better than her not being there at all. When we appeared, Macalister rose from his seat. Was this courtesy, or a power move? Royce stood as well, but his hesitation made it feel like an afterthought.

Her voice was as fragile as she looked. "Mr. Hale." Her gaze rolled over to his son. "Royce."

Macalister rounded the end of the table and strode toward her, his hand outstretched for a greeting. Earlier, he'd forgone a handshake when meeting a *nobody* like me, making it clear how much he preferred my sister.

"It's nice to see you again, Emily." There was no warmth in his tone, but I didn't think he was capable.

She opened her mouth to say something, but words did not come out. Instead, she heaved the contents of her stomach all over his offered hand.

# FIVE

My mother screamed. It was an awful sound, far worse than the groan from Emily as she tried unsuccessfully to cover her mouth and stop the catastrophe. The red dye from the sports drink she'd consumed was a sickly color when it came back up, like fake, garish blood running through her fingers.

The legs of my father's chair screeched across the hardwood as he leapt to his feet, yanked a cloth napkin off the table, and scurried to help his boss.

Macalister reared back. Red bile dripped from his hand, and he held it far away from his body. If he could have severed it clean off at that moment, he might have. Royce and I stood in stunned silence while everyone else buzzed around in a flurry of activity.

Emily muttered an apology and vanished. My father led his boss away to the nearest bathroom to wash off, while my mother chased down Delphine to clean up the puddle of vomit on the floor.

It left me alone with Royce, staring at each other from

across the expansive table my family hardly ever used.

"Hello, Marist. Or is it Medusa now?" His lips held the faintest of smiles. "Did you do what I asked?"

Air halted painfully in my body as everything constricted. I couldn't believe he had the balls to ask me that after what had just happened, after all this time, and to be so casual about it. Flames bloomed in my chest. "It's Medusa."

"Liar." He smiled so victoriously, I almost didn't catch the relief he was trying to hide beneath it. His gaze drifted from me to the door our fathers had disappeared through. "Is she pregnant?"

So much had happened in the last few seconds, I couldn't process. "What?"

He didn't repeat it, instead he let the question soak in silence.

Emily couldn't be pregnant. "She's not even dating anyone."

He arched an eyebrow. "Last time I checked, that's not a requirement for getting knocked up."

I couldn't manage my emotions. "She's not."

As soon as the statement was out, I began to question it. Whatever was going on with this insane wedding proposal, she hadn't confided any of it in me. My mouth went dry. She hadn't had anything to drink last night either. One of her friends had ordered celebratory tequila shots, but Emily turned hers down. She'd said she'd gotten sick off of Patron after finals week, and the smell made her nauseated.

Whatever expression I was making must have given away my thoughts because he looked smug.

"Fuck off, Royce," I snarled. "If she was pregnant, she'd tell me."

The door to the kitchen swung closed, announcing we were no longer alone. The cold draft of Macalister Hale was back, making the temperature in the room plummet until it was arctic.

"She's pregnant?" He appeared just as horrified as when my sister had thrown up on him.

"No, she's not," I answered quickly.

Royce shoved his hands in his pants pockets and rocked back on his heels like he found the whole thing amusing. "Go ask her. One hundred bucks says she is."

I didn't want to give him the satisfaction of running away, but his father had a way of making his desires known without saying a word. The set of his shoulders and the way he angled them toward me expectantly left me with no choice. I trudged back up the stairs with my hands balled into fists. I wished I could have reveled in the moment when someone threw up on Macalister, and if it had been anyone else not in my family, I would have.

She wasn't sitting on the bed this time, and I could hear her soft crying coming from the bathroom. She was bent over the sink, splashing water on her heated face. As soon as she saw me over her shoulder in the mirror, she straightened.

"Is it possible to die of shame?" She stared up at the ceiling, trying hopelessly to blink back her tears. "I want to. I'm so fucking embarrassed and miserable."

I had no idea what to say. I wasn't good at sugarcoating things, and my sister wasn't an idiot. She knew this wasn't something Macalister would quickly forgive or forget.

When I lingered awkwardly in the doorway, her expression changed to one filled with worry. "What now?"

"Are you pregnant?"

I'd whispered it, but her reaction was as if I'd screamed it at her. My sister's eyes expanded with shock, and then guilt spread through them like red wine spilled on a white tablecloth. Her gaze fell to her feet. "I'm . . . three weeks late."

"Three?" I had a million questions, but the practical one came out first and in a rush. "Shit, why haven't you taken a test?"

She shoved away from the sink and pressed the back of her hand to her lips. "Because," she said in a hush, "I know what it's going to say, and I don't want it to, okay?" Tears ran down her cheeks and dripped onto the travertine tile.

My heart broke a little. Not just for her, but selfishly for myself. She'd suspected for weeks and not confided in me. How many secrets was she keeping? "Whose is it?"

"I haven't told him yet."

"*Em.*"

"He's married. Oh, God, I'm a terrible person." She shut her eyes, squeezing out a fresh batch of tears. "It's . . . Dr. Galliat."

"Your psychology professor?"

She nodded. "What the hell am I going to do?"

"Well, you're not marrying Royce Hale, for starters." I put my hand on her shoulder and pulled her close, crushing her into a hug. "It's all right," I murmured. "Everything's going to be okay."

I held her reassuringly while the sobs wracked her body, not caring if her tears were staining my dress. I wondered if this baby could be a blessing in disguise. I certainly couldn't imagine Macalister as a father-in-law and didn't want us involved with the Hale family any more than we already were. It already felt like too much.

By the time I returned to the dining room, everything was back the way it had been at the start of lunch—except for the faint, lingering smell of disinfectant. Everyone was seated and appeared calm, but the tension was so strong, it invaded my senses like a thick paste.

"How is she?" my mother asked.

Royce took one look at me and smirked. "Pregnant. You owe me a hundred dollars."

Macalister didn't react with his face. He was perfectly composed even as he slammed a fist on the table so hard it created an enormous boom and made the silverware dance on the plates. Royce sobered, and for the first time I could remember, he looked nervous.

"That is unacceptable." Macalister's eyes were an intense Nor'easter, and I locked my knees before the hurricane-force winds knocked me down.

My parents were stunned, but the blow to the table seemed to knock my mother back to life. She pushed back her chair. "Please excuse me."

*"Sit down."*

At Macalister's snarl, she froze halfway out of her seat but then straightened until she stood tall, her backbone hardening. "No. I need to speak with my daughter."

"In a minute," he ordered. "You'll hear what I have to say first." His attention slithered my direction. "Take your seat. This involves you now, Marist."

He hardly ever said my name, and for that, I was grateful, because I always shuddered when he did. My feet moved independent of my mind to follow his order and bring me to my chair, and I fell into it while my heart rose into my throat.

"I'm not sure if you're aware," he adjusted the sleeves of his dress shirt beneath his suitcoat, "that the Northcott family has accrued so much debt, it's likely you'll declare bankruptcy by the end of the summer."

I let out a short laugh.

What the hell was he talking about? I glanced around our dining room. The ornate, hand-carved table had enough seating for sixteen, and the curtains were Dupioni silk. We'd just had a meal cooked by our private chef and served by our live-in staff.

We had money in spades.

Yet . . .

When I glanced at my parents, they both looked like they'd swallowed the canary, and choked half to death on it.

"I don't understand," I said.

My grandparents, the ones I'd been named after, had left their enormous wealth to my mother. Besides that, my father's annual salary was six figures. We had money in multiple markets. Property. Assets. There was no way bankruptcy was lurking around the corner. It just wasn't fucking possible.

"A decade ago," Macalister announced, "your father made a series of terrible investments. He chased the market for a while and dug a deeper hole. To stay afloat, they began draining their savings. You're a student of economics at Etonsons, correct?"

Hyperawareness inched over my skin, coupled with a terrible feeling of dread. "Yes, sir."

"Then I don't need to tell you how your tuition, plus your sister's, is more than Charles makes in a year. To keep you enrolled, he sold off his stock options."

My heart raced as the financial walls began to close in, making me swallow thickly. "But the house—"

"Was mortgaged three years ago and is now in default. I'm sure you know which bank holds the lien." He looked sickeningly pleased to tell me all this. "The fact is Charles and Delancey have been living well beyond their means for years. But that ends today."

I expected my parents to say something, to either defend themselves or say it wasn't true. But they were utterly silent, and the quiet grew more crippling with each breath I pulled in. All of our money was . . . *gone*?

Macalister spread his hands and placed his fingertips on the tabletop. "The only thing you currently own worth any value is your name and reputation." His statement was laced with a threat. We were all acutely aware he could take those just as easily as he could take the house. A single word from him and we'd be shunned.

"I'm going to make an offer," he said. "Only a fool

wouldn't accept it."

I dragged my gaze from Macalister, unable to look at him. I didn't want him to see the panic swamping in my eyes. Instead, I turned my attention to his son.

Royce sat perfectly still, one hand on the table, his fingertips resting against the edge of his folded napkin. The way he was unnaturally frozen in this casual position made me think it was for show. That inside he was tense and uncomfortable, and worried if he moved, he might give that away.

Macalister straightened in his chair, drawing my attention back to him. "When a new member is welcomed to the board, a woman plays an important role in the tradition."

My parents' shame had left them unable to speak, so I had to. "What kind of role?"

"She becomes his wife."

Oh, my God. The Hales had always been old-fashioned, but this was . . . *archaic.*

"Marriage is an important partnership," he continued. "And it's one the board needs to approve." He didn't notice the shock rippling through me. "Your parents were terrible with their finances, but they did a sufficient job raising their daughters. Obviously, Royce isn't going to marry Emily now, but your family name has enough status that, even though you're young, this pairing makes sense. And a Hale marrying a Northcott is what Royce's mother always wanted."

My shoulders rose and fell as I struggled to catch my breath. "You mean, Royce and I—?" My gaze flicked toward the man seated across from me. He hadn't moved, but there was an edge of excitement in his blue eyes.

An unwanted flash of heat coursed through me, when it should have been disgust.

"You will marry my son," Macalister stated flatly. "In exchange, I'll forgive your parents' mortgage and they can keep the house that's been in your mother's family for four generations. For appearances' sake, your father will continue at the company, but his finances will be taken over by a manager of my choosing."

Because he wouldn't want any scandal with his daughter-in-law's family, and more likely, because he preferred having total control.

My voice was hollow. "If I don't?"

"Charles will have to find employment elsewhere." Macalister's expression was a storm, and he dropped the pretense. "I'll foreclose on the house, and everyone will know how your parents squandered their money. When I'm done, you won't even have your reputation. You'll be left with nothing."

My mother burst into tears, and my heart tore down the middle. One side ached for her and this humiliation, and the other side was hot with anger. They'd seen this coming for years and purposefully kept it from my sister and me. They hadn't scaled back or tightened their belts. How could they continue living like nothing was wrong? Was it avoidance? Or pure denial?

I sucked in a breath through my teeth as another idea took shape. Perhaps they had a plan and had just been biding their time. Maybe they'd been counting on Emily marrying Royce and bailing them out.

It was the anger that gave me strength, although it couldn't be heard in my voice. I'd been told Macalister was a ruthless negotiator, but I was about to find out firsthand. "I . . . have a counteroffer."

His shoulders snapped back like I'd asked if his Cartier watch was a fake, but I sensed he was simply posturing. He probably enjoyed this sort of thing. "My offer was more than generous."

I ignored him. "If I agree to marry Royce," hysterical laughter bubbled in my throat, but I tamped it down, "we keep the house, my father keeps his job and agrees to the financial planner."

Macalister's irritation swelled to outright anger. "That's the exact offer I just proposed."

A tremble worked its way up my legs but was thankfully hidden beneath the table. Outwardly, I tried to match his merciless personality. I said it before I lost the nerve.

"And also, ten million dollars."

# SIX

A DEAL IS DEEMED GOOD WHEN NEITHER SIDE IS HAPPY AT THE end of negotiations, and right now Macalister Hale looked very, very unhappy.

I could relate.

My parents gaped at me. A stunned, short laugh came from Royce and hung awkwardly in the air.

Macalister's question was deadly quiet. It was scarier than if he'd shouted it at me. "Are you out of your mind?"

Obviously, I was, because I was considering this absurd deal. I had no desire to be married at twenty-one, and even less interest in becoming Mrs. Royce Hale. But what choice did I have? My entire family was broke, soon none of us would be employed, and it was likely my sister had a baby on the way.

I risked angering him further, and my voice warbled with a tremble. "Ten million isn't that much to you."

"*No.*" Rather than storm away from the table, he leaned over it, getting closer to me. "Understand something. I'm already forgiving a huge mortgage. I'm not stupid enough to extend your parents another loan."

"It wouldn't be a loan." I scrambled to come up with something. Anything to leverage. How deep did our money troubles run? What if my parents had years' worth of back taxes outstanding? Beneath the table, I balled my hands into fists. "Think of it as a reverse dowry. You'd be buying my silence and . . ." I choked it out, "loyalty to Royce."

Meaning I was essentially selling myself to him.

Macalister's eyes went thin as he evaluated it, and he made me wait a lifetime before speaking. "Five hundred thousand."

Relief and terror mixed inside my stomach. I was a freight train, barreling along much too fast and locked in on a path with one destination. Negotiations had started, and there was no turning back. I needed as much money as I could get. "Eight million."

His sneer cut me in half. "You think I'd be willing to pay that much? It's insulting."

"No more than your counteroffer."

The corner of his eyes crinkled. He was surprised I hadn't backed down, and perhaps intrigued. "I want this done. Two."

I was terrified to push my luck but went for it. "Five."

There was no emotion on his face. No hint of what he was thinking or what would happen next. He could laugh, he could curse, or he could walk away and leave us with nothing. I waited with painful anticipation.

"*Five million dollars*, Marist Northcott," he said, "and you better be the perfect, dutiful wife. You will look and act exactly how we tell you to. A paradigm of class, the girl who everyone looks up to and wants to be."

Oh, God. It was impossible to breathe. How was a *nobody* like me supposed to accomplish that?

"If you don't receive approval from the board, this offer is revoked. The house, the money, everything evaporates. You understand?"

I swallowed the lump in my throat and nodded.

"Then, we have a deal?" It was more statement than question from him.

"Marist." My mother's voice was a ghost. "We'll figure something out. You don't have to do this."

Who was she fucking kidding? Of course, I did. Up until now, my life had been easy. I'd been protected. My parents had spoiled Emily and me and given us anything we'd ever wanted. They'd ensured I'd never had to sacrifice or struggle.

I peered across the table at the man who looked a lot like his father but hadn't gained as hard of an edge yet. I traced the lines of Royce's fingers with my gaze and couldn't help but think about how he'd made me come. How he'd shattered me so completely with that same hand when he'd push me against the bookcase and jammed it inside my panties.

I could still smell the dusty, oaky scent of the library even now.

Agreeing to this was hard and unfair . . . but there were worse things than having to marry into one of the wealthiest families in the country. Becoming a Hale wasn't exactly a death sentence.

It wouldn't be—as long as I didn't lose who I was

along the way.

"Yes." I said it so softly it was impossible to hear, so I cleared my throat and strived for an even, sure tone. "I agree."

Royce's unexpected smile made my heart stumble. Was I reading him right? He looked pleased at my answer, like he wanted this. What kind of sense did that make?

His father's reaction was far more muted. Macalister was relieved to have an unpleasant task completed. He rose from his seat, reached across the table, and extended his hand. I smoothed my palms down on my skirt as I stood, wiping the sweat from them, and took the first handshake Macalister had ever offered me, sealing the deal.

His grip was overpowering and dominating, and I had the terrible feeling this was only a small taste of the control he craved. He held on to me as he spoke. "While I would have preferred you accepted my initial offering, I respect that you didn't. Maybe there's a brain in there beneath that ridiculous hair you've got." His compliment was mostly backhanded. Then he added, "I can see why Royce likes you."

Since he still had hold of me, Macalister had to feel the jolt traveling through my body. My gaze snapped to his son. Alarm blared loudly on Royce's expression but was shuttered instantly.

"I don't," he said quickly. "Like I told you before, either Northcott girl is fine with me."

My brain quit functioning, and the word fired off before I could rein it in. "*Wow.*"

As he retreated into his emotionless, statue-like state, I must have misinterpreted his reaction from before. He didn't care about my sister or me. We were interchangeable women to be married off. Merely a commodity.

*Aren't you?*

I'd just sold myself to him.

Turmoil churned in my belly, and for a moment, I wondered if I too would throw up all over Macalister's hand. I jerked back and forced my anxiety down. The full scope of what I'd agreed to hadn't hit me yet, and I needed to keep it together long enough until the Hales were gone. Then I could process the terrible decision I'd made.

A sinister smile lifted on Macalister's lips as he looked at his son, as if he wanted to see Royce squirm. "If that's true, what was all that on the car ride over here?"

"It was nothing." His voice was clipped. "I think it's time for dessert." When no one moved, he prompted my mother. "Mrs. Northcott?"

God, what an arrogant prick.

I didn't eat any of the chocolate tart Delphine served. My parents didn't either, unless my mother pushing around the raspberries with her fork counted. My family had no appetite following all the shit that went down. We sat as captives while Macalister laid out the instructions for the next month of my life.

An appointment was set up with Alice Hale. Royce's stepmother would meet me at her favorite salon and personally approve the "drastic changes" Macalister said were required to bring me in line with the Hale brand. Obviously, my evergreen hair color would be the first thing to go.

After coaching, which I was sure would be extensive, I'd sit for an initial interview with the board of HBHC. If I passed, a more extensive interview would be held just before the party celebrating Royce's new position. It would be lavish and extravagant, and the event of the year.

If I was approved, Macalister would announce his son's engagement to me during his toast that evening.

I saw my opening for a momentary escape when Delphine came in and began to clear the untouched desserts. I set my napkin on the table and seized my plate. "If you'll excuse me."

My legs wobbled as I pushed through the swinging door into the kitchen, and the plate clattered as I set it beside the sink. Delphine followed right behind me. Did she know? Did she have any idea my parents were in deep financial trouble and she could be out of a job very soon? Her questioning look was too hard to stomach, and I fled into the empty sitting room.

I shut the door and sank back against it, closed my eyes, and cupped a hand to my forehead. I fought my trembling bottom lip because I was on overload, but I refused to succumb to my emotions. I didn't want to face them again with a blotchy face and give them the upper hand, plus crying wasn't going to solve anything.

And it certainly wasn't going to undo what had been done.

Holy shit, I said I'd marry Royce. Until now, I'd spent my life obscured in Emily's shadow and I liked it that way.

There would be nowhere to hide once I became the princess of Cape Hill.

*Deep breaths.*

*You might not make it that far.*

If I couldn't win the ridiculous approval of the board, at least I'd bought some time to get my parents' finances in order. With a plan of action drafted up, the helplessness inside me dimmed just enough so I could straighten, press my cool fingertips to my warm cheeks, and calm down. I turned, pulled open the door, and buried my face in a dress shirt as I collided with a hard, male chest.

Royce's hands clamped down on my shoulders.

My gasp had no impact on him. He drove me back into the room and pulled the door closed behind us. His expression was . . . off. He had the audacity to look concerned.

"Are you all right?"

I blinked. "Are you fucking kidding me?"

"If it helps, I have about as much say in this as you do."

"No, it doesn't help, and that cannot be true." My shoulders tensed. Even though he was no longer touching me, the warmth of his palms lingered against my bare skin.

Frustration was an interesting look for him. The spoiled rich boy probably didn't have a lot of experience dealing with it. He always got whatever he wanted. Royce brushed back the sides of his suit coat as he rested his hands on his hips. It showed off his trim form and the curves of his powerful arms.

*Stop looking at him like that.*

"Believe what you want, but it's true," he said. "I do what I'm told because there's no alternative. Everything is planned or scheduled. I don't get to make decisions because my entire fucking life has already been scripted."

I didn't want to believe him, but it echoed true. Macalister's controlling personality was everywhere. My father had told me a story once how his boss had dictated what each staff member would wear during an audit.

Royce's expression warmed unexpectedly, and his voice dipped low. "But you and me? I was . . . hoping for this outcome."

Did he think I was stupid? "You literally said '*either Northcott girl is fine.*'"

"I said that to protect you." His tone was sincere. "It was a lie, Marist. Like I told you last year, I'm not interested in your sister."

At the memory, the room seemed to grow smaller the longer Royce and I stood alone in it. "Protect me from what?"

He gave a pointed look, as if the answer were obvious.

He was protecting me from his father. I sucked in a breath and matched his gentle tone. "Why?"

"I don't have time to explain right now. I need your phone. I told them we were exchanging numbers."

I begrudgingly dug it out of my dress pocket and passed it to him. "Right. Because you should probably have your fiancée's number."

He ignored my sarcasm and typed in the new contact, then texted himself from the phone. When done, he held it out to pass it back. Only he used it as an opportunity to jerk me close. His free hand slipped onto my cheek, forcing me to meet his intense gaze.

He was so close, a kiss threatened, and although our lips hadn't touched, it was powerfully intimate.

"You're not my fiancée, Marist. Yeah, you made the deal out there, but I haven't asked you to be my wife." His gaze roamed across my face, like he was memorizing each detail, before finally ending on my lips. His whispered words brushed over my sensitized skin. "Not yet."

Was he talking about proposing?

Or kissing me?

He carried out neither threat. Instead, he abruptly released me, and my body was bereft in his absence. Everything was off-balance. And like he'd done last time we'd been alone, he turned on his heel and was out the door before I could utter a word.

Numbness took up residence in my heart that afternoon after the Hales left.

Emily cried as she told our parents she thought she was pregnant, but her shame at disappointing them shifted to fear as they confessed how much financial trouble we were in. I emulated Royce and sat eerily still on the patterned couch in the front room, an emotionless expression slathered on my face like the makeup I'd been asked to wear.

It was the first time I'd seen my father break down, and it was unnerving. Once again, I didn't want him to surrender so quickly. Why didn't he fight or defend himself?

Horror splashed across Emily's face as my mother

explained—in between her choked sobs—the deal I'd made with Macalister to try to save us. My sister leaned across the couch and seized my hand in a vise-like grip. "Marist, no. You can't marry him."

My voice was detached. "Sure, I can."

My lack of emotion only increased hers, and panic flooded her face. "*No.*"

"Why not?"

She glanced at our parents before returning her focus to me. "You don't love him, and he's a Hale. They can't love anyone but themselves."

Was that true? Was Royce capable of loving another person, or was he Narcissus? In the myth, he'd refused all others and wasted away staring at the only thing he'd been cursed to love—his own reflection.

"There are worse things than marrying Royce Hale," I said.

"Like what?" she snapped.

I lost the reins on my emotions for a moment. "Oh, I don't know. Being pregnant and homeless?"

Her eyes went white from the pain I'd inflicted, then filled with tears.

"Shit." Shame poured onto my shoulders, weighing me down. "I'm sorry, I didn't mean—"

Emily shook her head, silencing me as she brushed the tears away that had collected in her eyes. I didn't want to be mean. I understood everyone was fragile, but we didn't have time to sit around feeling sorry for ourselves. My parents had squandered that time just as they had their money.

Thanks to Royce's cruel comment about me while I was

in high school, I'd survived on the fringe of high society. I was certain the rest of my family wasn't strong enough to do the same.

If our name was all we had left, then—*fuck*—I'd do everything in my power to keep it.

# SEVEN

DIAMONDS AND SAPPHIRES GLITTERED IN THE GLASS BOX IN front of me, and the modern crystal chandelier overhead sparkled, radiating rainbows down on the carpet. The store was decorated in creams and grays so it wouldn't compete with the breathtaking gems on display. I was at the back, waiting patiently on the edge of my seat for the owner to meet me. For once, traffic had cooperated and the drive into Boston had only taken forty-five minutes, which meant I had arrived early for our appointment.

It forced me to stare at the jewelry locked in the case before me. The gorgeous diamonds were so clear, they looked cold and heavy. Was that how it would feel when Royce slipped an engagement ring on my finger? Like an anchor? I swallowed a breath and tucked a lock of my doomed green hair behind an ear.

"Ms. Northcott?"

The warm, male voice caused me to turn in my seat. "Yes. Sorry, I'm early."

"No, you're fine."

The owner was in his fifties with thinning hair on top, but I liked how he'd buzzed it close rather than grow it long and comb it over. He wore wire-rimmed glasses and a jet-black suit that fit him perfectly.

"I'm Richard Costolli. It's so nice to meet you." When I pushed to my feet, he smiled. "Please, keep your seat. I was honored when your mother called."

"She planned to come, but something came up," I lied. "It's just me. I hope that's okay."

The truth was my mother found this too difficult. It made our dire situation "*too real.*" My blood had run hot through my veins. I was doing everything in my power to bail them out, and I was pissed that still, I was the only responsible one.

"Of course. I hope everything is all right." Mr. Costolli took the empty chair beside me, put one elbow on the glass case, and leaned forward. His expression was full of anticipation.

"Oh," I said, glancing around. "Do I . . ."

"Right here will be fine." His eyes gleamed just as much as the jewelry we were surrounded by. "I'm dying to see it."

I bent down and pulled the blue, leather-bound case from my purse and set it on the glass counter. He ran a hand reverently over the top of the lid, trailing appreciative fingers over the embossed silver logo.

My mother had done the same this morning before handing the box to me, only her fingers had been forlorn, and her eyes filled with unshed tears.

"May I?" he asked, motioning to open it.

I nodded.

There was a sharp intake of breath as he lifted the hinged lid and gazed at the necklace seated on velvet. His voice dropped to a hush. "It's stunning."

"Thank you," I said, my throat tight.

He was absolutely right. The diamond wreath necklace resting below the Harry Winston logo was the most beautiful piece of jewelry I'd ever seen. I'd never worn it, other than the few times growing up when my mother let me try it on.

The diamonds were set so they looked like vines covered in exquisite, faceted ice.

I didn't know why I felt compelled to tell him, but the words tumbled from my mouth. "My great-grandfather surprised my great-grandmother with it to celebrate their twentieth anniversary. She nearly had a heart attack because I'm told he was . . ." I lowered my voice, "well, a cheap bastard."

Mr. Costolli laughed, and I gave a forced smile, not wanting him to see how hard this was.

It must not have worked because he turned serious. His solemn expression said he understood whatever figure the necklace appraised for, its sentimental value to my family would far exceed that.

"My mother only wore it once, on the day she married my father," I added.

Emily and I had both hoped to wear it on our wedding day. I didn't want to sell it, but we were strapped for money, and insuring a necklace that appraised in the six figures was one of the many expenses we had to cut. I needed to soften the fall for my family if I failed to hold up my end of

Macalister's insane deal.

"This is a very special piece," Mr. Costolli said quietly. He pulled out a jeweler's loupe and examined the stones while I retrieved the envelope from my purse that contained all the paperwork he'd need to hold the necklace while it was prepared for auction.

When it was done, I took a final look at the necklace. I tried to ignore the pang of sadness lining my heart as I climbed to my feet. I said my goodbyes to Mr. Costolli, shouldered my purse, and headed for the entrance.

A whisper of something caught my attention. I turned and glanced at the case closest to the door. The rows of engagement rings glinted back, mocking me. I paused then changed course and went to the case.

The settings ran the gamut. Some were simple and understated, and some had no center stone set in them yet. Others were enormous or encrusted with jewels in elaborate designs.

Ever the salesman, Mr. Costolli's tone was light, but hopeful. "See anything you like?"

"Just looking." I gave a vague smile.

I wasn't about to tell him the display filled me with dread. Besides, what I liked was irrelevant. I had no doubt Macalister would have a say in the ring I'd be forced to wear.

After rinsing the dye from my hair, the stylist sat me in his chair and swiveled it away from the mirror, wanting to give me the "grand reveal" when he was done. He'd been blowing out my hair for at least thirty minutes, and every now and again I'd get a flash of a newly-dark lock before it was brushed out of my line of sight.

"I'm sorry, Marist, but this is a mess." Alice Hale stood across from me, clutched my phone in her hand, and used a manicured finger to scroll through my Instagram profile. Each swipe she made only deepened the crease in her forehead. "It's all mythology stuff and random pictures of food. This tells me nothing about you. What's your color story?"

"Color story?" I repeated over the incessant hairdryer.

Alice was classically beautiful. Her look was timeless, with her long blonde hair, big doe eyes, and skin that glowed. I'd swear she had a filter, like I was constantly viewing her through an old timey camera lens. She was luminescent.

Macalister's second wife was ten years younger than he was, barely in her forties, and although she looked like a trophy wife, Alice was anything but. She was the vice president of marketing at HBHC, a creative genius, and one of the few people at the company who didn't cower in fear of the boss. It helped she was sleeping with him.

But being married to Macalister came at a price, and she often searched for it at the bottom of a bottle of vodka. Her last stint at rehab seemed to take, though. She'd been 'on' and focused the whole time we'd been at the salon, and it had taken a while to cut and color my hair.

"Are you ready?" the stylist asked, but I wasn't sure if he was talking to me or to Alice. In any case, he didn't wait for an answer. The chair spun and, as I found my own gaze in the mirror, my lips parted on a deep breath.

"Well?" his voice teemed with pride. "What do you think?"

Alice glanced at my reflection, scrutinized his work, and nodded her approval. "So. Much. Better. Thank you, Sebastian." She leaned over my shoulder, bringing her face beside mine in the mirror. "Now you look like—"

"My sister," I interrupted.

"What?" Alice turned and peered at me with new eyes, considering my statement, but shrugged it off. "No. You look *better* than her."

I had no idea how to feel about that.

Now that my hair was done, the makeup artist on stand-by stepped in like a surgeon waiting for the patient to be transferred to their care. She discussed palettes with Alice, and the women found the perfect day-to-evening look for me, all without having to address me directly. My input was not needed.

I wasn't a tomboy. I liked dresses, and makeup, and feeling feminine, but there was no joy in this unwanted make-over. It wasn't just my appearance, it was my whole persona they were determined to manipulate. To manufacture. I'd had to give her access to all my social media accounts so she could rebrand them.

It left me powerless as she stripped away one thing after another that made me unique. That made me, *me*. As Alice's personal shopper arrived with bags of dresses to try on, each one too sexy, or bold, or edgy . . . anxiety needled up my spine.

If I wasn't careful, I'd become a Stepford wife. My personality would be hollowed out to make room for their brand,

and I'd exist as a shadow of a real woman.

No.

I was determined to play this game until I found a way to beat it.

It wasn't all that warm outside for late May and there was a breeze, but I was already sweating as I walked up to the restaurant and put a clammy hand on the door handle. The air conditioning slammed into me as I stepped inside and caused a shiver.

Or perhaps it was the man waiting in the foyer for me.

Royce had his back to the door, but he sensed my arrival. He turned, and his intense gaze swept down over my frame, taking in the new, repackaged me. My hair was now back to my natural shade, the color of dark chocolate, and had been curled into soft waves. My eyebrows had been waxed into perfect arches.

Other parts of my body were still pink and raw from wax as well, but they were hidden beneath my lace skirt.

I couldn't tell from his expression if he liked my new look, or if his smile was fiction. "You look nice," he said simply.

"Thank you," I parroted back. "You too."

He had on a navy sport coat and a check-patterned shirt over his blue jeans. Business up top and casual below, but at the same time, he looked like he could exist in both worlds without any effort. Maybe Alice had helped him find his day-to-evening look too.

Every pair of eyes in the restaurant was on us as we were led to our table for dinner. Probably not *every* pair, but God, it felt that way.

"Is it just me," I asked over the top of my menu, "or is everyone staring at us?"

Royce was indifferent. "They're staring at you."

His statement rattled me. "Why?"

"Because you're here with me." His gaze never lifted to mine, like he couldn't be bothered. "Or more likely, because you're fucking gorgeous. Who knows?"

Breath halted in my lungs. "You can't just say shit like that."

The leather-bound menu holder dropped onto the table with a thud, and I was met with the full power of Royce's irritated stare. "That you're beautiful? You are. Get over it."

Dismay twisted my lips into a frown. "Please, don't. I don't need bullshit lines from someone like you."

"It's not a line, and . . . someone like me?" More annoyance darted through his eyes, but intrigue too. "What's that supposed to mean?"

How was I going to put it into words? "You're a 'haver.' I mean, you could have any woman in this room if you wanted, and probably some of the guys too. You're young, hot, and filthy rich."

His irritation vanished. It was replaced with an arrogant expression that said none of this was news to him. I pushed forward, gathering steam.

"Me?" I said. "I'm a 'have-not.' I'm sure you didn't intend for it to happen, but when you said I was a nobody, you made it true. No one will touch me."

"I touched you."

He was immune to my scorching glare. "You wanted to know why I was still a virgin last year. Well, there's your answer. You're the reason, Royce. Nobody would be caught dead with me."

He considered the accusation I'd lobbed at him. "You're wrong," he said finally. "I was aware what was going to happen. It's exactly why I said it."

My head turned into a void. "What?"

He leaned over the table to ensure he had my full attention. "I saw you at the bar with your sister that night. You were swaying to the music, all happy, and pretty, and it pissed me off. My father had already laid out plans for me. I was supposed to be with Emily, but that wasn't what *I* wanted."

I clenched the menu in my hands. I sensed where he was going, but I couldn't wrap my head around it. My heart chugged along, thumping loudly in my ears.

"So, yeah. I knew you were behind me when I called you a *nobody*. I did it on purpose, because I couldn't stand you with anyone else. I wanted you for myself."

"Oh, my God." My body flushed hot, although I didn't know if it was with anger or excitement, or a deadly combination of the two.

"I'd tell you I'm sorry if that was hard for you, but honestly?" He tossed a hand up. "I'm not. I take my victories where I can get them, and I don't regret what I had to do to earn it. It's win-at-all-costs in the Hale family. You'll learn that soon enough."

Catching my breath was impossible. "You're making this up."

He looked dubious. "Seriously? Why would I? I went out with Emily once. Did she tell you about it?"

"She said," I swallowed thickly, "you were a jerk."

"Is that it?"

When I didn't answer, he sat back in his chair and crossed his arms, looking at me like I'd just proved his point.

"I wasn't aware that was something you could turn on or off." My tone was dry. "I thought it was a default setting for you."

He chuckled. "See? You're like me. You say what you're thinking, and no one talks to me like that. It's one of the reasons I like you. Everyone else has their nose so far up my family's ass it's uncomfortable."

*One of the reasons.* What were the others? "She also said you had zero chemistry."

The corner of his mouth quirked. "That should have been a dead giveaway. Because you and me, Marist? There's no fucking issue of chemistry. I still remember what you taste like."

Oh, Lord.

I put my hands on the linen tablecloth because the world was spinning too fast and threatened to hurl me off. The naïve part of me wanted to believe everything he'd said, but my brain didn't trust him. He was a master manipulator.

The waitress appeared. "Have you decided?"

"I'm not hungry." Because what I was interested in wasn't on the menu.

Royce gave her a strained smile. "We'll each have the filet, medium rare, with a Caesar salad." He snatched up the wine list and pointed to an entry. "And this bottle of wine, please."

She was gone almost instantly.

"I said I'm not hungry," I repeated.

"And this is supposed to be a date, not a business meeting, so maybe start acting like it."

Our evening tonight was to lay the groundwork that Royce and I were a couple, so when our engagement was announced next month it'd be less of a shock. Cape Hill wasn't large, and news of our evening would spread quickly.

Especially since the girl two tables over from us had snapped a picture. It was probably already up on Instagram.

At least, if it fit in with the girl's color story.

"It'd be more believable if you didn't look like you hate my guts," he added.

"I don't," I said and frowned. "Honestly? I have no idea how to feel about you."

A playful expression crossed his face. "I think you like me. You just don't want to."

"God, you're cocky."

He grinned widely, and I did my best not to let it get to me. A weaker woman would have swooned at that smile. "It's not cocky," he said, "if you can back it up."

I rolled my eyes. "That's exactly what a cocky person would say."

He laughed. It was a pleasant sound. "Can I tell you something?"

"Go for it."

"You look great," he said, "but I miss the green hair."

The momentary lightness in me faded. "Yeah, well, it wasn't exactly your father's cup of tea, was it?"

The muscles along his jaw flexed like he was gritting his teeth. "Nothing is. You'll get used to it after a while."

Although the way he'd said it made me think otherwise. Like Royce was still struggling not to disappoint his father. I ran my fingers along the edge of my silverware. "You said you were protecting me the other day."

His expression glazed over. "I don't want to talk about it."

I sighed. I was so very tired already, when I knew I still had a long way to go. "Please? Can we be honest with each other and—"

"Everything I have was given to me," Royce said. "He never stops reminding me and Vance of that. It all came from him, and he can take it away from us at any time."

His hard, serious expression made my insides cold.

"Which means," he continued, "everything that's mine? It's *his*, according to him." His gaze captured mine and refused to let go. "So, if I show an interest in something—let's say a particular Northcott sister—he might decide to take her away from me, just because he wants to make sure I remember who's in charge."

"Holy shit." Every muscle in me locked up. I had my doubts about a lot of things he'd said, but this I believed. Royce liked to mess with people, and he'd learned it from his father.

Macalister was Zeus. He fucked with the mortals just for the fun of it.

For *sport*.

Which meant everything was more dangerous than I realized. If Macalister decided to "take me away" from Royce, that meant the deal would be off and my family would be left with nothing. Anxiety fluttered in my chest. I would have to depend on the man sitting across from me to guide us through the next few weeks.

"We shouldn't talk about it right now." Royce's gaze dropped to the table and focused on something. "He has at least a spy or two here."

He plucked a non-existent piece of lint from his sleeve and flicked it away. It'd been a normal gesture, but I didn't miss his meaning. He'd used it to motion toward the couple sitting a few tables away.

One of whom was the girl who'd taken a picture of us. The idea of spies sounded ridiculous, but the Hales had a stupid amount of money, and it made them paranoid.

The wine arrived. I sat awkwardly still as the server poured Royce a sample, and my gaze followed the swirl of the red wine in his glass before it was set against his lips. When his throat bobbed with a swallow, a pulse deep between my legs mirrored it. Was that why he'd made a move on me in the library last year? Had he been sampling me? Making sure he wanted to buy the entire bottle?

He nodded his approval to the waitress and the wine was poured in both our glasses, and he didn't speak again until she was gone.

"Come home with me tonight."

I choked on my wine, coughing and sputtering.

"So we can talk about it freely," he offered over the rim of his glass.

Oh, he was smooth. My body clambered for it, but I shoved the desire down. "Right." My tone was drier than the wine. "Talk."

He sounded innocent, but his smile was sinful. "Did you have something else in mind?"

I crossed my arms and leaned on the table, not allowing myself to slide into his trap. "Do you think that's a good idea? I thought we didn't want to give your father the wrong impression."

He waved his hand dismissively. "It's fine. He knows I'm not going to fuck you."

The wine in my glass sloshed as I jerked. "What?"

It was amazing how I wasn't interested in that . . . until it was suddenly off the table. "Do you need board approval for that too?"

Darkness seeped into his eyes and turned them stormy, but he slowly blinked it away. "No. I don't fuck on the first date."

It was a lie. I knew it not because rumors were legendary about how fast he could get in a girl's pants, but from his stiff posture and the fist he'd unknowingly clenched on the tabletop. Interesting. Whatever the truth was, he didn't want to say, or perhaps he couldn't. Maybe I'd get more out of him when we were away from the invasive eyes of Cape Hill.

"All right." And then I said the words I never expected to utter in my lifetime. "I'll go home with you, Royce."

# EIGHT

I FOLLOWED THE BLACK TOWN CAR DOWN THE LONG DRIVEWAY, circled the fountain, and parked in the empty space beside the garage that had once been the Hale carriage house. I'd offered to give Royce a ride in my Porsche Cayenne and let his driver leave early, but his phone had chimed as we were leaving the restaurant. He'd said he had to make a work call to straighten someone out and he'd meet me at the house.

I was a little relieved he'd declined. It gave me time on the drive over to rerun the evening, regroup, and prepare. Once I'd agreed to come home with him, our conversation had turned to lighter topics. We knew the heavier stuff was to come later.

He didn't ask about my family, so I didn't ask about his.

We talked about his job and mine. I volunteered as a tutor at the community college over the summer, mostly to look good on my resume, but I enjoyed it. We chatted about my classes at Etonsons and other safe things like music and movies. It wasn't . . . unpleasant. For me, conversation came easier with him than it did with others.

He walked toward my car as I climbed out. He'd taken off his sport coat and folded it over an arm, but rather than look relaxed, he seemed anxious. His hair was mussed, like he'd run a hand through it in frustration.

"Everything okay?" I asked.

"Fine." His tone said otherwise, and I gave him an expectant look. He let out a breath. "There's some stock I bought recently, and it's underperforming. My broker wasn't paying attention, so we had to have a conversation about it." Like this was a normal problem for a twenty-five-year-old to have. He tipped his head toward the front door. "Come on."

I walked beside him up the stone staircase and tried not to think that this might someday be my home. *Our* home. Unease churned in my stomach. As we got close to the front door, there was a metal click as the lock disengaged with his keycard.

The entryway was quiet and dark as we stepped inside. "What, no one is going to announce me?"

Royce quirked an eyebrow in a silent question.

"Last time I was here—your graduation party? There was a man at the door, announcing everyone when they came in."

He gave a short, amused laugh. "Yeah, that sounds like some pretentious shit my family would do."

He was halfway up the grand staircase before he realized I hadn't followed. He stopped and turned, one foot on the step above the other, casting his intense look down on me. He was framed perfectly on the stairs, and if my heart weren't already racing, this would have made it. He was a beautiful man, surrounded by danger.

"Where are you going?" My voice came out sounding unsure, and I hated it. What if Macalister was up there? No amount of work could mentally prepare me for it.

"My room," he said. When I didn't move, he took in a deep breath. "Just to talk, Marist. We can go to the kitchen if you want, but I'm pretty sure everyone's home."

Meaning he wouldn't be able to say everything he wanted.

I nodded, placed a hand on the smooth banister, and made my way up to join him on the landing. I followed him as he led us deep into the heart of the house, not knowing which room was his. Was last year the first time I'd been upstairs? Most of the times I'd come here, it'd been for some event, and they were usually held in the gardens out back. His graduation party would have been too, except it had rained.

We passed several guest bedrooms as we made our way to the end of the hall, and then a closed door on the right. "Vance's room," Royce said. "Although he's probably in the theater room downstairs, playing PlayStation. His door has to stay closed because Lucifer isn't allowed in there."

"Lucifer?" Was this some sort of cruel nickname for someone on his staff?

"As in the devil?" A smile hinted on Royce's lips as he put a hand on the small of my back and guided me through the open doorway to the left.

"Actually, in mythology, Lucifer is the morning star."

The room he'd led me into looked like a luxury hotel. The walls were paneled in rich, dark wood. There was a sitting area with a light gray couch, a black coffee table in the middle, and two chairs upholstered in smoke gray on the other side. Beyond that was the king-sized bed. Its linens and headboard were done in the same light-to-dark gray scheme. Even the sleeping black cat curled into a perfect circle at the foot of the bed matched.

When Royce shut the door and closed us in, the cat lifted its head and gazed at me with apple-green eyes. It scrutinized me with a discerning look then moved on to the man. A half-second later it was on its feet, vaulting toward him and landing on the carpet with a soft *meow*. Like a dog who was happy to see its owner, the cat hurried to him and brushed against his leg.

"Are you allergic?" Royce tossed his sport coat onto one of the chairs. It was so his hands were free and he could reach down to grab the cat.

"No," I said.

"Vance is." I'd expected him to go to the door and set the cat outside of his room, but instead he held it in his arms and scratched its cheeks.

"This is Lucifer?" My brain short-circuited while watching him with the gorgeous cat, who was clearly loving the attention. A loud, steady purr rumbled from the animal.

"Yeah. My father hates him."

"I'm surprised he lets Alice keep him."

When he set the cat down, Lucifer wasn't pleased. He snaked between Royce's legs, meowing his protests. "He's not Alice's."

That was . . . surprising. "Really? You don't strike me as a cat person."

He lifted a shoulder in a shrug and motioned toward the sitting area. "I found this kitten beside the dumpster outside my college apartment. His back leg was broken." His tone turned playful. "Fucker cost three grand at the vet and sheds everywhere, but the upside is—as I mentioned—my father hates him."

Royce dropped down onto the couch, which was more of a loveseat and didn't leave much room for me. Not unless I wanted to sit close. I eyed the chair across from him and took it. "That's an upside?"

Lucifer looked delighted Royce's lap was unoccupied and immediately jumped onto the couch. The miniature panther draped himself across one of Royce's legs, demanding more attention.

As he stroked the cat, Royce's gaze didn't leave mine. "I like to go off-script sometimes."

The way he stared at me charged the room with electricity. His subtext was clear. Like this cat, I was not in the first draft of his scripted life, but he was happy with the revision. I crossed my legs, feeling uncomfortably hot and exposed. And *needy*.

"Well," my voice was unnaturally tight, "you've got the whole villain look working for you with that cat on your lap. Like you're plotting world domination."

"I have been for a long time."

I laughed, although I got the feeling he wasn't joking. I teased, "Have you?"

"When my father steps down, I'll be the head of HBHC." His gaze dropped to the cat who stretched, revealing his claws as he did one paw and then the other before curling back into place. "Everything I've done is so that will happen. My whole life has been leading up to it, and it's been the only thing I've wanted for so long, I don't know if I can care about anything else." Royce's tone was deathly serious. "I want to be honest. You should know what you're getting with me."

Pressure squeezed my body, turning me immobile.

My sister's words flitted through my mind. *Hales can't love anyone but themselves.* Even here in Royce's bedroom, it felt cold and impersonal. There weren't photographs of his family, not even his mother who'd died when he was young. Just the pet, who seemed to be a tool of defiance against his father.

But . . . I appreciated him being upfront. Macalister had said marriage was an important partnership, and I believed it. I wouldn't want to work with someone who didn't respect me or refused to see me as an equal. I believed Royce did.

"You took my father's deal for a reason," he said, "and the same is true for me. Securing my future as the head of the company is all that matters." His hand froze mid-stroke on Lucifer's back. "There are a lot of hoops I still have to jump through, now and even after I'm on the board, and . . . I'm going to need your help."

I swallowed a breath. "How so?"

"Win at all costs is the Hale family motto, so there will be times I'm going to say or do things you're not going to like." His expression was resigned, like a doctor delivering tough news. "I'll be mean, Marist. Maybe even awful. I'll tell lies, and when this is all over? You might think I'm worse than my father."

My hands, which had been resting in my lap, tensed into fists and my mouth went dry.

"But," he continued, "you'll know it's lies. Anything I say or do when other people are around, don't believe it. That's not me. It's a character I've invented to help me win the game. The person I am with you is different than the one outside."

*Whoa.* I sipped in air through my parted lips. He'd already shown me this a little, hadn't he? That day of the dreadful luncheon, he'd been a completely different person in my family's sitting room when it had been just been the two of us. His night-and-day personality was by design.

"You have to adapt constantly if you want to survive. You never know with my father, because he can change his mind in an instant, and everything he's promised? It's gone. He says he's a man of his word, but it's always going to be your word against his, and who do you think wins there?"

"He does."

Royce threaded a hand through his hair, which fell back into its perfectly messy style. "You're smart, Marist. I probably don't need to tell you, but you should do the same. Be the girl he wants when people are watching. When it's just you and me? You can be the girl I found in my library with green hair, buried in a book when there was a party going on downstairs." He gave me the full intensity of his stare, the one that saw all the way into the depths of me. "You can just be *you.*"

"Okay," I whispered. There was no other answer. I was vaguely aware I was sliding under his spell, but I was powerless to stop it.

I hadn't noticed the tension he was holding in his shoulders until he released it on a heavy breath. "Good."

There was a series of windows on the far wall, and since the sun was setting, the garden lights outside flickered on, catching my attention. A century ago, the sprawling acres of the Hale estate might have been cornfields, but now they were landscaped gardens and a meticulously maintained hedge maze.

When I was little, I'd hunted for eggs in the maze every Easter Sunday with my sister and the other HBHC executives' kids. The golden egg had five grand in it, but I'd never been lucky or fast enough to find it.

As a girl, I'd been insanely jealous of Royce and Vance. If I'd had a hedge maze in my back yard, I'd have played in it all day. I'd have lived my *Labyrinth* fantasies with Jareth the Goblin King and never come out when my parents called. Neither of the Hale boys seemed to care about the maze at all. Maybe they'd seen *The Shining* too many times.

I hadn't seen the gardens or the hedge maze from this vantagepoint before. It was much bigger than I would have thought. The exterior was square, but the maze had curves and lines and dead-ends decorated with statues or stone urns. The thick, evergreen hedges were well over six feet tall, separated by narrow pebble paths, and in the center, a three-tiered water fountain glowed.

The carefully executed maze was a daunting work of art.

Even now, a part of me still longed to go searching for David Bowie, where he'd seduce me into being his queen and take me to the masquerade ball.

Royce leaned back and cast an arm over the back of the couch, relaxing. It looked like an invitation, and I wasn't opposed to it. The deal had been made. There was no harm in enjoying the benefits.

"This won't be easy," he said. "If you ever need anything, just say the word. I'll do my best to help."

"Okay." I lifted my chin and smoothed my hands down my skirt. "You can actually help right now."

He gave me a questioning look.

"I waited a year, Royce. Touch me."

His blue eyes widened with surprise, then heated. A seductive smile spread slowly on his lips. He tipped his head down toward his lap, then back to me in a gesture that said, *what are you waiting for?*

I shook my head. There was a cat currently where I wanted to be, plus this was a power move. I'd given up so much already in this deal. He could give up something.

"Oh, you want me to come to you?" His tone was silk.

He was the only person besides myself who'd made me come, and my sex-starved body demanded his attention. I wasn't a prude. I was very interested in learning about sex and had no one to explore it with, and that was mostly his fault. My frustration had reached critical mass.

"You owe me."

"I do," he agreed.

He undid the button of one of his cuffs and worked back the sleeve. One careful fold, then another, moving at a painstaking, deliberate pace to roll up his sleeve. And when that one was done, he did the other, watching me the entire time.

Seeing him prepare to touch me was the most delicious kind of foreplay I could imagine. Lust coiled inside me, winding tight as a spring. He rose from the couch and moved toward me, a stalking predator, and I was his prey too enamored to run. When I uncrossed my legs, he licked his lips, and the pull in my center was so acute, it verged on pain.

God, how I wanted him.

When I absolutely shouldn't.

He'd literally told me he'd never put me first, and here I was, throwing myself at him anyway. Begging for his hands on my body.

He leaned over and gripped each armrest of my chair, trapping me beneath him. He looked down his long nose at me, his eyes gleaming like the Big Bad Wolf. "Do you still taste as good as I remember, Marist?"

"Find out," I ordered.

There was just a flash of his smile, all sharp teeth, before his lips crashed to mine. It ignited a fire between us that instantly burned so hot I worried I'd vaporize. His hands were in my hair and his tongue filled my mouth, and every cell in me cried out with relief.

"*Fuck*," he groaned, catching his breath before going back for more. His knees thudded to the carpet before me, and inside I was dying. Kissing me had literally brought Royce Hale to his knees. It was ridiculous and wonderful.

No one would believe it.

I could barely, and I was witnessing it firsthand.

His mouth moved against my lips, persuasive and commanding. His tongue slicked over mine, and when I moaned, he jerked me closer to the edge of the chair. My legs parted around his hips, and the champagne-colored lace skirt I wore rode high across my thighs.

It'd been a year since we'd kissed, but our bodies remembered. He curled a hand under my knee and pulled me closer still, until there was no space left and we were connected, his chest to my heaving chest.

His palm remained against the bare skin of my leg as he waged war with his mouth. He tasted like sex. Like uncontrolled, dangerous desire. And as his hand inched up my thigh, he ratcheted up the intensity of his brutal kiss.

Everything was moving too fast and not fast enough. My heart raced like a jet engine, but his fingers moved at an irritatingly slow crawl. I ripped my mouth away from his and sucked in a ragged breath, only for him to steal it when his hand curved inward, going exactly where I wanted it to.

"Better?" he asked on a low, husky voice. He wasn't breathing as hard as I was, but he did struggle. He brushed a thumb over my panties, massaging me through the thin fabric.

"*Yes*," I hissed.

Thanks to Alice and her salon of torture, I'd had my first ever Brazilian wax this afternoon. I was still a little warm and tender, but I'd grin and bear it. I was too desperate not to.

"Such patience, waiting for me." He nipped at my earlobe.

I growled it out. "You better make it worth it."

A sound of amusement drifted from him, but he made a silent promise with each fiery kiss he dropped in a line down the side of my neck. Lust was thick, choking the air swirling around us.

"Sit back," he commanded.

I swallowed thickly, and as soon as I was slumped against the chair back, he followed my command. I'd ordered him to touch me, and he delivered. He slid a hand beneath the hem of the silk top I was wearing and coursed his palm over my trembling stomach. As his hand moved up, so did my top, bunching over his forearm and revealing more of my skin.

Royce had one hand on my bra and the other on my underwear, massaging and teasing, but it was his dark, focused gaze that possessed me. I'd sold myself to him, and this was the first moment I felt truly owned.

I didn't mind the feeling. I liked it, maybe a little.

His lips were turned up in a shadow of a smile. He spent so much of his life under his father's command—did he revel in having control over someone else? Getting to give the orders rather than having to follow?

I arched into his hands, stretching and writhing and needing his touch to survive. The cup of my bra was pulled down and my pebbled nipple exposed to him. First to his gaze, then his fingers to pinch, and lastly his hot mouth.

"Oh," I sighed.

It felt good, and even better when he hummed his satisfaction. I'd had fantasies about this on nights when I was tired and weak, and just wanted to get myself off quickly. That was the only time I'd allowed myself to think about Royce over the last year. But those fantasies weren't nearly as good as this.

I stared in fascination as his tongue explored my flesh. It flicked my nipple, and I felt the snap of pleasure *everywhere*.

His fingers pressed to me, deep in the cleft between my legs, and the steady slide back and forth caused goosebumps to lift on my thighs. Heat built and swelled from his touch.

"Jesus, you're sexy," he murmured when I swiveled my hips, wanting more friction, and his statement went straight to my head. He'd said his words would be lies when other people were around, so did that mean I'd always get the truth when we were alone together?

He jerked the crotch of my panties to the side and plunged a finger deep inside me in one swift move. The shocking invasion made me ball his shirt into my fists, pulling so hard I was lucky I didn't rip the buttons. The stretch of his thick finger was uncomfortable but followed immediately by warmth and satisfaction. "Oh, oh, *oh!*"

His lips curled in a victorious smile as he sat back on his heels, focusing on his task. He used one hand to hold my panties out of his way and thumb my clit, while he turned the other palm up to the ceiling and eased his middle finger in and out of me.

"So smooth," he commented.

Because he was looking at the most intimate part of me, all bare and exposed. He sounded appreciative, and that made sense, didn't it? Wasn't my forced makeover today partially for him?

He worked his finger in and out of me, moving faster with each thrust, until my whimpers and gasps weren't the only sound in the room. Wet skin slid through wet skin, and the slick noise heated my cheeks. I was so turned on. Was that normal? I threaded my hands into my newly-dark hair and closed my eyes, unable to watch for a moment. I needed a break from the sight that was so erotic, I was going to tip over.

And I wasn't ready to lose control.

I wanted this to last. To be able to commit it to memory, because every moment with Royce was full of peril. If Macalister found me lacking in any way, all this would be over. He'd take Royce from me and give him someone else to play with.

That thought made my eyes pop open. I didn't want that. I shook on the deal and had promised myself to Royce, but that meant he belonged to me too. I reeled until I found his gaze, which was locked on to me. He was enjoying watching the pleasure wring through my body and twist on my face.

As if it weren't enough, he bent and brushed his lips on the inside of my thigh, close to my knee. It was a chaste, sweet kiss, and the juxtaposition with what his hands were doing made me spiral. Up I went, climbing toward the end I wasn't ready for.

Tremors bubbled up my legs, and he knew he was the cause. A deep smile widened on his lips. "You like this?"

I didn't answer his rhetorical question. I simply hung on to his shoulders, my fingers twisting the dress shirt fabric as I hopelessly chased my breath. My pulse roared in my ears and my vision narrowed.

His finger pushed deeper, reaching somewhere new, and coupled with his insistent thumb rolling on my clit, I was doomed. When I gave a sharp gasp, he sank his teeth into the spot he'd just kissed on my thigh, and this soft, playful bite pushed me over the edge. My toes curled inside my sandals as my body jerked, overwhelmed with sensations.

I came—and left no doubt about it—because I shuddered wildly and let loose a bliss-soaked cry. It was a half-sob wrenched from my chest like part of me was dying and being reborn.

He stilled as the orgasm rocked through me in waves and slowly subsided.

When I returned to reality, he was waiting patiently on his knees, and my heart thudded faster, skipping a beat.

"That wasn't very good," I whispered. "Try again."

He laughed, and the deep, warm sound was addictive. "You're so full of shit." His eyes were alight with humor, but sex simmered as well.

I pulled my top back into place but was interrupted when he yanked me into a surprising kiss. It was blistering. Mind-numbing. I could do nothing but tilt my head and receive it. I'd expected lust from Royce, but not passion. I thought he'd be the hurried and inconsiderate prince of Cape Hill, but as he'd admitted—that wasn't *him*. I'd only met the real version of Royce a handful of times.

This version was . . . easier to imagine marrying.

Kissing, along with most things involving boys, wasn't something I was practiced in, and he seemed content to let me find my way. I strayed from his lips, moving over his cheek, and enjoyed the sensation of his whisker-dotted skin.

I had a flash of him standing at a bathroom sink, shirtless with a jaw covered in shaving cream and a razor gleaming in his hand. He'd probably done it right before our date because his skin was soft and smooth until I went against the grain. Someday soon, perhaps I'd see that domestic, every-day image for real. That thought should have scared the hell out of me.

But it didn't.

I used the tip of my tongue to trace the edge of his ear, mimicking the techniques he'd used on me. Satisfaction swelled as he let out a soft sigh. His hands tightened on my waist and pressed me into him . . .

So I could feel every inch of my effect.

It was powerful and intoxicating, and the courage that had waned after my orgasm started anew. I pushed a hand down his chest, tracing the line of buttons on his shirt as I headed for his belt, and appreciated the hardened form of his muscles beneath my palm.

He smelled like pine trees and something else. Like I imagined sex and desire would if they had a fragrance.

"You smell so good," I whispered into the crook of his neck. I hadn't intended to say that out loud, but my brain-to-mouth filter wasn't operating at full capacity. I'd given exactly one hand job in my life, and I was pretty sure it hadn't been good. I wanted to be better.

When I eased my hand between our bodies and traced the outline of him with my fingertips, his heavy breath filled my ear. He held perfectly still as I cupped him through his jeans and brushed my palm over the bulge.

Was my touch too timid? He reached down and placed his hand on top of mine, making me hesitate. Alarm shot up my back. Was he stopping me because I'd done something wrong?

No. He held on to my hand as he stood and then used it to help pull me up to my feet as well. He'd grown tired of kneeling, I realized, as he led me to the couch.

"Get lost, cat," he said.

Lucifer lifted his head, eyed his master, and begrudgingly jumped down from the couch when Royce gave him a gentle nudge. Once the cockblocking cat was gone, Royce sat and tugged me down beside him. He guided my hand back to where it had been, encouraging me to use more pressure.

As I leaned over, he slipped a hand behind my head and resumed kissing my neck. It was seductive. He used his tongue and the edge of his teeth, and bliss buzzed through me as a fast-acting drug.

He undid his belt with one hand and unzipped his fly, giving me better access while also making it clear what he wanted. I was happy he was taking the lead. Would he mind giving me more direction if I asked?

"So, um . . ." I whispered as I slipped my hand inside his undone jeans, caressing him through the soft, black underwear he wore. "You might have to tell me what to do. This will be the second hand job I've ever given, and the first one was subpar."

A laugh cut off in his throat as he froze. "Subpar," he repeated in disbelief. But then Royce was there, cupping my hand and guiding me again to stroke him. "Not fucking possible, unless you tried to squeeze his dick off." His lips against the side of my neck curved into a smile. "Did you?"

My eyebrows pulled together. "I don't think so."

"Show me how hard your grip was."

I did.

"Oh, you're adorable." He licked a line up to my ear, drawing a shudder from me. His voice was encouraging and persuasive. "Do it like you mean it."

He jerked down the waistband of his underwear, and his dick popped free. I palmed it and was surprised at the soft skin, yet how rigid he was beneath. Stone sheathed in velvet. I closed my fingers around him.

"Harder," he encouraged in a hush.

His palm moved to my wrist and urged me to slide up and down. The thick head of his dick pushed through my fist as I pumped back and forth on long strokes. I sat up so I could do it better.

His chest moved rapidly on his quickening breath, and the muscle along his jaw ticked. Royce's eyes hazed. This was more reaction than I'd gotten last time, so I was doing something right.

"Who was it?" he asked between two heavy breaths. "The guy you were with?"

Was I supposed to talk about someone else when I had a guy's dick in my hand? "Uh . . . Richard Shaunessy."

"Liam's son?"

I'd forgotten Richard's father was a board member. I bit my lip. "Yeah. It was one time, and he wasn't—"

"Nope." Royce's tone was clipped. "I don't need to know. I shouldn't have asked."

Richard had been my prom date my senior year. We'd gone as friends, but when I'd made a move that night in the back of the limo, he hadn't refused. Halfway into it, he'd explained we couldn't tell anyone. *It'll be our little secret,* he'd said. His embarrassment of me had been such a turn-off, I'd told him I'd changed my mind, and that his micropenis would *be our little secret.*

Surprisingly, Richard and I hadn't spoken since that night.

Royce wasn't nervous or shy. In fact, I'd been the one last time to demand we couldn't tell anyone. It didn't seem to bother him.

It was hard to move my hand inside his jeans. I grabbed the undone sides of his pants and tugged hesitantly. "Is it okay if I—"

One corner of his mouth turned up in a sly smile. "Yeah."

He slipped his hands under the waistbands, lifted his hips, and down everything went. As I gazed at his nakedness, I sensed his gaze burning right back into me. He was curious what my reaction would be, and I was . . . just curious. Tan legs gave way to lighter thighs in an ombre effect.

He was beautiful like this.

"Hmm, okay," he said, grinning widely as I moved off the couch and onto my knees before him.

"It seems like it'll be easier this way."

His eyes were electric. "Please know I'm not complaining."

I smiled as I used both hands to grip him. "Are two hands okay? Or too much?"

He sucked in an enormous breath, but his words were still tight with satisfaction. "No, that's good."

Since his pants were down around his ankles, it made it difficult to kneel right between his legs, but it was better than leaning awkwardly over him. I stroked both hands together from tip to base, and back up again.

"Tighter, if you can," he said softly. I clamped my hands and dragged my fists down. He groaned and tipped his head back. "*Fuck*. Atta-girl."

*Oh, my God.* I snickered. I was on my knees with a guy I didn't really know, his dick was in my hands, and I wasn't sure what I was doing. This was supposed to be awkward. Or hot and heavy. It wasn't supposed to be intimate like this or enjoyable in this way. His easy, supportive attitude gave me the confidence to keep going.

His hips moved subtly with the tempo of my hands, but his chest? That moved much faster. He sighed and shuddered as I twisted my hands. I wrung a moan from his lips when I let one hand drift lower and explore, cupping him. His hands were splayed on the couch cushions, but they curled into fists as I worked him over.

I'd thought the sight of his finger sliding inside me was hot, but this? Him throbbing in my hands as I stroked him, all while he struggled to hold in his moans, was lightyears beyond that sexy scene. It forced me to squeeze my knees together, and an aftershock of pleasure shot through my center.

"Faster." The word from him danced the line between an order and a desperate plea.

I picked up my rhythm. Dark satisfaction sped through me as he lost the battle and a loud, deep groan slipped past his restraint. He seemed to like it went I paid attention to the tip, so I brushed my thumb over the head, swirling around the drops of moisture there.

He said it as a warning. "Keep that up and you're gonna make me come."

I stared up at him. "Can I put it in my mouth first?"

He jerked in my grasp. "Fuck, Marist." His smile was brilliant. "Did I create a monster when I asked you to wait?"

I slowed to a stop, letting him pulse in my grip. "I thought I already was. You said I was Medusa."

"Wait." His face went blank and his body tense.

I was stunned he was being indecisive about my offer, but I was even more shocked when he abruptly stood and yanked at his pants. The action knocked me backward, and I fell on my ass with a hard thud. I glared up at him, but he ignored me. Instead, he hurried to do up his zipper and re-fasten his belt.

I hadn't heard the approaching footsteps, but the abrupt knock on Royce's door was loud and short.

It was the only warning we got. I had just enough time to turn and see the door swing open, revealing Macalister Hale standing in the hall.

# NINE

Royce was twenty-five, but age didn't seem to matter when he was being caught by a parent. He sank onto the couch, snatched up a throw pillow, and set it in his lap to cover his erection.

Abandoned on the floor, I scrambled to my feet, and my face flamed to a million degrees. So much for protecting me. Yes, I had all my clothes on, but it was obvious what we'd been doing the moment before his father appeared.

Macalister surveyed the room the same way I assumed he'd search for a redundant employee to fire. His gaze missed nothing as he stood in the doorway, one hand still on the doorknob. He had on slacks and a button-down shirt, and it was the closest to a relaxed outfit I'd seen him in.

"I came to ask how your dinner went," he said, "but I see it's still going."

The sharp edge of his words gave me a thousand invisible cuts. I dropped my gaze to the floor, wanting to find a throw pillow like Royce had, only one big enough so I could hide behind it completely.

"Yeah," Royce said, acting disinterested. He threw his arm over the back of the couch with the same ease he'd had with me earlier. "We were just talking."

I traced the pattern on the rug, but the tense, heavy silence said Macalister wasn't buying his son's bullshit. A blast of cold wafted over me, and I knew his focus had shifted my direction.

"Alice showed me pictures, but since you're here, Marist, let's have a look at you."

My gaze crept hesitantly back up. I was frayed and raw but did my best to stand straight and meet Macalister in the eye, whether I was ready for his evaluation or not. I had no idea what making out with Royce had done to my hair or makeup, or if his father would notice my flushed cheeks and kiss-swollen mouth.

I'd bet money he did—if I had any money to my name.

Macalister's eyes were blue like his sons', but much darker. They were the color of the Atlantic in January, and just like the ocean, they were volatile. They could be calm one minute and ferocious the next. They were intriguing and haunting. His gaze tore down from my dark hair to my newly pedicured toes, and then worked its way back up at a measured pace.

"Turn," he said.

I was a purchase being assessed, and it was humiliating, but Royce's advice played on a constant loop in my mind.

*Be the girl he wants you to be.*

I forced out a smile and turned slowly in place, an

expensive toy on display, spun so he could see the details from all angles. When I came back around, I felt just as hollow as the smile on his face.

I was the girl who didn't care what anyone thought, and with a cruel twist of fate, now this man's opinion meant everything. So much rode on it.

"Very nice," he said. "Alice worked a miracle."

Tension snapped through me, but I didn't react. It was like my spine had broken but as long as I stood perfectly still, no one else would know. I could hold myself together with the strength of the shell of my body.

As the quiet stretched in the room, it became evident he was waiting for a response from me.

"Thank you," I bit out.

"I'm sorry I interrupted your evening."

"It's fine." Royce sounded bored. "She was just leaving."

*What,* I almost demanded, but caught myself in time. He'd switched so fast into the other version of himself I had whiplash, but he'd had years of practice. He was an expert at it by now.

I straightened and tried not to look uncomfortable. "Yes. Thank you for dinner."

He rose reluctantly from the couch. "I'll walk you to your car."

Macalister followed us down the hall until we reached the landing at the top of the staircase. "Good night, Marist," he said.

I held in the shiver at my name in his voice. "Good night, Mr. Hale."

"You may call me Macalister. We might be family one day, after all." It sounded like a threat.

I nodded since my throat had closed up, preventing me from speaking. I turned and controlled my descent down the stairs when I wanted to run. His calculating gaze bore into my back as I took every step, and I felt it in the marrow of my bones all the way home.

The headquarters of the HBHC was a rather plain-looking tower of steel and glass, but it had a strange greenish tint to it, like it had been stained with the same ink that was used to print money. The building didn't stand out from the other skyscrapers in downtown Boston, but it was easy to identify by the glowing red and black logo at the top.

There were glass elevators in each corner of the building, and sometimes from the street you could see them whisking people up and down, but only the executives with offices on the top floors were allowed to use them. The rest of the employees used the bank of elevators in the middle of the tower.

A week ago, I would have been thrilled with a job offer from HBHC after graduating from Etonsons. I would have strived to work my way toward a glass elevator job, just like my father had. But now, as I sat waiting in the atrium of the building, my future was unclear.

*Perhaps being Royce's wife will be your only job.*

I stared glumly at the water feature in the center of the atrium. It was a glass wall with the HBHC logo etched on it and water cascading down both sides. The water flowed in waves, rippling down the glass, and it was a nice effect. Pretty and—

*Oh, shit.*

I dug my phone out, flipped to the camera app and snapped a few pictures of the water wall. I'd been busy yesterday helping my students find different tutors since Alice demanded I quit my summer job. I'd forgotten all about her Instagram assignment.

I held the phone at a crazy angle, hoping for an artistic shot when my father appeared. He put his hands in the pockets of his suit pants, like he wasn't sure what else to do with them. "Sorry for making you wait. The morning meeting ran long."

"It's all right." I stood, and my father's eyes widened.

He gazed at the outfit Alice had instructed me to wear today. It was a white, sleeveless blouse with pin-tuck details at the neckline and paired with a navy skirt and nude heels.

"You look nice."

I pasted on a smile. "Thanks, Dad."

"Come on. I'll take you up."

We rode in the glass elevator, and all the space we didn't take up was filled with my father's shame. I hated how everything had changed between us. No matter how much I wanted to, I'd never be able to see him as I once had. My parents' lie had cost so much more than just money.

The elevator car stopped one floor from the top, and my father navigated us through the hallways until we reached Alice's assistant's desk.

"Since you're already in the city," he said, "do you want to grab lunch when you're done?"

No, I didn't. I was sure as soon as my appointment was over, I'd want to get the fuck out of the building. When I hesitated, hurt washed over his expression.

I gave him a sad smile, trying to show he wasn't the cause. "I'd like to, but I don't have any idea how long this will take."

"Okay, I understand." My father straightened the coat sitting on his shoulders as he prepared to head to his office. "Text me if you change your mind." His gaze flitted to Alice's office door. "Good luck."

"Thanks."

He put a hand on my arm to give me support, and then he was gone, moving down the hall. His posture indicated the guilt he was carrying was heavy. I tried not to think about it. I needed to focus.

"Hi," I said to the pretty woman seated at the desk across from Alice's office. "I'm Marist Northcott. I have a ten-thirty with—"

"Go right in." The woman waved her hand toward the door. "She's ready for you."

Too bad I was nowhere near ready for her. But I rapped my knuckles on the door anyway, waited for Alice's permission, and when it was granted, I turned the handle.

Her office was exactly how I expected it to be. It belonged on Pinterest boards and Instagram feeds. The side wall was all windows with natural light and a view of the bay. Her workspace was organized and tastefully decorated in soothing grays and greens. Even the clutter on her side table felt 'right,' as if it had been placed just so.

*Manufactured.*

"Oh." Alice froze mid-step and a frown cast on her face. "What are you wearing?"

I glanced down, checking to make sure my clothes hadn't magically changed during the elevator ride up. "Um . . . I thought this was what you said I should wear."

"Hmm." She evaluated my outfit and tucked two fingers under her chin. "That white's not right on you. You look washed out."

She pointed to one of the chairs in front of her desk, indicating where I should sit as she moved to the closet. A few backup outfits on hangers hung there, over bins with labels on them. She rifled through her choices and selected an ivory top.

"I think we're close enough in size, this should work." She thrust the silk fabric into my hands.

I stared down at it, then lifted my gaze to her. She peered back at me impatiently.

*Oh, God.* "You want me to change right now?"

Her expression said I was being weird, and the idea of me taking my shirt off in front of her was *wasn't.*

Her tone was matter-of-fact. "We're both girls."

"Right." Except she was a woman, one who was twenty years older than I was and potentially going to be my stepmother-in-law.

I shoved aside the icky sensation in my stomach, draped the top over the back of the chair, and gripped the hem of my shirt with nervous hands. She appeared disinterested in watching me change, but also made no attempt to turn or give me privacy, so I turned in place. I wasn't ashamed of my body, but this was an office, not a locker room.

Once I'd slipped into the new top and tucked it into the skirt, I shifted back to face her and awaited approval.

She nodded. "Yes, that works." She brightened abruptly. "How did you do with your assignment?"

It was a foreign feeling to not put my best effort forward. I was suddenly the kid who forgot to turn in their homework. "I might need another day or two."

Her expression was pointed. I knew what she wanted, so I unlocked my phone and reluctantly handed it over. She wasn't going to be happy with my feeble attempt. As I sank into the chair, Alice scrolled through my album.

"Oh. What's the story with this necklace?"

I'd forgotten that was in there. I frowned. "It was my mother's."

She glanced up from my phone. "Was?"

"I mean, it is. I took it Costolli's to be"—I searched for something other than the truth—"appraised."

Her eyes softened with understanding. Her attention went back to the screen, and as she scrolled, each picture seemed to increase her irritation.

"What are these at the end?" she asked. "The fountain downstairs?"

"I thought it was pretty."

Her look was pointed. "Okay, but this doesn't work. It still doesn't tell me who you are, Marist."

I bit my tongue so hard it was a miracle my mouth didn't

fill with blood. The problem was she actually wasn't interested in *me*. I had no desire to live a carefully curated life of picture-worthy moments, hoping to impress others. The real me posted random shit of mythology and pretty plates of food.

"Don't slouch," she said, correcting me like a schoolmarm. I straightened my posture, and she pressed her lips together, considering. Her tone was conversational, rather than adversarial. "Maybe you think all this is silly or pointless, but I need you to understand . . . this is important to Macalister."

"Why?" I wished instantly I hadn't said it, but she didn't seem offended by the question.

"Because he's trying to improve the dynasty that is the Hale family. He has a legacy to protect, sure. But he's also thinking bigger. He wants to be a recognizable, elite brand. Part of America's new royal class, like the Kennedys."

My pulse quickened. "He's considering politics?"

"Macalister? God, no." The thought was humorous to her. "But Vance will have a degree in political science next year, and his father has big expectations."

Oh, I bet he did. If Vance was going into politics, his father would want to see a President Hale in his lifetime.

Alice had said the magic words when she'd told me this was important to Macalister. I hoped she'd believe my eagerness. "I can try harder."

"Good. Tomorrow you'll have better shots, I'm sure. Today you'll post the picture of the necklace and tag Costolli's in it." She took her seat behind the desk, opened a drawer, and passed a folder to me. "Before we get started, this is a nondisclosure agreement. It's standard stuff. Anything said or witnessed when you're with the Hales is confidential."

I flipped open the folder and was assaulted by a dense contract. My eyes glazed over just scanning the first paragraph. There was no sound in the office other than Alice absentmindedly tapping the edge of the pen she'd picked up against her blotter while I looked over the NDA. I hurried through the reading, not wanting to keep her waiting. I selected a pen from the holder, uncapped it, and leaned over to sign—

"Stop," she said abruptly. Her hand shot out and grabbed my wrist. "Marist, did you read all of it?"

I parted my lips to say something, but she already had her answer from my reaction. I hadn't.

"You're so young." Her voice went soft. "I'm going to give you some friendly advice I wish I'd gotten, and it's advice you're going to need. Read *everything* before you sign. Take as much time as you need. If you don't understand, you ask questions." She gently squeezed my wrist. "Promise me."

"I promise." I nodded, and when she was satisfied, she released me.

After reading it line-by-line, I picked up the pen and signed. I understood that I couldn't discuss anything with anyone outside the family, and there would be steep fines and legal recourse if I did. Alice made a copy for me, and I slipped it in my purse.

"All right," she said, tucking a lock of her blonde hair behind her ear. "Do you know how many board members there are here?"

"Nine."

She looked pleased with my correct answer. "Do you know any of them?"

"No, not really. I've met Mr. Shaunessy a few times. I went to prom with his son."

Alice's expression was strange, like she'd swallowed wrong—but the feeling seemed to pass quickly. "Okay, then, we'll start there."

It took nearly an hour to go through the file of Liam Shaunessy that was stored completely in Alice's head. First, it was his basic history. Where he went to school, how he came to HBHC, his ascension to the board. Next came the personal. He was married with two kids, both boys, which I already knew. He lived in Cape Hill and enjoyed golf and duck hunting.

Finally, we moved onto social politics. There'd been a squabble between his wife and another board member's over an interior designer, something about using the same upholstery patterns. As a result, they didn't speak to each other, and it was imperative they not be seated together at any events.

I wanted to rub away the pain it caused in the front of my forehead, but I sat dutifully and listened as Alice laid out all the skeletons and drama associated with the Shaunessys. Thankfully, her desk phone rang with an urgent call, and I was dismissed until our appointment tomorrow.

I practically leapt from the chair and hurried toward the door—

"Marist?"

I froze, halfway to freedom, then slowly turned to face her. She clicked a button on her phone to mute the call and picked up a black journal, a place marker ribbon trailing out the bottom.

"Can you drop this off at Royce's desk before you go? It's some of my ideas for his party."

I took the journal with a tight smile. "Sure, but where—"

"His office is three doors toward the elevator." Her focus shifted to her computer screen. "See you tomorrow." She pressed the button on her phone and went back to her conversation. Task accomplished, I ceased to exist to her at that point.

I folded my arms over the journal as I strode down the hall. It was quiet on the floor. Most people had their doors closed, either in meetings or out, which made sense. It was close to lunchtime. The desk across from Royce's office was empty and not in use. Had they not hired an assistant for him? Or did he not need one?

The door to his office was ajar. I went to knock, but my knuckles hovered at the wood when his brusque voice rang out. "And how long is that going to take?"

A male voice was piped through the speakerphone. "If you want me to move on it now? A few weeks. It might raise flags."

"I don't care," Royce said. "Just get it done."

My hand moved of its own volition, nudging the

door open.

The layout was the same as Alice's office. The back wall was all glass and had a view of the harbor, but otherwise they were completely different. His furniture was masculine and traditional. Ornate scrolls were woodworked into the side of his dark oak desk. Like his room at home, the space was devoid of personal items. Only one piece of framed artwork decorated the wall, and I recognized the crimson Harvard logo.

Maybe he didn't hang artwork on the walls because, like the jewelry store, it couldn't compete with the most beautiful thing in the room—him. Royce stood at the side of his desk and leaned over it, his hands in fists resting on the top. He wasn't wearing his suit coat or his tie; both hung on the back of his chair. The sleeves of his shirt were undone and rolled back, his collar undone.

With his terse conversation over, he stared down at the desktop, head hung and lost in thought. The corded muscles traveling along forearms twisted, the line broken only by the expensive watch on his wrist. The sight of him so contemplative and backlit by the windows was breathtaking. It looked as if the fate of the world was on his shoulders.

I snuck my phone out of my purse, hurrying to capture the image. In my rush, I'd forgotten to put it on silent, and the electronic shutter clicking made his gaze snap to me. His eyes were wild and furious until he realized who he was seeing. His expression quickly morphed to confusion.

I lowered my phone and tried to act natural.

"Marist?" He straightened from the desk. "What are you doing here?"

"I had an appointment with Alice. She asked me to bring you this before I left." I held up the journal and gave it a small shake.

"What is it?"

He hadn't invited me into his office. It felt rude to charge in, so I stayed in my place. "She said it was ideas for your party."

"Oh." He held out his hand, curling his fingers in a *come closer* gesture. "Shut the door."

I inhaled deeply, did as he said, and handed him the book, only for him to toss it with a thud onto his desk.

"I'm sorry about the other night."

An apology from a Hale? I didn't think remorse was something they could experience. I didn't want him to read any emotion on my face. "Telling me to leave? Or the stuff that happened before?"

He cocked his head to the side and shot me a look that said I was being silly. "I meant how I had to kick you out. I'm not sorry about anything else." He made a face. "Well, maybe that we were interrupted."

He leaned back against the desktop and crossed his arms over his chest. As his unhurried gaze worked over me, I shifted my weight on my pumps. It was strange to be standing alone in his office in the middle of the workday.

I didn't belong here.

He didn't seem to feel any of the discomfort I did. "What was your appointment with Alice about?"

"Prep work for the interview."

A muscle along his neck twitched. Or . . . had I imagined

it? He painted on a smile. "I can help with that if you'd like. Come over tonight."

I tensed, unsure if I was even allowed to say no. "I have plans."

"This weekend, then. I'll send my driver."

"You don't have to do that. Besides, I like driving."

It was like I'd just told him his account was overdrawn. Skepticism wrinkled the bridge of his nose. "Really?"

"You don't?"

"No. I mean, I don't know. I don't drive."

What? I'd assumed he had a whole fleet of sports cars, and some days his hardest decision was which one to take for a spin. "Like, ever? Why not?"

He tossed a hand up in the air casually, then used it to rub the back of his neck. "I've always had a driver, so I guess I never saw the point in learning."

Shock bolted through me. "You don't know how?" I would never want to be that dependent on someone else. "Oh, my God, you should learn. I think you'd really enjoy it. When I've got my favorite song on and it's just me in the car? I love it. That's freedom."

I snapped my mouth shut, realizing too late that I sounded like an idiot. But he didn't act like he thought that. He considered my statement, and it seemed to grow more appealing each second. "Freedom, huh?"

"Yeah," I offered. "I could teach you. You help me with the interview, I show you which pedal's the gas."

He arched an eyebrow. "I know which one's the gas, thank you."

Royce pushed off the desk, rising to his full height. Even though I wore heels, he was still two inches taller than I was, and as he closed the distance between us, my eyes grew large. He was dangerous like this. Confident and powerful while in his own domain, all of Boston at his feet.

His voice was smooth like the glossy lacquer on his desktop. "All right. Sounds like a deal to me."

I'd expected a handshake, but instead he brushed his knuckles across my cheekbone and lowered in, sealing our deal with a slow, lingering kiss.

# TEN

Alice was able to cover a lot more ground at our next meeting, which was good. She had a work trip to the Chicago branch next week and would be out of the office until Wednesday. Coordinating the schedules of the eight current board members was no small feat, and the only workable date was Thursday.

Which meant I'd have to clear hurdle number one and face the board in less than a week.

I'd learned about almost all of the men who sat in the coveted positions—all but Macalister himself. I wasn't sure if Alice was saving him for last, or not going to cover him at all. She was cagey whenever I asked for details about the interview. It was clear she wanted me to do well when I sat for it, but she also wouldn't give me a clue about what kind of questions they'd ask.

That made it nearly impossible to prepare.

Friday morning, while I was stuck in Alice's office learning that Mr. Powell raced sailboats and competed in regattas, my mother and Emily went to the doctor and confirmed she was pregnant. Apparently, the relationship between her and her professor had ended as quickly as it had started, and once she told him he was the father, he calmly offered her five thousand dollars to take care of it and not tell his wife.

I loved my sister, but—Jesus. She had the worst taste in men.

I was still incredibly hurt that she'd kept so much from me. She'd tried to talk to me, but I'd used my meetings with Alice as an excuse to avoid her. I just needed more time to get over it. Emily was fragile right now, and I didn't want to say anything that would upset her.

On Saturday, I arrived at the Hale estate after lunchtime. I'd spent the morning making my way through my family's finances. The head in the sand approach wasn't working. I told them I'd rather face it head-on, no matter how bad it was. I'd go into it with eyes wide open.

Royce saw my Porsche pull up in the circle drive and came out to meet me. He wore shorts and a t-shirt, looking much more his age than when I'd seen him at the office two days ago. I'd snapped the picture of him that day for myself, but Alice posted it to my account. She'd tagged him in it and used a million hashtags, and as a result, I had a hundred new followers.

All of Cape Hill knew we were dating. They believed the lie that Royce Hale was into me.

Although, as he made his way down the stone steps and opened the passenger door of my SUV, he flashed a genuine smile, and I wanted to believe the lie too. Just for today, I told myself.

It was a manufactured whirlwind romance, so why did I struggled to find the deception?

"Hi," he said as he climbed into the passenger seat. "You look nice."

Perplexed, I glanced down at my basic top and pair of jeans. I'd put on makeup, but nothing special. I simply looked like me. "Hey. Thanks."

He buckled his seatbelt. "Where are we going?"

"The old mall that closed down. They have a big, empty parking lot you can practice in."

He nodded his approval, and then we were off.

Royce was quiet for the first few minutes. An angsty love song crooned from my car speakers and I thought about changing it, but he didn't seem to mind. He stared out the window and watched Cape Hill speed by.

"Where did you leave it with Alice?" he asked finally.

"She's told me about almost everyone on the board, so I think I'm in good shape? I don't know. It's weird. Sometimes it feels like she's purposefully keeping me in the dark."

He didn't turn to look at me, so I couldn't see his expression, but he kept his voice even. "Maybe she's trying to protect you."

Well, that was cryptic. "Protect me from what?"

"I don't know. I'm not on the board yet. It's not official until my initiation is done." His words died off at the end. This was something he wasn't supposed to say, or I wasn't supposed to know.

"Initiation?" I struggled not to roll my eyes. "Is there a

secret handshake and decoder rings too?" I wanted to study him closer, but I needed to keep my attention on the road.

He'd probably been aiming for a casual tone, but it came out forced. "Forget I said anything."

"Okay." The silence between us dragged, and I felt compelled to fill it. "So, the only person she hasn't talked about is your father."

The mood in the car plummeted further. "What do you want to know?"

I shrugged. "Anything, I guess. I'm going to be honest— he scares the hell out of me."

Royce was quiet.

The tension got to me. "So, do you like Alice?"

"I do." He sounded sincere.

"How'd she get together with your dad? I mean, he's her boss."

He relaxed on a breath. "She's like him in a lot of ways. When she wants something, there's no stopping her. That woman is relentless. For example, you say he scares you? Lots of people are terrified of him, but not Alice. She'd been working at the company a week when she walked into my father's office and told him he needed to get rid of his brand manager. She asked him to fire her boss and showed him all the reasons why." Royce fiddled with an air vent before continuing. "That took guts. He respects her."

Macalister's marriage wasn't about love but finding a partner he respected. They made it work. Did he assume the same would happen for his son and me?

The conversation lulled for a moment before Royce

added, "When they first got married, they used to fuck like rabbits."

*What?* Was he trying to deflect?

"Lovely," I gritted out. Macalister was handsome and powerful, but I couldn't imagine wanting to sleep with him.

"It drove Vance and me nuts, but it kept him occupied and off our backs."

I hesitated. "He always seemed pretty involved in your lives."

"Ever since my mom died, yeah."

The Hale estate used to have working stables because Elizabeth Hale loved horses. She'd been riding one when it spooked and threw her off. She hadn't been wearing a helmet, and when she fell, her head slammed into a stump.

She hadn't died right away. It'd been three agonizing days for the Hale family as she deteriorated in the hospital before she was gone. I'd been six when it happened and barely remembered her, but she'd been nice and pretty, and Macalister hadn't seemed so scary back then.

Maybe when she died, all he felt he had left were his sons and his legacy.

After several laps in the parking lot, Royce said he felt confident enough to try driving on some back roads. I agreed. He'd been surprisingly easy to teach. I would have thought he'd shrug off my instructions, not just because he was older and a man, but because he'd acted most of his life like he was better than everyone else.

My assumptions about him were wrong. He really had been acting, putting on fake bravado so he wouldn't appear weak in his father's eyes. Today he listened thoughtfully and took directions, and had no problem asking questions. There didn't seem to be any worry that he might look stupid or make mistakes and I would judge him.

Behind the vacant department store on one end of the mall, the parking lot let out into a neighborhood, and beyond that, away from civilization. The heavily wooded sections of the curvy road were broken up occasionally by farmland, but otherwise the trees, flush with the first leaves of summer, closed in around us.

"I see what you mean," he said abruptly. "It's nice."

He subtly relaxed his grip on the steering wheel but kept his hands at ten-and-two. We weren't going very fast as he navigated the curves and gently slalomed through the forest. I smiled. "I thought you'd like it."

He took his gaze off the road for a second, and when he turned his head to look at me and smile, his hands followed, moving slightly to the right.

The road was narrow. A single strip of white paint outlined the edge of the pavement, and there wasn't a shoulder. Only some gravel and grassy weeds. The car drifted just enough to edge off the pavement, crunching rocks and earth noisily under the tires.

"Shit!" Royce's focus snapped back to the road and he jerked the wheel.

But he overcompensated, and we swerved into the

oncoming lane. No one was coming—the road had been empty the whole time we'd been on it—but we were at the base
of a steep hill and couldn't see what lay ahead. He yanked
the steering wheel back the other direction, once again with
too much aggression, and the tires dipped off the road a
second time.

I punched the nonexistent brake in the passenger seat
with my foot, wanting to slow us down, and Royce must
have had the same thought. Only in his panic, he pushed the
wrong pedal and the car lurched forward.

The engine screamed as he slammed his foot on the
accelerator.

My hands flew out, bracing myself in my seat. "Brake!"

He twisted the wheel wildly as we bounced further off
the road, the nose of the car pointed straight for a line of
trees that looked like they'd been there a hundred years.
Tires churned on the uneven ground, and we swung wildly
back toward the road.

*"Brake!"* I yelled again. We shot across the pavement
in a blink and were on the other side of the road, barreling
toward a deep ditch. Oh, God. I shut my eyes and held my
breath, preparing for impact.

But abruptly, the car turned. It rumbled to a shuddering
stop like it was on a hook being pulled the opposite direction.

He'd finally found the brake.

I heard the gearshift move as he put the car into park.
It was silent except for the music wafting from the stereo,
which was slow and smooth in stark contrast to the pulse
hammering in my body.

Air burst from my lungs as I opened my eyes. We were sitting on a grassy bank beside the creek, facing the opposite way we'd been driving and on the other side of the road. My Porsche seemed to have survived unscathed, we were all right, and to anyone who passed by, it would probably appear like we'd intentionally pulled off the road to park here.

Royce didn't look at me. He turned the engine off, pushed open his door, and climbed out. Was he running away? Where the fuck was he going? My seatbelt was made of concrete and weighed me down. I couldn't move. I sat dumbfounded as he disappeared behind the back of the SUV.

A shadow fell across me and then my door was tugged open, bringing in cool air and the scent of the woods. I lifted my gaze to stare up at him. He had one hand on the door frame and the other on the roof, trapping me in. His face was streaked with worry. "Are you all right?"

I blinked. "I'm fine. Are you?"

"I'm fucking embarrassed." He sucked in a deep breath as he stepped back. "I could have killed us."

Since it no longer weighed anything, I undid my seatbelt and stood, my knees wobbling. "We're okay."

I'd disliked him for so long, and now everything was upside-down. His eyes were full of shame and his lips twisted downward in a frown, and I hated the way it looked on him. I even preferred the cocky version he pretended to be over this.

"You did pretty good up until the end, there," I said, desperate to relieve the tension, "but maybe don't fire your driver."

A faint smile warmed his lips. "Do you want to know what my final thought was when we were headed for that creek?"

*Please say something sexy.* Because my heart was still racing, and adrenaline filled my bloodstream. "What was it?"

"That this is all your fault."

My mouth dropped open. "My fault?"

The heat in his eyes was the only hint he wasn't being serious. Or perhaps he wasn't talking about the near crash but was accusing me of something else. I didn't get time to think about it. He used one strong hand to grip my waist and pull my body crashing into him, and the other to cradle my face, angling my head so he could claim my lips.

Our last kiss had been restrained since we were in his office in the middle of the work day. Now there was no one around to interrupt the intense, wild way he kissed me. His tongue pressed at the seam of my lips and demanded entrance, which I gave with a soft sigh. Warmth bloomed in my center and spread along my limbs, heating me to my toes and fingertips.

Our kiss started with passion, but it morphed into something different the longer our mouths were melded. It became harder. Darker. Reckless.

His hand twined in my hair, tugged at the strands, and moved right to the edge of pain. I put my hand on his shoulder and sank my fingernails into the meaty part of his arm. He escalated by sliding his hand down my back and gripped my ass so hard, I rose up onto my toes, pushing deeper into him.

I'd kept my raw, primal desire for Royce contained for a year, but this kiss? It unleashed all of it. Lust poured out of me in a throaty moan. It ached and throbbed between my legs as an empty feeling I was desperate for him to fill. And it intensified as he abandoned my lips and nipped at my neck, yanking so hard on my hair it stole my breath.

His teeth said he was angry with me, like he was mad about how much he wanted me, but his lips replaced the sting and wordlessly showed me he wasn't. Using his hold, he moved us one stumbling step so he could pin me flat to the backseat door.

Sunlight dappled through the trees. Birds called out. Cicadas buzzed their deafeningly loud hum from seemingly nowhere yet all around us in the forest. It fed into the belief that Royce and I were entirely alone. The last two souls on the Earth.

He worked a hand up my shirt and raked his fingers over the cup of my bra, trying to get inside. I wanted to take everything off and give him free rein over my body. I wanted him to *have* me, and I'd waited a year for this.

"I want you," I whispered.

"What?" He growled it in my ear. He'd heard what I'd said but demanded I repeat it anyway. And to distract me, he adjusted his stance so his leg was between mine and his thigh pressed at the junction of my legs. Pleasure was hot lighting coursing through me as he ground against my center.

"You could have killed us, and I would have died a virgin."

He stepped away from me so abruptly, I nearly fell to the ground without his support. He stroked a hand over his lips, like he was wiping away the taste of my kiss. His expression was hard, and chaos swarmed in his eyes. "You're not going to."

"Great." My word was sharp like the need he created

inside me. I kept my gaze fixed on him as I grabbed the handle and wrenched open the door to the back seat. "Then, let's do this."

Anger tensed every muscle in him. His chest expanded as he pushed forward and got in my face. "Oh, believe me, Marist. I'm going to fuck you. But not today."

What the hell was his deal? He wasn't a virgin, and he was obviously interested in me. I wasn't asking him something difficult. "Why not?"

"Because," he said with exasperation, "I'm not taking your virginity in the back seat of your Porsche."

That problem was easily solved. "Okay. Let's go back to your place."

"No. Why are you in such a hurry?"

A noise of frustration seeped out of me. "Oh, I don't know—because I want to know what it's like? I'm ready. I did what you asked. I waited, Royce. *For you*. For a whole fucking year where it was all I could think about, and I don't understand how you're not dying like me."

The words had run out of my mouth before I could stop them, and I swallowed a breath at what I'd revealed.

His hard edge softened and blurred until it was gone. He motioned to the open back seat. "Get in."

*Yes*. I scrambled across the leather bench seat and was relieved when he followed, folding his long legs into the small space before shutting the door behind himself. He turned to me, and his lips parted, but nothing came out. There was something he wanted to say but couldn't find the words. Or perhaps they were choked in his throat.

His hesitation made me nervous.

He smoothed his hands along his thighs and finally found his voice. "In my experience, the first time is uncomfortable for girls."

I lowered my chin so I could look at him with a plain expression. "Deflowered a lot of virgins, have you?"

"Some, yeah. I want to give you . . ." his lips pressed together as he struggled, "the best chance for you to enjoy it the first time."

He was so serious, and it was sobering. "Okay, sorry. I'm not following you. What do you—"

He moved quickly. His mouth was hot and urgent, thrust to mine. His hands went to the snap of my jeans and made quick work of dropping my zipper. I still didn't understand what he'd meant, but he seemed to be on board now, so I let it go. There was awkward twisting and fumbling as we sat side by side and struggled to push the denim down over my hips and legs. I hadn't gotten the jeans past my ankles before he shoved a hand down the front of my panties and touched me.

I gasped and latched a hand on his forearm. Not to stop him. It was instinctual from the sensation he caused. It felt so good. A featherlight caress over my swollen clit, but it packed a punch of pleasure, and a shudder rattled through me.

It was warm in the car, but not terribly so. Still, sweat blossomed on my skin. Royce's distracting mouth on mine and his hand grinding against me caused my knees to fall open as wide as possible with the jeans still wrapped around my ankles. I looked ridiculous like this. My shirt was on, and it couldn't look sexy, me in this state of half-undress. But his hand moving inside my black satin underwear? That was undeniably hot.

I broke the kiss and pressed my forehead to his. His dick was already half-hard, straining against the fly of his shorts. I whispered as I reached for him. "Let's get naked."

But he shifted to prevent my touch and slid a finger past my entrance. I was already breathless and coming apart, but his voice was low and solid. "I'm dictating how this goes, Marist."

His thick finger slipped further inside, making me freeze. Like last time, his gentle, slow thrust felt uncomfortably tight but also weirdly good. I liked the stretch of my body as it got used to him.

I let out a shuddering breath as he leaned over and pulsed his finger in and out, going a little deeper with each pass. He stopped kissing me abruptly and withdrew. It was so he could jerk the front of my panties down. When I understood what he was trying to do, I closed my legs and lifted my hips, helping him work my underwear down until it was also caught around my ankles.

This time, when he plunged his finger back inside me, he wasn't gentle. He asserted his ownership of me, and my body responded, clamping down. He let out an appreciative groan, and the corners of his mouth turned up in a wicked smile.

He rocked his finger in and out, picking up the pace as he studied me. That dark, intense stare of his was as fiery as the sun. Now, it was sweltering in the car. Sweat dampened my temples and the nape of my neck.

I tipped my head back, letting it rest on the seat as

trembles inched up my legs—

"Oh," I said on a shallow breath.

One finger felt good, but two fingers . . . were too much, too fast. I had a hand on his shoulder, but I curled my fingers into a fist. My body tightened with discomfort. I knew I'd get used to it, but I needed a moment.

"Uh . . ." I started.

He blinked slowly. "Too much?"

I bit my lip and nodded.

He stilled, leaving his fingers lodged inside me. "My dick's bigger than two fingers," he whispered. "You sure you still want it?"

My mouth rounded into an 'oh' as I realized what he was doing. He was hoping I'd back down from this challenge, but it wasn't going to work. I wanted it too much. "I'm fine. Just go slow."

It was strange how he could look disappointed and re-lieved at the same time. His fingers moved, unhurried and deliberate, working the tension loose from my muscles. The dull ache of fullness eased, and it wasn't long before I began to rock my hips in time with his thrusts.

The air in the car was so humid, I was breathing in liquid. I closed my eyes as Royce planted a kiss on my lips. I couldn't watch the corded muscles in his arm flex as he sawed his fingers deep between my legs. He mouthed more kisses on my chin and down my neck.

"When I put a ring on your finger," he murmured in the hollow of my throat, "I'll fuck you non-stop. I'm going to get inside you, Marist, and probably never want to leave."

My eyelids burst open.

"But not until then," he added.

Before I could process what he meant, he wedged three fingers inside me, driving deep and hard. My body jerked, and I hissed loudly. This wasn't discomfort.

It was *pain*.

A hot, intense sting, like a bandage being ripped off in a quick, unapologetic jerk.

I seized his wrist with both hands and shoved him away, but it was too late. His fingertips came away smeared red with my blood.

"I'm sorry," he said quickly.

His apology had sounded genuine, but there wasn't shock or surprise in his voice—like he'd expected this to happen. His words from earlier finally made sense, how he'd wanted to give me the best chance for me to enjoy my first time.

He'd broken my hymen just now, and he'd done it intentionally.

# ELEVEN

I STRAIGHTENED IN MY SEAT AND STARED AT ROYCE. INSIDE MY head, I cursed his stupid handsome face and what he'd done. My cheeks burned a million degrees. I didn't want to look at his fingers, or down at my legs. The ache was either subsiding, or I was too scattered and embarrassed to notice it anymore.

"Why?" I demanded.

His Adam's apple bobbed with a hard swallow, and guilt rushed through his expression. "Are you okay? I didn't want to hurt you, but I thought this might make our first time less traumatic."

"*Traumatic?*" Jesus. "It's just sex, Royce. Not war."

He had no response to that. Maybe he was thinking I was a naïve virgin and he knew better. Was I Medusa now? He sat in the tense silence, utterly still. Even in statue form, he was beautiful. I wanted him to pull me into his arms. He needed to do something fast, because emotions roiled in my belly, and I worried I might start to freak out.

"Are you all right?" he asked softly.

"I changed my mind." I didn't want to show weakness, but all the desire in me had fled. Now I just wanted to be dressed as quickly as possible and pretend this never happened. I leaned forward and grabbed the jeans wadded at my feet. He nodded in understanding and leaned between the front seats, reaching to grab the package of tissues on the tray in my console.

"I thought you might. You still haven't answered me, though." He pulled out a tissue for himself and handed the pack to me. "Are you okay?"

"I'm fine," I said curtly. I was aware I was being unfair to him. I'd asked for this, and although he'd been misguided, he *had* been trying to help me. Part of me was relieved to have this part over with. "I can't stand the sight of blood."

His gaze left mine and drifted down to the tissues in my hand. "Do you need me to—"

"Nope," I said.

*God, no.* He didn't seem squeamish or fazed by this, but I wasn't about to accept his help cleaning me up. When we both finished our tasks and I was buttoning my pants, my confidence inched back into place.

"You should have asked if that was how I wanted it done."

His gaze was heavy. "You're right. I'm sorry."

I sighed. "It'd be easier to argue with you if you'd stop agreeing with me."

"I know it's fucked up, but I was trying to help." He turned to face me, bringing one of his legs up onto the seat and propped an elbow on the seat back. "Are *we* okay?"

Were we? I stared at my knees, unable to hold his gaze.

"I don't know," I said softly. I wanted us to be.

He reached out and grasped my chin, turning me to look at him. His fingertips slid over my cheekbone so he could cup my face.

"This whole thing?" I continued. "The situation we're in . . . *it's* so fucked up."

His chest expanded as he took in a deep breath. "Yeah."

I could read the thought he had loudly on his face. What he really wanted to say was, *you have no idea.* But he didn't. Instead he moved in until there was no space left and captured my lips with his.

It was sunny but windy outside, and the water on the bay was tumultuous. I watched the whitecaps froth on the waves through the window in Alice's office, and it matched the emotions swirling inside me. I sat alone, waiting with my legs crossed and my foot bouncing with nerves.

I hadn't seen Royce since Saturday afternoon. He had corporate events and business dinners, and obligations he promised to fulfill on his father's behalf. He'd texted me a few times during the week under the guise of quizzing me on board members, but I believed it was really an excuse to talk to me.

I kind of liked it.

Would I see him now before the interview? Or would he be in the room as well?

I was sure I didn't have time to text him and ask. Alice

had left me in her office while she went to check on the board-room and make sure everything was set up. I drummed my fingers on the armrests of my chair. I'd sat for interviews be-fore, but they had been for summer internships. Not some-thing where the stakes were so high.

No matter how much I'd tried to tighten finances and forced my parents to squirrel money away, my family would struggle if I failed.

"They're ready for you."

I swiveled toward Alice's voice and gazed at her as she stood in the hallway, her gray dress matching the steel sky-scrapers outside. My heart stayed in my seat as I stood and filed out of her office, clutching the handle of my purse so tightly, my hand ached.

"Do I look all right?" I despised how timid I sounded, and I knew better. If the wind had destroyed my hair or I'd smeared my lipstick on the elevator ride up, Alice would have told me when I first arrived.

I'd spent the last five years learning how not to care about other people's opinions, and it was impossible to un-learn it in ten days.

Her smile was all brilliantly-white teeth. "You look lovely."

I fell in step with her as we went down the corridor, marching toward the biggest conversation of my life. It was sure to be hard, but if this went well, I'd be able to finish my degree and save my family, and as a bonus, I'd end up with the prince who dominated my thoughts.

The same prince who was waiting beside the door, his arms folded across his chest and leaning against the wall. He

wore a black three-piece suit and a green tie, which perfectly matched the emerald green dress I wore. It had to be intentional on Alice's part. It made us look like we belonged
together.

Like a couple.

"You look nervous," was the greeting he gave me, which
didn't help my anxiety.

Alice lifted her gaze to the ceiling, annoyed. "Don't tell
her that. She looks perfect."

His focus slid down me, tracing my curves appreciative-
ly. The dress was simple. One deep color and cut modestly,
but tailored so it flattered my figure. Conservative but not
stuffy. *Professionally feminine*, Alice had called it. That was
what she wanted my brand to be.

"I look nervous," I said, "because I am."

He straightened from the wall, and his shadow fell on
me. "Don't be. You'll be fine."

Alice was less convinced. "Just answer the questions
honestly, even if some of them make you uncomfortable, and
it shouldn't take long."

Alarm pricked at me. "Uncomfortable? Like, what?"

Her face went blank. She was a computer accessing files
from the archives. "Medical history. Personal stuff."

"Oh." My apprehension grew.

"I'm going to introduce you," Royce said, "but I can't
stay." He gave me a final once-over. "Ready?"

*No. Not at all.* "Yes."

"Good luck." Alice flashed a supportive smile.

He took my elbow and guided me through the door,

keeping his voice at a hush, only for me. "You don't need luck. You've got an ace up your sleeve."

I glanced at him in surprise. "I do?"

It was too late for him to explain. We were now in the boardroom and the interview had officially started.

There was a lot to take in. The ceilings were tall and the room wide, but my eye went to the long conference table and the reflection of the Boston skyline in its glossy finish. The outer wall was all windows like the offices, but since we were on the opposite side of the building, the sun-drenched city stretched out for miles beyond the glass.

Eight pairs of eyes sharpened on us as Royce urged me deeper into the room.

Four men in suits sat on one side of the table, three on the other, and Macalister presided at the head. Was it another Hale tradition to have his chair sit taller than the rest, to make him more impressive and opposing? Because it was working. He held dominion over the room.

"Gentleman," Royce said straight-faced, "may I present Marist Northcott for your consideration?"

I strangled back the nervous laugh that wanted to escape. He was mocking them, or his family's ridiculous tradition, or both.

He pulled out the chair for me at the other end of the table, which left a buffer of several empty seats, but put me directly across from his father. I strode toward it, determined not to look intimidated even as my insides quaked. I would do as Royce did. Be a different person when others were around.

Adapt to survive.

The evaluating stare of the board members made it cumbersome to move, but I lowered into the seat, kept my chin up and my gaze firmly on Macalister. I was smart enough to know the chairman was the only one whose opinion mattered, and I was already starting behind since I wasn't my sister. If I lost his approval, I'd be doomed.

A hand gently clasped my shoulder, and I turned to look up at Royce. His expression made his thoughts clear. *You've got this.* My heart skittered from his small, supportive gesture, but when I faced the board, the action hadn't been lost on Macalister. He eyed his son with interest.

Or perhaps suspicion.

Footsteps carried Royce away, and no one spoke until the door was shut behind him. Alice's voice filtered in my mind. *Mind your posture. Smile. Hands in your lap.*

"Welcome." Macalister's voice was fixed and even. "Thank you for taking the time to meet with us."

I hoped my smile wasn't unnatural. "Thank you for having me."

As a whole, the board was rather young-looking, and it was by design. Years ago, they had created a rule that each member would retire from their seat by sixty-five. Macalister had argued it was to keep the members fresh and sharp, but I suspected he'd done it to force his own father to relinquish his seat and allow Macalister to take over sooner.

The two members who'd come from outside HBHC were in their early fifties. Both men had made hundreds of millions on companies they'd taken public, retired from, and now held seats on the board. They drew cushy salaries for four meetings a year, plus a few events. It was a sweet gig.

Macalister turned to the members, one side and then the other as he spoke. "I believe most of you have already met her. She's Charles Northcott's youngest daughter."

Heads nodded in agreement.

His cold stare returned to me. "But why don't you indulge us and tell us a little about yourself?"

I adjusted my posture as my shoulders were already slipping. At least this was a question I was prepared for.

"Of course," I said. "I'm twenty-one and will be starting my final year at Etonsons this fall. I'm studying economics with a minor in history. I've interned at Marche Risk Management and volunteered at the Museum of Natural History." I took in a breath to transition from my schoolwork to my daily life. "I'm a voracious reader and collector of books, preferably—"

He lifted a hand, silencing me. I had ticked the box and supplied a satisfactory answer, and he wanted to move on.

The next few questions were also as I expected. My career goals. Strengths and weaknesses. How I dealt with conflict and failure. After that, the group shifted to my personal life. I was asked about loyalty, and what was the most important thing to me.

"Family," I answered.

"Are you an organized person? A planner?" Macalister asked.

"Yes, sir." I always looked ahead.

"So, tell me. How do you find the planning is going for Royce's celebration?"

"Royce's party?" His question tripped me up. "I haven't been involved with that."

Displeasure painted his face an ugly color. "It's the biggest event of my son's life—the man who's to be your husband. You don't care enough to be involved with that?"

The disapproving expressions swept through the board members like a cold chill, and excitement lurked in Macalister's eyes. This wasn't an interview, it was an interrogation. I needed to be extra careful. He was going to ask questions he already knew the answers to.

I swallowed hard but kept my chin level, scrambling to find the right response. "I figured it was best to wait for board approval before asking to be included. I didn't want to overstep." The lie came out sugary sweet. "Of course, if he'd asked me, I would have been thrilled to be included."

The dark expressions around the table faded, but the chairman's eyes narrowed. He'd meant to fluster me, and his plan had failed.

"Do you want children?" Mr. Geffen asked.

There was a pang in my chest. Of course he asked this question. Alice had told me how he and his wife tried IVF several times but had not been successful.

"Yes," I said. "Eventually."

I'd been so caught up in the immediate part of the arrangement, I hadn't considered children. Did Royce want them? We were compatible on a basic level, but what if we weren't on something else? What if it were a deal breaker? We'd known each other our whole lives but—God—we had so much left to learn.

"And you're healthy?" Mr. Geffen was reluctant to ask it. "Everything seems to be okay in that department?"

I gave a pained smile. "Yes, sir."

"Are you on birth control?" Macalister asked abruptly.

The air solidified, leaving nothing left to breathe. "Excuse me?"

All the way on the other end of the room, I could sense his irritation. It rolled down the table at me like a pen on a slant, picking up steam as it went. He weighted each word. "Are you on birth control?"

My breath came rapid and uneven. "Yeah. I mean, yes, sir."

"What kind?"

*Seriously?* I had terrible cramps, and the pill was the only thing that saved me. I hadn't had a period in a year. Did they want to know that too? My tone was clipped. "The pill."

"And how many sexual partners have you had?"

I should have sensed this coming. With how conservative and controlling Macalister was, he'd want to know. He'd need every detail. My spine hardened into steel. "I don't sleep around."

"That's good to know," Mr. Shaunessy interjected. "But it wasn't what Macalister asked, was it, dear?"

My jaw ached to hold in the words I wanted to say. As I stared at the man seated at the head of the table, my blood heated until it ran scalding through my veins. I wanted to wipe the smug expression off his face. He wouldn't call me a slut outright, but he would imply. He'd use whatever number I gave him to shame me in front of the board.

Except the trap he'd laid was going to backfire. This was a question he *didn't* know the answer to.

There was probably a flush on my cheeks, but I calmed and blinked a cold stare at the sea of older, pale faces. "Zero."

Mouths dropped open. Mr. Geffen stopped mid-sip of his glass of water.

Macalister scowled and sat back in his chair. "Don't lie to us."

"I promise you, I'm not." I couldn't have sounded more sincere if I'd tried.

It looked like Mr. Burrows believed me. He was the oldest member at sixty-two, but he looked at least ten years younger. Alice told me he ran a four-hour marathon.

He leaned forward in his chair. "Are you waiting for marriage?"

"No, sir. I mean, I wasn't intentionally." My mouth had gone dry, and I eyed the water glass in front of me longingly, watching a drop of condensation trail erratically down the side. But I knew if I reached for it, they might see how I was shaking. "Honestly, I didn't date much in high school or college, and when I did, it just . . . never went that far."

Mr. Lynch, who was seated to Macalister's right, turned his stunned gaze to his boss and said it with awe. "She's a virgin."

Macalister wasn't having it. "You're a gorgeous girl from a wealthy family. You really expect us to believe no one has touched you?"

With everything he'd said, it was his compliment that threw me the most. "I didn't say no one has touched me, but

I haven't—"

"I see. What exactly have you done?" The corner of his mouth lifted in a smile. It screamed, *gotcha*.

My gaze dropped to the blank notepad before me and the pen with the HBHC logo printed on its side. There was no point in lying. Macalister had nearly caught me with Royce's dick in my hands.

I was supposed to play my part and be what Macalister wanted, but it seemed like what he wanted most was to tear me apart. To break me down and prove I wasn't worthy of entry into his family.

Alice had won him over by standing up to him. It was incredibly risky, but if I was going to lose, at least I could say I went down swinging.

I filled my lungs with air, using it to inflate my confidence. From this point on, I needed to be unsinkable. "I've been intimate with two guys."

His lips parted, probably to ask for specifics, but I cut him off before he could.

"Hands," I said, "above and below the waist. That kind of thing."

Mr. Lynch didn't seem to be aware this conversation was truly between Macalister and me and interrupted. "No oral sex? Ever?"

My gaze was locked onto Macalister as I answered his lackey. "No, sir."

In my peripheral vision, I saw the rest of the board members exchange looks with each other.

"Who were the boys?" asked Mr. Shaunessy.

"Do you really want their names?" It was clear they did. "Well, Royce. And, um . . . Richard."

Mr. Shaunessy flinched. "My son?"

The king, sitting on his throne, stared at me. He didn't care about who, only why I was still a virgin. To him, I was a puzzle to solve. "Are you not interested in sex?"

"No, I am." I wasn't going to play his game and let him embarrass me for something that wasn't shameful. "Very interested, actually."

"Is that so?" His eyebrow arrowed upward. "Then, I assume you masturbate?"

A few of the board members gasped. Mr. Geffen coughed as he choked on his own spit.

Inside I was dying, but I refused to show it. *Be unfazed.* Besides, I read the challenge in Macalister's words and would meet it head-on. My voice was loud and strong. "Nearly every day."

Some of the board stirred in their seat. But Macalister? The shift was subtle, barely noticeable. His lips parted and heat flared in his eyes. It wasn't judgement or disgust causing it—this fire was something far more insidious.

*Arousal.*

My heart thudded to a stop.

His broad shoulders tilted as he leaned on one armrest of his chair, and his lips peeled back into a smile. "I'm sorry if you find my questions frank, but I believe sex is an important aspect of a healthy marriage. Most girls your age have already had some experience with it."

"I am not like most girls."

His smile widened, stretching into his eyes. "No. No, you're not. I see that now." He thumbed the underside of wedding band on his finger. "You're attracted to Royce? Sexually?"

I would have thought that was clear, but I humored him. "Yes, sir."

"That's good. However, I'd prefer if the two of you don't go any further until we've finished this approval process."

Yet another instance of Macalister trying to assert absolute control, but it wouldn't work. Royce had already told me he wouldn't take my virginity until we were engaged. "I've waited a year for him, I think I can wait another . . ." *Shit!* What was I doing? "I mean, I've waited this long, it's fine."

My attempt at backtracking was futile. Macalister latched on, intrigued. "What was that?" When I said nothing, he prodded, "Go on. You said you waited a year for him. What did you mean?"

My hesitation wasn't helping, but it was hard to admit. "Last year, Royce . . . he asked me not to sleep with anyone."

His expression didn't change, but behind his eyes I could see him working through it. "He wanted to be your first."

It had felt like I had been winning the battle up until this point, but now I was losing ground. I said it so softly, it barely traveled the length of the room to reach him. "Yes."

"And you waited. He could have been off with a dozen different girls, and yet you stayed faithful. Why?"

We'd come full circle. Macalister had returned to asking questions he already knew the answers to. My pulse thundered, making blood whoosh loudly in my ears. I didn't want to say why I'd waited for the boy I'd grown up disliking. I didn't want to admit to myself why I'd turned down the stranger who'd asked for my number at the coffee shop this past spring.

"She's in love with him." Mr. Shaunessy acted like this was a fact he'd been clever enough to discover.

"No," I said instantly. "No, definitely not. I barely know him."

Mr. Shaunessy took on an all-knowing look. "All right. Infatuated with him, then."

That one was harder to argue against, so I fell silent. I risked a glance at Macalister, who seemed pleased. I knew in my gut it wasn't how his son and I had made a connection, but that this information gave him more leverage over us.

Mr. Burrows set down his water with a thud, the ice tinkling against the glass. "Well, she's loyal, and you can't buy that."

Macalister's attention snapped to him. "There's no problem too big that money can't solve. You, of all people, should know that."

Mr. Burrows reacted as if his boss had slapped him across the face rather than just verbally. He sank back in his chair, and I doubted he'd say another word the rest of the time he was in the room.

Macalister's focus crept back to me. "He's not wrong, though. I respect honesty and loyalty, as both are difficult to find these days. Do you feel you would make a good wife?"

Alice had told me to control my hands, so I resisted the urge to tuck my hair behind my ear. "I don't know how to answer that, other than to say I would try my best."

Macalister nodded. "Well, that's all we can ask of someone, isn't it? Thank you, Marist. Please shut the door as you leave. The board and I have a lot to discuss."

# TWELVE

THANK FUCK THE OFFICE HALLWAY WAS EMPTY WHEN I LEFT the boardroom. I put one hand on the wall to lean on, and the other in the center of my chest, and willed myself to keep it together. A million emotions churned inside me.

Relief it was over. Proud I'd survived. Fear at what I'd revealed. And, most of all, anger. All that preparing, and it had been pointless. I'd been ambushed by the questions.

I took a moment, sucking in air to steady myself before launching down the hallway toward Royce's office. There was no assistant to stop me, and his closed door wasn't going to either. I seized the doorknob, turned it, and stormed inside.

He was alone in his spacious room, typing on the keyboard and his gaze fixed on the computer screen. The other monitor beside him scrolled real-time data from the markets.

"Did you know?" I demanded, startling him. My voice cracked and lost its power. "Did you know what he was going to ask?"

Concern had Royce shooting out of his seat. He came to

me, pushing his office door closed with one swift hand and sweeping me into his embrace with the other. His tone was hushed and soothing. "It's okay."

"The fuck it is!" I glared up as he loomed over me, taking up all my space. "I just told a room full of men that—oh, let's see. I'm a virgin. I've given hand jobs to you and Richard Shaunessy, whose father asked for the names, by the way." My stomach flipped over on itself as I declared the worst part. "And I masturbate nearly every day."

"You do?" Lust pooled in his expression. "That's hot, Marist."

"*Royce.*" I was in no mood. Didn't he see how serious I was about this? His comment only made me angrier. "This might be a game for you, but it's my fucking life."

He stiffened. "I'm sorry, you're right."

"Some of them are my father's coworkers, and *his boss.*" I twisted out of his arms, needing distance. I didn't want his touch to disarm me. "And you didn't answer me. Did you know?"

His expression glazed over, and he hesitated before speaking. "I had an idea, yeah."

I had to stare at the ceiling to drain back my tears of frustration. "You should have warned me."

"I wasn't allowed." I could hear how torn he was. He'd at least *wanted* to tell me. Did that count for something? "If I had prepped you, they would have known, and then they wouldn't have believed any other answer you gave."

The jerk was probably right.

When it was safe, I put my gaze back on him and pinned

him in place. "It screwed with my head." A tremble rumbled through my shoulders, so I cross my arms to hold it in. My voice dropped to a whisper. "I think I fucked up."

Alarm rushed through his expression, but he tried to downplay it, being strong for my benefit. Once again, he moved in and put his arms around me. "I'm sure you did fine."

It should have felt weird, but I welcomed his offer of comfort. I'd pushed him away the first time, but now I desperately needed it. I gripped the lapels of his suit and peered up into his piercing eyes. They were like multifaceted jewels. Pale blue, and then ringed with dark sapphire at the outer edges.

"I told them I waited for you."

He took in a deep breath, but otherwise he didn't react. "So?"

"So . . . your father knows you asked me to wait because you want to be my first."

Again, there was little reaction from him, but movement sparked behind his eyes, like he was entering crisis mode. "That's fine."

"You should have seen his face, though," I warned.

He shrugged it off. "Whatever happens, we'll figure it out."

My heart beat a little faster. He could have easily said *I'll figure it out*, but instead he'd said *we*. It had rolled so naturally off his lips. He saw us as a pair.

The phone on his desk rang in a jarring trill, forcing him to release me. He walked to it and punched a button. "This is Royce."

Macalister's voice filtered through the electronic speaker

and turned my bones to ice. "You should have told me she was a virgin." I pictured the irritation on his face. "Of course, they ate that up. The board loves her."

Royce glanced over his shoulder and flashed a sly smile. *Oh, my God.* This was the 'ace up my sleeve' he'd mentioned. Once again, I was annoyed by how big of a deal men made about women's virginity.

"I guess it went well?" he asked his father.

"She was . . . surprising," Macalister said. "I told her this already, but just to be clear—you don't touch her before the initiation."

Royce's smile soured. "I understand."

There was rustling on the other end, followed by a distinct click as his father hung up.

I stood in the dressing room of the designer dress shop, watching the Instagram notifications blow up my phone.

The week following the interview had been worse than the previous.

My preparation lessons with Alice had been replaced with meetings about Royce's party. Since I had passed the first stage of the approval process, things grew more serious. Being Royce's wife basically meant I'd be a project manager. I'd be tasked with planning events and making all the decisions he couldn't be bothered with.

This was my audition.

I'd sat in on meetings with florists about centerpieces

and inspected table linen samples, all while Alice watched over and second-guessed every decision I'd been forced to make. I didn't care whether the tables were round or long rectangles, or if the invitations were embossed or letterpress.

But I pretended I did. I smiled and nodded and Instagrammed what she encouraged me to. I developed the narrative of the happy girlfriend swept away with excitement at planning a celebration for the man of her dreams. I played the role everyone wanted me to be.

Everyone, except for me.

Each selection I made felt like I was blindly filling in a test answer bubble, praying it was right. Once the RSVPs started to come in, it became more complicated. Everyone wanted to be there. This was going to be the party of the decade. It had been thirteen years since anyone had ascended to the board, and Royce wasn't going to be just any board member—he was supposed to take over for Macalister when his father retired.

Media outlets wanted in on the celebration. Once it was clear I was Royce's girlfriend and in charge of his party, I'd started getting requests from everywhere. People who'd shunned me in high school were suddenly obnoxiously friendly. Style editors and Instagram influencers followed me and sent direct messages, hoping to score an invite.

I tried not to let it go to my head, but it was a trip.

All those people who had treated me like I had a social disease were suddenly climbing over each other to be my friend. The petty part of me enjoyed it a little.

Alice's favorite designer was in Boston for a trunk show,

and she'd scheduled an appointment for both of us this evening. I hadn't known Royce was coming until he'd appeared on the couch in the lobby of the store, looking annoyingly sexy. He'd come straight from the office, and his tie was stuffed haphazardly in the pocket of his blue suit coat.

"Why are you here?" I made a face. I hadn't meant for it to come out so forceful. I was tired, and I didn't like him seeing the person I had to be when Alice was around.

He smirked, unfazed by my tone. "I need to know what you're going to be wearing so I can coordinate."

"I'm sure I could send you a picture."

He tossed up a hand in surrender. "Okay. I wanted to have a say in the decision."

Like his father, Royce liked having control.

Donna Willow, the dress designer, was the embodiment of her name. Her head was a mop of wispy white hair and she was so slender, the collection of bracelets jangling on her wrists looked like they might break her arms. When Alice introduced us, Donna gave me a once-over and a pleasant smile.

"My fall collection is all jewel tones," she said, nodding to herself. "Lots of options, but I already have a dress in mind for you."

Gowns were pulled for me to try on, and then I was shepherded toward a dressing room.

"This is just to get an idea. I've got clips for whatever is too big." She pointed to the glittering, fluffy assortment of dresses hanging on the rack. "I'm confident the red strapless number will be your dress, but we'll start with the blue one just for fun." Her eyes sparkled. "We don't want this over too quickly."

I gave a smile and hoped she couldn't see it was pained.

Once the door shut, my face fell. I should have been excited. This was basically every little girl's dream, trying on fancy dresses for the big ball. I even had the Prince Charming already lined up.

Except it was fabricated.

Would my relationship with Royce grow to become more than just fiction?

I retrieved my phone from my purse, snapped a picture of the rack of gowns, and posted it to my feed. I fed the lie with a question of which dress I should try on first, followed by a bunch of happy, vapid hashtags.

"Nice," Alice said when I emerged from the fitting room wearing the blue mermaid style dress.

I went up the step to stand on the platform in front of the mirrors and take it in. Its high neck had beaded embellishments that wrapped around my throat and I couldn't help but feel strangled.

Alice sat on the cream-colored couch and Royce in a gold armchair beside it, and his gaze met mine through the mirror.

"It's just okay to me," he said.

"Agreed," Donna concluded. "Try the black one next."

The second dress was far more comfortable, but I didn't have to see my reflection to know it wasn't right. Three frowns greeted me when I appeared from the fitting room.

"No," Donna said, before sending me back. "The waistline is too high."

I stood in the small, mirrorless room, staring at the

notifications as they popped up on my screen, one after another. People seemed to like the curated Marist Northcott a
hell of a lot more than the real one. I hurled my phone in my
purse and reminded myself it was pointless to be upset. I was
doing what I had to. Macalister's deal said I was supposed to
be the girl everyone wanted to be.

My gaze landed on the red dress.

Frowns weren't waiting for me when I rounded the corner and stepped into view. Alice inhaled sharply and clasped
a hand to her chest. Donna's proud smile was enormous. I
didn't risk a glance at Royce at first. Instead, I grasped the
sides of skirt and stepped up onto the platform, took in a
breath, and raised my eyes to the mirror.

My own reflection turned me to stone.

The strapless dress was the color of power and sin. Below
the waist, the red corseted bodice burst into tulle rosettes in
varying shades of crimson and scarlet, flowing down to the
floor and trailing behind me in a short train.

Who knew fabric could be so transformative?

I suddenly felt like I could do this. I could wear this
beautiful costume when it was announced to the world I was
about to become the princess of the Hale dynasty. That Royce
had chosen me. I'd don a smile on my face that wouldn't be
much of a lie, and it was because of the way he was looking
at me right now.

His lush lips parted, but he didn't seem to be breathing.
He stared at me as if the world turned at my command. I'd
always thought his eyes were hungry, but that hunger was
the hunt for signs of weakness. For mistakes and dark secrets

people hoped to conceal.

His hunger now was something else entirely.

Unabashed desire drenched his expression. He held my gaze so long my knees softened, and my cheeks warmed with a flush. Had he forgotten we weren't alone? It was indecent the way he stared at me. There was no mistaking what he craved.

Perhaps I wasn't Medusa, but Persephone. Royce was Hades, the king of the underworld. He'd come to carry me down into his dark world, make me his unwilling bride and his queen.

*She didn't stay unwilling, did she?*

The myth said once Persephone had been granted her freedom by Zeus, lovesick Hades tricked her into eating pomegranate seeds. This meant she had to return to her husband in the underworld.

In some versions, Persephone ate the seeds knowingly. She wanted the excuse to return to him.

The women in the room were thankfully oblivious. They both rushed toward me.

"You'll wear your hair up," Alice said. She gathered my hair in her hands and held it against the crown of my head.

Donna's cold fingers slipped into the back of the dress and tugged it tight. "It'll have to be taken in."

"Earrings?" Alice asked the designer. "Or necklace? I don't want to ruin the neckline."

There was no discussion if this was the right one, and Royce hadn't given his approval. I turned and looked at him over my shoulder while the women continued to fuss at me.

"Do you like it?"

"I do." His voice was thick like honey. "Very much."

*God, that stare.* My mouth went dry.

For the first time ever, I wanted the initiation to get here quicker. All the sooner we'd both be able to satisfy our cravings.

I stood in the kitchen and lay my hands flat on the countertop to prevent myself from hurling the stack of envelopes at my mother. I was *livid.* So angry, it solidified my muscles and made my back ache from the weight of it.

It had been a month since Macalister had shattered my world. And in that time, miraculously, no bills had arrived.

Last week I'd started going through the mail as soon as I was home from my appointments with Alice or the event coordinator. But there'd been nothing. Not even an electric bill.

Something wasn't right. Macalister had said the house was in default, so there would be notices. Foreclosing wasn't something that just happened overnight. It was a long, tedious process with a paper trail. Even if he'd stopped his bank's foreclosure, it'd take days before the system processed it.

This morning I'd told my family I'd be gone all day, but I'd lied. At one o'clock, I'd lurked in the guest bedroom upstairs that had the best view of the driveway, and I waited. The mail truck rumbled up twenty minutes later and deposited a thick stack of envelopes into our mailbox. It had only just pulled away when my mother walked down the drive.

My suspicions rose exponentially as she stood at the mailbox, sorting the letters into two piles. Maybe she was weeding out the junk mail, but in my gut, I knew it was wishful thinking. As she disappeared from view and back into the house, I closed my eyes and said a little prayer.

Downstairs, there were footsteps as my mother moved around in the kitchen. A cabinet door creaked open and then thumped shut. More sounds as the water ran in the sink.

I'd seen my mother do dishes before, but up until recently, it had been a rare occurrence. Delphine had been let go, and we were all feeling the loss, but my mother had been hit the hardest. Not just in housework and meals, either. Delphine had been part of our family.

I forced myself to sound light and casual. "Hey. Did the mail come yet?"

"Oh, I didn't know you were home." She bobbed her head in a nod. "It's there on the counter." She used one wet hand to point to the stack, and a sickening, sour taste filled my mouth.

"Where's the rest of it?"

"What?" she asked over the running water.

My voice was loud and pointed. "The rest of the mail, Mom."

She stilled. Slowly, she turned off the water and turned to face me, her panic barely disguised. "I don't know what you mean."

Shit, she was a terrible liar. I strode over to the cabinets that weren't used often, throwing open the doors, one after another, searching.

"Marist, stop," she cried.

It only fueled me to keep going. When I reached for the next one, she sucked in a deep breath. It was because when I jerked the door open, I was meet with several shelves of mail. The cabinet was *fucking full*.

Weeks' worth of bills had been hidden here.

I scooped out a stack of letters in disbelief, some of them spilling onto the counter below. There were red 'past due' and 'urgent' stamps on a few. Not a single one had been opened. I set my hands on the counter, infuriated and crushed with disappointment.

She whispered, "I know you're upset, but—"

"Yes." The voice that spoke didn't sound like it belonged to me, but it couldn't have come from anyone else.

Her bottom lip trembled. "It's just . . . you have so much on your plate right now, and your father and I didn't want you to worry."

"Oh, my God," I snapped. "That's such bullshit."

She scowled. "Don't talk to me like that. I'm your mother."

I snatched up one of the bills before me, tearing open the envelope as I spoke. "Except I'm the only one with any responsibility around here. What are you thinking? You can't just ignore this and believe it's going to go away." Tears of anger burned my eyes, making my vision bleary and the credit card statement I'd opened hard to read.

"We're not ignoring it, we just need a little more time."

"Time for what? For Macalister to write me a five-million-dollar check?"

It looked like I'd kicked her in the stomach, but it was hard to feel much sympathy for her right now. My anger burned so hot inside me, it consumed all other emotion. I stared at the charges printed on the paper and my focus zeroed in on the date.

"What the fuck is this?" I jammed the statement at her, my finger on the line pointing it out. "You spent four thousand dollars at Chanel last week?"

A range of emotions played out on her face. Surprise, followed by guilt, and then defensiveness.

"You don't know what it's like!" Tears spilled down her face. "It's so overwhelming. I feel awful all the time, Marist. I'm miserable every second of every day, and I just . . ." She tipped her head back and stared at the ceiling. "I needed some relief, all right? I saw the bag, and I just wanted to be happy for two seconds. I needed an escape. I'm sorry."

I swung away, unable to look at her, but there was no escape for me. The Etonsons crest was on one of the letters in the pile. It was far too late to apply for a student loan, and who would give me one, anyway? My family was supposed to be American royalty with coffers full of money.

"I'll take the bag back," she mumbled.

Like that would solve anything. My mother had lived her whole life as an entitled and privileged woman. Her behavior would never change.

I said nothing to her. I simply stared at my family's financial ruin and tried not to cry. In five days, I would be armed with Hale resources and this would be a mountain I could climb. My silence drove my mother away, and I was grateful she wasn't near. I assumed she went to her room to feel sorry for herself some more, rather than do anything about her situation.

I pulled down the ignored bills and notices, flinging them to the floor until they were a puddle of debt at my feet. I dropped down beside it, my back against the lower cabinets, and began to open each one.

Some time later, Emily found me there, neat piles sorted by priority gathered around me. She barely blinked at how I was sitting on the floor of the kitchen or what I was doing. It wasn't all that surprising. My parents had passed on the avoider gene to her. She'd put the pregnancy test off for weeks so she wouldn't have to face reality.

As she slid down the cabinets to sit beside me, I sighed. I was still upset with her about what she'd kept from me. She was supposed to be my best friend. Did she feel like she couldn't trust me? That I'd judge her? It *hurt*.

But this wasn't the time to talk through our issues. Couldn't she see that? I was frayed and raw, and there were bigger things to worry about than my feelings.

"You've been avoiding me for weeks," she said. "And I've been avoiding this too, but we *have* to talk."

"I know, but not now, Em." I scanned the papers surrounding us. "Just let me get through this weekend, and then everything's going to get better."

"No, it isn't. I shouldn't have let this go on as long as it has. I should have told you weeks ago." She grabbed my arm to let me know she was serious. My breath cut off as her expression turned to desperation. "You can't marry Royce."

My pulse slowed to a crawl. Hyperawareness tingled across my skin, warning me something big was coming.

Oh, God. Was this where she told me she was secretly in love with him?

My voice wavered. "Why's that?"

"Because for him to join the board?" Her hand squeezed so hard it was uncomfortable. "He has to fuck you in front of them."

# THIRTEEN

INCREDULOUS LAUGHTER WELLED UP AND ERUPTED FROM MY throat. Emily's joke was so ridiculous it wasn't even that funny, but I needed the stress relief, and it felt good to let it out.

My sister didn't laugh with me. Her eyes were full of fear, and—damn—she was really selling the joke.

"Stop it," I said. "Where'd you even come up with that?"

"Marist, I'm serious." She frowned, trying to assemble convincing words. "I thought it was like an urban legend too when I heard it. You know people talk all sorts of shit about the Hales. But this? It's true."

"Okay." I patronized her with a look. "Sure."

Yet an unwelcomed sensation folded my stomach in two. It whispered to listen to my sister.

"My friend Jenny," she said, "used to babysit for the Scoffields. She said one night when they'd come home after a party, Mrs. Scoffield was shitfaced and started screaming at her husband about how she let him fuck her while they all watched."

I pressed my lips together. "She could have been talking about anything."

Money made people crazy. It lowered inhibitions and sent them on power trips. Everyone knew there was a seedy underside to Cape Hill. Plenty of the higher-ups had been caught in compromising positions. Everything from under-age drinking and affairs, to drugs and prostitutes.

I was sure there was kinky shit going on as well. Most of the executives at HBHC acted like the Gods on Mount Olympus. They did whatever fucked-up thing they wanted and didn't worry about consequences.

My sister shook her head. "Mr. Scoffield gave Jenny three hundred dollars that night. He said it was a joke and not to repeat it to anyone." Emily's focus left mine. She pulled up her knees and stared at them as her voice sank further. "I asked Royce about it when we went out last year."

I tensed. She made me wait a decade before elaborating.

"He'd been an asshole to me all night, but when I told him I'd heard a rumor about it, he changed. It was like he became a completely different person. He said it wasn't true, of course, but he spent the rest of the night wanting to know *exactly* who I'd heard the rumor from." Her gaze wandered back to mine. "He was angry, Marist. And I think he was scared." Her blue eyes had been soft, but they turned hard. "He was terrified I knew the truth."

I shifted uncomfortably on the floor, wanting to get away from what she was telling me. The whole thing was fucking insane.

Yet . . .

Why did I think there was even the tiniest chance it could be true?

My gaze swiveled to peer through the open kitchen door that led to the dining room. Macalister had sat there last month and announced his family had a tradition, and a woman played a significant role in it. How the board needed to approve me before I could become Royce's wife. There'd also been the invasive questions during my interview.

And Macalister had lectured me about sex being necessary for a healthy marriage.

I scrambled to my feet, knocking over some of the piles I'd spent more than an hour organizing. "If it was true, Royce would have told me."

Even as I said it, I knew it was a lie.

All the Hales had only given me the information they thought I needed to know. Surely, Royce wasn't allowed to tell me. If he had, I could have bolted, and they wouldn't want that. A lot of time and money had been invested in me, and besides—it was win at all costs. It was the Hale family motto, he'd said.

"Oh, my God," I whispered. I pressed a fist into my stomach, desperate to feel anything other than the nausea sweeping through me. I settled on anger and whirled to face my sister. "Why are you telling me this *now*?"

She climbed to her feet, scattering more of the bills around us. "I tried, and . . ." She looked lost. "I thought you'd back out, or it wouldn't get this far."

My rage went from scalding hot to icy cold in an instant as the realization hit me. "You thought I'd fail."

"No," Emily said quickly, but it was pointless. I could read it all over her face. "No, but I . . ."

She might have said something else in her defense, but I didn't hear it. Instead, Royce's comment in the back seat of my car flitted through my mind, how he'd been worried our first time would be *traumatic*.

There was so much he wasn't telling me, how could I believe anything he said? A lie by omission was still a lie. Yet the way Royce had looked at me as I tried on the red dress—even if everything else was manipulation, that moment was real, wasn't it?

"What are you going to do?" Emily asked, jarring me from my thoughts.

I didn't know.

If it was true, could I actually go through with it? Let Royce take my virginity as the rest of the board watched? Including his father? Oh, my God.

The whole idea was like something out of the myths I enjoyed. A dark ritual of sex and power, and I'd be at the center. It made me shudder. Mostly in fear, but the part of me that loved the twisted, fucked-up stories in Greek mythology, it found this appealing.

Jesus, what was wrong with me?

I had to focus. It was too late to turn back, and there were no good options. I stood in the nest of bills, put a hand to my forehead, and closed my eyes. Emily had asked me what I was going to do, and I gave her the best answer I had. "Whatever I have to."

This was the last time I'd see Royce before my final meeting with the board. The initiation, as he and his father had called it. He'd had his driver pick me up, and we rode in the back of the car alternating between stilted conversation and uncomfortable silence. Royce seemed as agitated as I was, but he did a better job at trying not to reveal it.

Maybe he was nervous about the promotion, and not whether he could perform in front of eight other dudes, one of whom was his father.

I was under no delusions what this "date" really was—a photo op. A show. We would get ice cream, then go for a hand-in-hand stroll down Cape Hill's main street to maximize viewing opportunities for the public. Some of the guests for Royce's celebration had already arrived, and since the town was small, it was likely we'd run into people.

"Are you okay?" he asked, stabbing his spoon into his hot fudge sundae. "You seem weird."

"Yeah," I said coolly. "You too."

He frowned, pressing his lips together.

The shop was decorated like an old-fashioned ice cream parlor. It had pink and cream striped wallpaper and white wrought iron chairs with patterned seat cushions. The ice cream dishes were tulip shaped and footed. It was like the 1950s, and I didn't need a reminder of a time where wives were expected to be subservient to their husbands.

"Saturday's going to be difficult." He wiped his face with his napkin, wadded it up, and tossed it on the table. Then he leaned back in his chair and gave me a serious look.

My breath caught. "Difficult how, exactly?"

"We hate parties, remember?"

"Oh. Right." My mood worsened. For a hot second, I'd thought he was going to tell me. But, no.

Last night as I lay awake in my bed, I came fully to terms with it. I'd adapt. I'd give him every opportunity to confess what was going to happen, but if he didn't—I wasn't going to let on that I knew. Information was power, and I'd hold on to it as long as I could. Let him see how much he liked being left in the dark.

I tried to envision what the initiation would be like. It lined my stomach with lead, but also made me uncomfortably hot. Tension wrapped around my body, cinched me tight and kept me still as I burned from the inside out. It was scary and wrong, and I was willing to admit to myself a little exciting too. The big picture was I'd get what I wanted.

Maybe I was prepared to win at all costs to get Royce.

It was June and summer was in full swing, and the ice cream place was busy. I hadn't noticed the blonde girl waving at me until we locked eyes. I wanted to turn and look behind me to see who she was waving at, until I remembered we were seated in the corner and there was no one else it could be.

Noemi Rosso was waving at *me*.

She rose gingerly from her seat, careful of her pregnant belly, and made her way over to me.

"Emily, right?" she said, extending a hand.

My smile froze. Of course, she thought I was my sister. I'd only met the heiress a few times. Her father owned a media empire, and like Royce, she was poised to take control when he retired. Rosso was as much a household name as Hale was.

"Actually," Royce said, turning in his seat, "this is Marist, not—"

He blinked at the sight of the woman, and a smile flashed across his lips as he pushed back his chair to stand.

"Noemi." His tone was warm. "Good to see you."

"Royce." She grinned.

Although they clasped hands in a businesslike handshake, it all seemed so *familiar,* and an unwanted emotion spiked through me. I'd never seen him act sincerely friendly before. It probably didn't help that Noemi was beautiful. She was close to him in age, maybe the same or a year older.

"Congratulations on the promotion," she said. Her hand fell to rest on her belly, and the wedding rings glittered on her finger.

"Thanks. I was surprised you decided to come."

"Of course. This worked out great. Joseph and I wanted to get out of Chicago for a weekend while it was still just the two of us." She gave a sly smile to the man I hadn't noticed standing beside her until now. "I don't think you've met my husband. This is Joseph Monsato."

The men engaged in a cursory handshake and exchanged hellos.

I didn't follow the gossip rags, but there was no avoiding the story. Noemi's husband was at least fifteen years older than she was, and soon after they'd eloped, she'd gotten pregnant. The tabloids accused him of seducing her for her money, and most of the stories downplayed how he had money of his own.

Joseph's dark eyes followed his wife with reverence, and it was obvious to me their marriage had nothing to do with money.

Was it possible the same would ever be said of mine?

"This is my girlfriend," Royce announced. "Marist Northcott."

I pushed to my feet, squeezed out a smile, and shook the couple's hands while Royce's statement buzzed in my brain. *Girlfriend.* Once again, it had come from him so quick and naturally.

I had to remind myself to be careful. He was a spectacular liar.

"Nice to meet you," I said.

"Marist," Noemi repeated. "We've met before, right?"

"Yeah. I think at the HBHC golf classic last year." And a few other events before that, but I wasn't going to point it out. She wouldn't remember me.

"Ah, yeah. Didn't you have green hair, or am I totally making that up? Sorry, pregnancy has eaten my brain."

"No," Royce said with a chuckle, "that's her."

Noemi's gaze turned to him. "Well, it's nice to see you both again. We didn't mean to interrupt. I was craving some mint chocolate chip and thought I should say 'hi.' I'm sure we'll see each other this weekend."

"Yeah, of course." Royce nodded.

She gave a final smile, took her husband's hand, and then they disappeared out the door.

It made sense Royce would be friends with her; they had a lot in common. They were from two of the wealthiest, most powerful families in America and pseudo celebrities. I'd never experienced that.

As we slid back into our seats, Royce's tone was matter-of-fact. "If my father could have picked any woman in the world for me to marry, it would have been her. He pushed her dad for her to apply to Etonsons, but I don't think she got in."

My jaw fell open, but I promptly shut it. The two of them would have been a great couple. Noemi's family had a ton of prestige and power, and she was gorgeous and Royce's age. But I didn't like the thought of them together at all. I was glad she hadn't gotten in to Etonsons, stayed in Chicago, and the two of them never became more than friends.

It worked out better for everyone this way.

*Oh, my God.* The possessiveness I felt toward Royce was staggering. I'd never thought I'd be a jealous person, but one simple conversation showed me otherwise.

"You should know," he said, using the same straightforward tone, "if my father had asked me to pick, I'd have chosen the one sitting across from me right now, not eating her ice cream and looking pissed."

I thought I'd erected all these defenses, yet he punched right through them. I couldn't tell if this was manipulation or real, but I *wanted* it to be the truth. It was painful to look at him.

"Promise me," I said abruptly, my words whisper quiet as I stared at my melting ice cream, "that you're not going to hurt me."

His eyes widened and he drew in an enormous breath. The silence stretched between us until every part of me ached. I longed for him to say something. Anything. His expression was heartbreaking.

"I can't promise you that," he matched my hushed voice, "but I promise I'll try my best not to."

I parroted back the same words his father had given me. "Well, that's all you can ask of someone, isn't it?"

On Saturday, I nearly threw up on the solo car ride over to the Hale estate. I'd been too anxious to eat all day, and now acid roiled in my stomach. Maybe I could ask Alice for some toast when I got there. And perhaps I could get some Xanax sprinkled on top too.

She'd insisted I come over by three p.m. to get ready. Thursday, the preparations had officially begun. I'd visited her salon of torture, been given another painful Brazilian, and Sebastian refreshed my hair color. Yesterday, it had been manicures, pedicures, and a spray tan.

This afternoon, two chairs had been brought into one of the guest suites, and Alice and I sat in them while her team of stylists went to work, twisting and curling and pinning until our hair was stacked high on our heads. Conversation wasn't difficult. I was too nervous to speak, and Alice talked non-stop, rattling off all the guests I needed to make sure I mingled with tonight.

I'd been so focused on the initiation, I hadn't given much

thought to the party afterward. Was it possible to dread that more than the impending sex?

When our makeup had been expertly applied, Alice set her hand on my shoulder and leaned over, putting her face near mine. She held her phone out, high above us and angled down.

"Smile!" It came out light and breezy, but I heard the demand in it all the same.

I pulled my lips back, showing my teeth.

"No," she scolded. "Smile with your eyes too."

I forced myself to look happy and carefree, and it must have been satisfying enough for her, because she snapped a few and then airdropped the best photo to my phone in my lap. She didn't have to tell me what to do next. I opened the Instagram app.

The picture I was about to post gave me pause. There Alice and I were, looking excited and like new best friends, who'd just enjoyed getting their makeovers together. The whole thing was so fucking deceitful.

And yet, I posted in anyway.

*Win at all costs.*

The red Donna Willow dress had been altered to fit me, but I held my breath as Alice finished tugging the ribbons tight at the back. Last time I'd had the dress on, I'd felt powerful, and I hoped the magic was still there. I needed every ounce of strength today.

I stared at the finished product in the full-length mirror. I barely recognized the girl staring back at me.

Alice sighed wistfully. "It's like she made the dress

for you." Her expression was full of admiration. "You are breathtaking."

I swallowed hard. "Thank you."

She turned to leave, but I did something I'd never done before. I reached out and grasped her wrist to stop her. To make her feel a connection. I wasn't sure who it startled more, me or her. Her wide eyes went from my grasp to my face.

"Thank you for everything, Alice."

Did she know what I meant? I'd done my best, struggling through what they wanted, and although at times she'd been aloof and direct, I wouldn't have gotten this far without her. I wanted her on my side.

The corner of her mouth twisted up into a half-smile, but it looked like she didn't know whether to laugh or apologize. Her normally confident voice faltered. "You're welcome."

There was a knock at the bedroom door, followed by a male voice. "He's asking for her."

Suddenly, I was pulled close. Panic swamped her face and her words were urgent and low. "Try to enjoy it."

"What?" I reared back. Had she really just said that?

But the nervous Alice disappeared. She hardened back into her veneer, returning to the cheerful woman from twenty seconds ago. "Come in," she called.

The door swung open.

Vance Hale looked similar to his older brother Royce. He had the same long nose, blue eyes, and brown hair, but he was taller. More lanky and slender, like a long-distance runner without an ounce of fat. It made his high cheekbones look razor sharp.

The guy's social calendar put Alice's to shame, and I hadn't seen him in ages. His hair was different from before. It was neat and tidy, and he looked so polished and comfortable in his tuxedo, had I not known him, I would have wondered if he'd been born in one.

As I assessed him, he did the same. His curious gaze raked down me and back up again, and his smile was easy. "Hey, Marist. Pretty dress."

"Hi." I was so nervous, I was vibrating. "Thanks."

"You ready? Royce wants a word."

My feet wouldn't move. I was rooted to the carpet. Worse, my mouth filled with glue and wouldn't work. Fear gripped me in its vise. It told me as long as I stayed where I was, I would be okay.

His head tilted to the side in confusion.

"Marist?" Alice prompted.

No. I wouldn't be an avoider like the rest of my family. I willed my feet to begin moving. I ordered my heart not to beat too fast and make me lightheaded. I demanded my lips and tongue do my bidding. When I'd stepped into the red dress, I'd pulled on the other version of myself—the girl the Hales wanted me to be.

The girl who could handle anything.

"Sorry." It was surprising how normal it sounded from me. "I'm ready."

Vance escorted me along the hallway, and when we reached the top of the grand staircase, I grasped a handful of the skirt to lift so I wouldn't trip. I wasn't expecting him to take my other hand and help guide me. The gentlemanly gesture was . . . nice. His hand was warm and steady, and it distracted as we descended the stairs.

"I'm glad it was you," he said at the bottom. His face shifted from serious to playful. "I had such a crush on Emily. This would have been weird."

Did he know what was about to happen? "Right," I said. "Because this isn't weird at all."

His surprised smile was wide. He nodded toward the closed door ahead of us, the one which led into the formal dining room. "You better get in there. He thinks I can't tell, but he's nervous."

Vance pulled open the door for me and waited beside it.

The heavy curtains had been drawn closed, and the extravagant crystal chandelier that loomed over the dining table wasn't lit. The room was naturally dark, paneled in walnut that was so deep in color it was nearly black, which made the formal space somber and cold. The red rug, trimmed in gold, beneath the huge dining table did nothing to warm it up.

The only source of light came from the flickering, five-arm candelabras around the room. Long, white tapers burned, and crystals dangled from each base. There were two candelabras spaced evenly apart in the center of the table, one on the side buffet, and one tucked in the arched, built-in alcove.

It transformed the dining room into a shadowy cave. If I hadn't been filled with apprehension, I might have laughed at how over the top it was. But this wasn't a space for laughter. It was ominous. Its walls held secrets of perversion.

Royce was waiting beside the buffet table, and I was drawn to him. My dress fluttered around me like moth wings, and he was the flame I couldn't resist, even if he was going to be my downfall.

He was spectacular, wrapped in a classic tuxedo without a vest, a black bow tied at his neck, and a glass of champagne in one hand. When the door was pulled closed behind me, it drew his attention. He lifted his gaze to meet mine, and for a long moment we simply stared at each other from across the room, drinking in the sight of the other.

His shoulders pulled back as he straightened, and his intense eyes went wide. He liked what he saw, but it also seemed to be hurting him. I understood. I felt the same ache down to the marrow of my bones.

There was awe in his voice. "You are devastating."

My knees weakened. My entire body wanted to go soft and puddle at his words. He could have said I was beautiful, but no. He'd chosen a word that gave me power, saying I could lay waste to others. I was too tense to respond with words. I swallowed and nodded, hoping he could read the gratitude in my eyes.

Royce picked up a second flute of champagne from the side table and strode toward me. As I reached out to accept it, he caught the subtle tremble in my hand.

"You're nervous," he said. It wasn't a question, just him stating facts.

I took a tiny sip of the champagne, letting the bubbles work my tongue loose. "Yes. It's better now that I'm here with you."

Because it felt like I'd crossed the point of no return. I was locked in, and he was with me. It alleviated the anxiety about whether I could back out and run. All I had to do now was get through it.

Being around him helped me, but was the opposite true for him? As I settled into my choice, he seemed more nervous. Like now he was thinking about backing out and running. Instead, he set his glass down on the dining table and pulled out one of the chairs.

"We need to talk," he said. "And you're going to want to sit down for this."

His expression announced he was so uncomfortable, it verged on pain, so I took the offered seat. He grasped the back of the chair beside me, dragging it away from the table, but he didn't sit. Instead, he returned to the buffet and retrieved something.

"Before we get into it, I have something for you."

He set the black box down in front of me and dropped into his seat. If this was an engagement ring, it must be enormous. The box, tied with a red satin bow, was as big as a hardcover book.

My hands shook as I unknotted the ribbon and lifted the lid, my breath held.

One look inside and I burst into tears.

# FOURTEEN

ALL THE EMOTIONS I'D BEEN TRYING TO AVOID POURED OUT OF me now in one uncontrollable instant. I gripped the lid of the box so tightly, the cardboard bent in my hands. Tears streamed hotly down my cheeks, likely destroying the make-up Alice's stylists had applied.

Royce looked terrified. "Oh, shit. Please don't cry."

He had no idea how to deal with me, but it didn't matter. At that moment, he could do nothing wrong. I stared at the Harry Winston necklace I thought I'd never see again, letting my gaze trace the delicate cluster of diamonds.

I could barely whisper. "This is for me?"

"Yes. It's yours."

I wiped away my tears with my thumb, and even though I was crying, I laughed in amazement too. "How? How did you . . ."

"Alice showed me the picture on Instagram. Costolli let me buy it before it went to auction."

I had to look up to the unlit chandelier to keep from

spilling more tears. "Oh, my God, Royce."

Confusion spread across his face. "You don't like it?"

"Are you kidding?" I dropped the lid and turned in my seat, gripping his face in my hands. "Thank you. My God, I can't even find the words." Now this heirloom could remain in my family. "You don't know how much this means to me."

His hands gently cuffed my wrists, and his eyes melted. "Tell me."

"It was my great-grandmother's." I struggled to rein in my emotions. "My mom wore it when she married my dad, and I hoped I'd get to wear it on my wedding day."

"Well, now you can." He let go and drew back out of my hands, his expression shuttering. "Even if it's not to me."

"Why wouldn't it be to you?" My heartrate inched toward the chandelier.

He ignored my question. Royce grabbed the box, dipped a hand inside, and gently lifted the necklace out. He unclasped it and stood, draping it down over my front. The cold line of diamonds kissed the sides of my neck and I held still as he fastened it. It was heavy, but it belonged. I hadn't felt like something was missing until it was there, completing me.

His hand lingered at the nape of my neck, fingers trailing down the line of my spine. It gave me a delicious shiver.

"There's a mirror," he said softly.

It hung over the banquet, and I rose from my chair. He followed alongside, and when I gasped at the sight of the glittering necklace, his eyes filled with pride. I slipped a hand up to curl around the back of his neck, fisting his hair and pulled him into my urgent, grateful kiss.

Even though our lips were pressed together, he held himself back from me. The kiss was . . . reluctant. *Guilty*. Like he thought he had no right to accept it from me, when it should have been the other way around. He'd spent a fortune on this necklace, and if I wasn't so desperate, I should have refused.

When he ended the kiss, the mood in the room shifted, and in the flickering candlelight, his hesitation made him look like a statue. "I need to remind you of the non-disclosure you've signed, because what we're going to talk about can't be repeated. Ever."

He motioned to the chairs, all businesslike. I shook my head. "I think I'd prefer to stand."

He looked pained all over again, a frown twisting the lips I'd just kissed. "Marist, please. This is hard for me, and if you could—"

"I know," I interrupted. I gave him the most serious look I possessed so he would understand. "I *already* know."

His eyes narrowed with distrust, disguising his worry. "What do you think you know?"

"You're going to take my virginity in front of them."

He flinched and went wooden.

Whatever was going on in his mind, I couldn't read it. His expression was devoid of emotion. The longer he stood there, simply blinking at me like I was a ghost he couldn't believe he was seeing, the more upset I became.

I'd held out hope that he would laugh and tell me I was being ridiculous. Or that he'd say he'd found a way out. He could forgo the archaic and insane tradition.

That hope died earlier when I came into this room. I

sensed it in the air and tasted the hint of promised debauchery. Plus, it was foolish to expect any other outcome. He'd made it perfectly clear he was willing to do whatever was necessary to get what he wanted. He wasn't going to give up a seat with the board to save me.

Royce looked like he wanted to ask a question, but he must have discovered the answer on his own. "Emily."

He'd been wondering how I'd found out. "Yeah," I said.

"Why didn't you tell me?" Betrayal colored his voice. It threw me off-kilter to see him look wounded. "For fuck's sake, Marist. Do you have any idea what this has been like? I didn't sleep at all last night. It's been fucking tearing me apart."

"Are you seriously upset with me for withholding information?" I scowled. "You don't tell me *anything*."

He jammed a hand into his hair, possibly to yank it out. "I couldn't tell you, no matter how much I wanted to. And— fuck—I wanted to so badly."

I sighed, not sure what to believe.

He took off and paced a few steps before coming to an abrupt stop. "Wait a minute. Why are you here?"

Had the champagne gone to his head and killed all his brain cells? "What do you mean, why am I here?"

"You know what's going to happen, and you're still . . ." He couldn't seem to process it. His dubious gaze trapped mine. "You're going through with it?"

I fought a losing battle to sound tough and unaffected. "I don't understand it, but unless you tell me there's another way, I came prepared to do what"—I struggled to find the words—"needs to be done." I gripped the elbow of my other arm in awkward posture that Alice would probably scold if she saw. "We both need this to get what we want, right?"

His chest expanded with a deep breath, and his voice was quiet. "I was sure you were going to say no. That you'd walk away, and I'd never see you again. It's why I wasn't allowed to tell you until today."

"Because what girl in her right mind would agree to this?" I said bitterly.

And then I was suddenly in his arms, his hot mouth fused to mine. He wasn't holding anything back this time. His kiss was desperate and full of passion, and it stole all the air from my lungs.

"I'll make it fast," he murmured as he peppered more kisses to me. "It won't count. We'll do it for real when it's just you and me. The real us. That will be our first time."

I found it oddly comforting to think of it that way. I wasn't losing my virginity while a bunch of other men watched—the fake version of myself would be.

"I need to know why it's like this," I said.

"I'll tell you, but there's something else." He closed his eyes and pressed his forehead to mine. Since I was fitted tight against him, I could feel how fast his heart was pumping. "Each board member is going to—"

The sharp, jarring sound of knuckles banging on wood made us jolt. Someone was knocking on the door.

Royce's thumbs brushed over my cheeks, hurriedly wiping away smudged mascara. "It's going to be okay, no matter what. I'm right here. Close your eyes, and it will be just us."

If his goal was to soothe me, it had the opposite effect.

It sent my stomach plummeting to my toes. When the door behind us opened, Royce separated from me. The boy who'd been kissing me seconds ago faded into the hard, selfish persona like a reverse cocoon. He turned his cold focus to the men sweeping into the dark room.

It was a parade of tuxedos and faces I recognized, but also ones who caused a cold sweat to break out and cling to my skin. They filed in without a word, moving like it had been practiced. Four men to the left, three men to the right.

Macalister was the last to step through the doorway, and when he pulled closed the heavy door, the click of the lock reverberated through my body. There were nine sets of eyes looking at me, but Macalister's glacial ones were the hardest to bear. My dress hid my shaking knees, but there was nothing to be done about my upper body. The dress was strapless, and he could see my trembling shoulders from where he stood.

In his refined tuxedo, he could have been a gorgeous advertisement for expensive watches or high-end liquor. But the one that fit best in my mind right now was he looked like a spy movie villain. The mastermind billionaire who could be charming, or sexy, or cruel depending on the scene.

His gaze worked over my dress, and satisfaction sizzled in his expression.

"I wasn't finished explaining it to her," Royce said. Irritation had him jamming his hands in his pockets. Had he done it to stop himself from balling them into fists?

Macalister's attention slid momentarily to his son as he waved the comment off. "It's fine. I'll handle the rest." He refocused on me. "Good evening, Marist. You look exquisite. Doesn't she, gentlemen?"

There were nods and sounds of approval from the pack. As their leader approached, my pulse skyrocketed and roared at breakneck speed. To anyone else, his smile would appear benign, but it only set me more on edge.

I stood still as he sauntered a slow circle around me, inspecting my body like an expensive cut of meat.

"You can stop this and leave at any time." His tone was firm. "It's important you know that. You can choose not to go further or change your mind at any point. No one is making you stay." He finished his circuit, stopping in front of me. "The decision is yours. So, tell me—who is in control?"

My throat threatened to close up, but I squeaked it out just in time. "I am."

He was pleased I gave the answer he was looking for. "Exactly."

His hand dipped into his tuxedo jacket, and a pen was extracted from his interior pocket. It was held out to me. I stared at it, unsure of what it meant. But it became clear when one of the board members placed a leather portfolio on the dining table.

"It's not a contract," Macalister said. "It's a release, simply stating you're here of your own volition."

They wanted my consent in writing.

When my gaze flicked to Royce, Macalister took a step closer, pulling my focus back to look at him. "We'll all be signing it."

The black pen was trimmed in gold, and it glinted in

the candlelight. When I took it, my fingers brushed his and gave me an unwelcomed sting of electricity. The room was charged with violent, sexual energy.

The black portfolio had been set on the table beside the giftbox and our forgotten glasses of champagne, and when I moved toward it, Royce attempted to clear them away. I grabbed my glass from him and took a huge gulp, watching him put the rest on the side table.

"Please, have a seat," Mr. Lynch said. He'd been the one to carry the portfolio in, which made sense. He was the chief financial officer at HBHC and the man Macalister worked the closest with.

I smoothed a hand down the back of my dress, lowered into the chair, and opened the portfolio.

Paragraphs of text filled the top half of the page, followed by ten signature lines beneath. My name first, and the nine who would make up the board after we were done in this room.

It was nearly impossible to read and comprehend the document as the men towered over me, waiting. I read through it halfway, set down my champagne flute, and tried again from the beginning. Whenever I found myself rushing, the promise I'd made to Alice echoed in my mind.

*Take as much time as you need. Don't sign what you don't understand.*

Macalister shifted his weight impatiently from one foot to the other. "Is there an issue?"

He was wondering what was taking me so long. A contributing factor was how it was all there, spelled out. It said

I'd willingly consent to the board witnessing Royce and I during sexual intercourse. That since I was on birth control and Royce had submitted to a physical proving he was free of any sexually transmitted diseases, there was no need for a condom to be used.

And that I agreed to this while not under any kind of duress.

It was true. No one was making me do this.

But if I walked away, I'd give up everything. There'd be no college degree from Etonsons. No chance to save my family from social and financial ruin. And definitely no Royce Hale.

I swallowed the lump in my throat, and the necklace bobbed with it. "Can you explain this line?" I read aloud from the document. "Each board member will have an equal opportunity to evaluate the participant."

A cold hand slipped onto my bare shoulder. "You will be naked."

I shuddered. Perhaps I should have been grateful for Macalister's grip because it kept me from bolting out of the chair, but his touch was unexpected. So different than his son's.

Like everything else about this day, I'd held out hope that what I suspected wouldn't be true. I'd feared this but expected it, especially with the insisted grooming I'd had to endure at the salon.

My voice was a ghost, too quiet to disturb the flames burning on the candles nearby. "Why?"

The fingers clenched tighter. Not enough to cause pain, just enough to remind me they were there. "So they may evaluate you visually."

"And other ways," Royce commented.

My blood turned to slush as Macalister tensed. The mood in the room was like the stock market had suddenly plummeted six hundred points.

"What other ways?" I demanded.

He gave his son a pointed look, irritated Royce had spoiled the fun. "Each member may use their hands and mouths."

*Hands and . . . mouths?*

I went wooden, and the word came out drenched in horror. "What?"

My gaze traveled the room, as much as it could with my shoulder pinned under Macalister's hand. The men staring back at me watched my reaction with curiosity. I was resigned to my fate with Royce, but this? Letting the rest of the board touch me? Kiss me? Just the idea of Macalister's mouth pressed to mine made panic crawl all over me.

As he released me, his fingertips traced a line along my back. "I know you have questions, but I think everyone will feel more comfortable once you've signed. I can explain when that's done."

"No," I blurted out. "You can explain right now."

He didn't like being told what to do, and certainly not by me. "If I don't?"

I closed the portfolio and went to stand, but this time, Macalister's grip was more forceful. "This tradition goes back a century, and it's one you already agreed to."

I turned under his hold so I could see Royce. He stood

beside his father, wearing an unreadable expression.

"You're all right with this?" I was filled with disbelief.

He was already okay with his dad and boss watching us together, so maybe additional stuff wasn't that big of a deal to him. Or maybe he'd had his whole life to get used to the concept.

Or perhaps this was a cost he was willing to pay to get the seat he wanted.

Candlelight flickered over him as Royce glanced at his father, and—was that malice echoing through his expression? His gaze landed back on me, and he emptied of emotion. "I'd rather my father not be involved."

I let out a tight breath. Removing Macalister from this part might make it . . . bearable. I tried not to look fearful as I peered up at him. "I agree with Royce."

Everything from his expression to his words were absolute. "I am the chairman of this board. It's my responsibility to protect its members, and therefore, my vote counts more than anyone else's."

"All right." I swallowed a breath. "Then make Royce your proxy."

My attention was locked onto Macalister, but out of the corner of my eye, I saw Royce straighten with surprise.

"No," Macalister said simply, as if overruling me were that easy. "I'm not relinquishing my vote."

I saw everything in his eyes. As chairman, he felt this was his God-given right. I was owed to him. He was willing to pay five million dollars for my participation, and he wasn't going to give up control. But had he forgotten what he'd told me?

"I won't sign this unless you do."

He leaned down and uttered it with condescension. "Then you'll leave here with nothing."

"If I walk out of here, we both lose. You'll have to tell your guests that Royce's promotion has been postponed."

Macalister let go of me and stared down, evaluating to see if this were a bluff.

It wasn't.

I'd put up with a lot, but this was my limit. Besides, the past month had shown me how important this was to him. He wouldn't give up a hundred years of tradition and look like a fool, just because he'd been asked to step aside.

He needed me as much as I needed his money.

It was a gamble because it might piss him off, but I went in for the kill. "Who's in control?"

A range of emotions flitted across his expression. Disbelief. Anger. Frustration. But the last one was harder to place. Begrudging respect?

He seethed as he said it. "You are." He tacked the final word on, and I didn't miss the danger that lurked in it. "Tonight."

I wanted to look at Royce and see his reaction but didn't dare risk it. Macalister was deep in thought, considering his next move.

Finally, he spoke. "If I do this, I'm not giving my vote to Royce for nothing."

It terrified me to ask. What did I have to offer that was of any value to him? "What do you want?"

"You need to understand something. There are only two

things in this world that are important to me. My family and my company."

I understood that perfectly, although I'd argue he had them in the wrong order.

"It would reflect badly on all of us if Royce's marriage were to fail." He delivered the statement as merely an observation and not the implied threat it really was. "It's best we figure that out before the vows, don't you agree?"

I wasn't going to like where he was heading. "Of course."

"It will take at least a year to plan the wedding, and you'll want to finish your degree beforehand."

"Yes."

"You'll use that time to see how compatible you two are long-term." The faintest of smiles curled on his lips. "We'll make arrangements to have your things brought to the house. You'll have your own room, of course."

The shocked word tumbled from my mouth. "What?"

His tone was plain. "You'll move in next week. It will give you more time with Royce and make you more accessible to Alice for the wedding planning. It's a shorter commute to Etonsons."

"No." It was a knee-jerk reaction.

Macalister lifted an eyebrow. "When you're married, you will live here. I don't see the point in delaying it."

It was difficult to decide which idea scared me the most. Being trapped under the same roof as him, or that I couldn't figure out his true agenda. Was he asking for this just because he knew I wouldn't want it? Or was it another way for him to have control of Royce and me?

"I'm not ready." I needed to be home with my family to help with the finances, but moreover, I needed to have a place to escape the Hales. I couldn't catch my breath, and the plea came out shallow. "Please, Macalister."

It was the first time I'd ever addressed him by his name, and I tightened, unsure how he'd react. His eyes widened and his lips parted to draw in a deep breath. He was off-kilter for a single moment, before his handsome face hardened. "I want to be clear. Royce will act on my behalf, but I will still oversee the initiation. In exchange, you will live here. That's my offer."

Like last time I'd negotiated with him, neither of us seemed happy.

"Do you agree?" he asked.

Was I trading one brief encounter with him tonight, only to give him a lifetime of more?

I clumsily uncapped the pen, and it took more than one attempt to rest the cap on the other side of it. Even though this wasn't a contract, and I could walk away after signing, there was a terrible finality to putting the ink on the paper. It was a stain that couldn't be washed away.

I couldn't stand not to look at Royce one more time.

He'd retreated so far inside himself I barely recognized the man I'd discovered hidden inside. There was only a flicker of him now, lurking in his eyes.

The flicker was just enough to make me scrawl my name on the line.

"Good. Royce?" Macalister prompted.

Royce took the pen from my hand and signed his name

with a quick flourish. He dropped it with a thud and gently grasped my wrist, urging me to stand. He moved me out of the way so the other men could form a line, and each signed in their place on the document. As I stood there watching it, Royce's warm hand remained curled around me. The connection between us was a closed circuit, and when he brushed his thumb softly over the inside of my wrist, electricity flowed freely between us.

Macalister was the last to sign. When he finished, he closed the portfolio, picked up my glass of champagne, and offered it to me. Yet, as his gaze etched over the necklace, seemingly mapping each diamond in the wreath, his expression darkened.

Royce released me, severing our connection, leaving me to step forward and take the flute of champagne from his father.

"Thank you," I said automatically.

"No, I believe it's us that need to thank you," Macalister said. He looked like he was going to say something else, but a distracted frown crossed his face. "Your necklace is very nice, but it's too much. Tonight is supposed to be about Royce, not you."

From behind me, Royce's irritated voice rang out. "It's at least a little about her."

His father didn't appreciate the tone and delivered a stern look to his son. "Take it off."

For a moment, no one moved. The Hale men were locked in a silent battle, but the fingertips at the clasp on the back of my neck announced Macalister had won this round.

The weight of the necklace shifted, one end coming loose and skating down my front before being pulled away.

I felt naked and exposed already, and it was the only thing to come off so far.

Footsteps carried Royce away, leaving me alone to face his father and the group of men gathered around us in a half-circle while he put the necklace away in its box.

"The Hale family," Macalister announced, "came here from Germany at the turn of the nineteenth century, back when our country was almost as young as you are. We'd been watchmakers, but Eduard Hale had a head for finance. He worked for years at different banking firms before starting his own, which eventually grew into the Hale Banking and Holding Company of today. I am the eighth Hale to head up the board." He pushed back one side of his black jacket and slipped a hand in his pocket, relaxing just enough to look less scary. "Royce, or Vance, will be the ninth."

I mentally tripped over the statement. It had always been a given to me that Royce would take control when his father retired, but then again . . . The brothers had received identical educations, and Macalister pushed both of his sons hard. He'd had no qualms pitting them against each other.

It added another layer to Royce's situation. Even after joining the board, would he still be competing for that top spot? All the way until his father stepped down?

"The company's history isn't perfect," Macalister continued. "After the Civil War, they'd pledged too much stock to back their loans. This was before the Federal Reserve existed. Being a student of economics, you might remember what happened in 1907."

I wasn't sure where he was going with this history lesson. "The Panic?"

Three weeks of turmoil had gripped America as people and companies made terrified runs to the banks to withdraw their money, and some were left with nothing.

Again, he was pleased with my answer. "The Stock Exchange plummeted. Banks weren't just going out of business in New York, they were failing all over the country. Wall Street was in crisis. When my company's loans were called, we nearly went bankrupt. But my great-great grandfather, Nelson Hale, was incredibly savvy. He consolidated investments, organized a merger between the railroads, and freed up enough capital to avert disaster." There was admiration in his voice. "He is one of the great men credited with stabilizing the US economy."

Macalister's lips turned up in an ironic smile.

"It's quite spectacular, all he accomplished," he said, "especially considering he suffered a debilitating stroke the prior year and was completely incapacitated."

"What?" I asked. "How—"

"His wife Alma, my great-great grandmother. With the help of the board, she saved the company. Nelson remained as the figurehead, but it was her pulling the strings while ensuring no one knew. For ten years she ruled in secret, and HBHC flourished. She made the board very wealthy, and they owed everything to her." Something dark and sexual swirled in the room, so powerful, it seemed to make the candles flicker.

"In return," he said quietly, "they showed her their appreciation in ways her husband no longer could."

*Oh, my God.*

His icy eyes wandered down over my frame. "Marriage is a partnership, and we need to know what kind of woman you are, Marist. If you would be willing to step in and do what needs to be done to protect the Hale name, no matter how hard it was." His inescapable gaze connected with mine. "Would you?"

I dragged air into my body. I wasn't touching Royce, but I could feel him near, lingering behind me. "Yes," I whispered.

This faint smile from Macalister was the most sinister of them all. "Then we ask that you prove it." He nodded to Royce. "You'll bind yourself not just to him, but to this board."

There was a tug at my back, and my eyes widened. He was undoing the knots on my corset.

*Holy. Fuck.*

Macalister pulled the untouched glass of champagne from my grasp. I'd forgotten it existed, and as soon as my hands were empty, I pressed them to the front of my dress. My chest heaved, but the dress was a skeleton of boning and fabric, caging me in. I fluttered nakedly inside my prison, not ready to be released.

I held the dress as the laces at my back were loosened, my gaze fixed on Macalister, although I sensed the other men as well. I felt their heavy eyes scouring me, waiting with bated breath.

The back of my dress was undone by Royce's sure hands, and with my flesh bared to only him, he took advantage. It was his favorite part of a woman, after all. His palms crept inside and slid over my skin just like he'd done in the library upstairs last year.

That night had been a century ago.

Neither of us should be those people right now. I was supposed to be the girl who could handle anything. But I came undone when Royce's lips ghosted a kiss against my back.

"Be Medusa," he whispered.

I sucked in a final breath, let go of my dress, and as it cascaded down my body, I unleashed my power, turning all the men into stone.

# FIFTEEN

THE RED DRESS COASTED DOWN MY LEGS UNTIL IT WAS A HEAP of satin and tulle at my ankles. I wasn't wearing a bra since the dress molded to my body and offered support. I stood before the board in nothing more that a pair of lace panties.

My mind was as motionless as the men looking at me.

Of course, it was Macalister who recovered first. His gaze washed down and hovered on my breasts. Invisible fingers slipped over me, tracing the curves of my exposed, sensitive flesh. His attention lingered on my nipples, teasing the distended tips with a featherlight touch.

It seemed to happen in slow motion. His hand extended to me in an offer. Or a demand. I was bashful and wanted to cover myself, but what was the point? I wasn't done until they'd seen it all.

I stared at his hand, unsure.

"I can't make him my proxy," Macalister said, "until we've begun."

Meaning the initiation hadn't officially started.

I didn't know how I had the strength, but I reached out and took Macalister's cold hand. He used his hold to urge me to step free of the dress, but once I had, he didn't release me. He squeezed my fingers and guided me to walk with him.

My breasts swayed with each inelegant step I took in the red bottomed heels Alice had dressed me in, and I held my body tight and careful. It was a sexual promenade to the far end of the enormous dining table with a court of hungry men in tuxedos trailing behind us. There was something darkly powerful about it. I was the queen, and their desire made them my subjects.

When we reached the head of the table, Macalister let go of me and pulled the large, ornate chair out of the way. More chairs scraped over the rug and hardwood as they were dragged away, making room for the board. Royce moved in, turning me so my back was to the men and he became all I could see. He smoothed his warm palms over my stomach, sliding them around my body until they came to rest on the small of my back. His eyes searched my face, desperate to make sure I was okay.

It was so much easier like this when he was all that existed. I pressed my body against his, flattening my breasts to his dress shirt. We couldn't stay like this forever, though. He'd come to me with a purpose, and his fingers hesitantly inched toward the lace. It was the last scrap of fabric hiding me from everyone else.

It had to be quite the image. I was nearly naked in his arms, while the men gathered around the table. Once again, four on one side and three on the other, the Hales and I at the end. It tasted like pennies in my mouth, which I found ironic until I realized I'd bitten the inside of my cheek so hard I'd drawn blood.

The question was loud in Royce's expression. He needed to know if I could keep going. I gave the subtlest of nods and closed my eyes.

Down, he pulled the lace, dragging it over my thighs and trembling knees. My breath went so shallow I was barely taking air into my body, and I swayed, a reed in the wind. One strong gust and I'd break.

The quick, uneven breath and shuffle of feet was the only thing I could hear when he bent, and my underwear dropped all the way to my ankles. Then Royce straightened, and his voice went nearly silent, like he didn't want to disturb me or the quiet in the room.

"Have a seat."

I had to open my eyes to do it. I put my hands down beside me on the tabletop at my back, and my bare skin squealed as I got up, sliding until my knees were at the edge, my feet dangling over the side. I pinched my legs together and my shoulders were tight to my ears. Tension twisted so hard inside me it made my chest hurt.

This command came from Macalister instead of his son. "Lie back."

*Oh, God.*

Trepidation was strong, but so was relief. It wouldn't be long now, and the sooner we started, the sooner it would be over. I'd waited so fucking long, the darkest part inside of me no longer cared how it happened. I was eager for Royce to make me his.

The table was a hard slab of concrete against my heated skin. My shoes and panties were removed, and I curled my awkward hands in fists, resting them tensely over my stomach. I couldn't really see the Hales at the end of the table, but the other men? They stood shoulder to shoulder at the sides of the table, their curious and thirsty gazes exploring the naked landscape before them.

"Are you comfortable?" Macalister's tone was pleasant and off-putting.

"Yeah," I said, punctuated by a nervous, sarcastic laugh. Being naked was beyond disorienting. "This is great."

Although I couldn't see him without lifting my head, I felt Royce stiffen at my flippant tone. I wished I could take it back. If the board found me disrespectful, would I lose their approval? I pressed my lips together to keep anything else unfiltered from coming out.

Rather than look upset, Macalister appeared understanding and turned to his son. "There's a pillow in the cabinet with the hourglass."

Right, I wanted to say. A pillow was going to make all the difference. I stared up at the chandelier, ignoring the eyes leering down at me. I'd never really been naked in front of the opposite sex. Royce had seen all of my body, but not at one time, and now there were nine men seeing me at once.

*Try to enjoy it*, Alice had said.

Had she done this? Lain right here on this same spot while Macalister fucked her? Had she been special enough to warrant a pillow? I wanted to giggle inappropriately. My emotions were all over the place.

My eyelids fluttered closed as I drew in a deep breath through my nose and pushed it out slowly through my mouth, hoping to center myself. A cabinet opened and clicked closed, followed by rustling. Then fabric, covering a male form, leaned into me.

"Marist," Royce whispered.

There was a gold throw pillow in his hands, and when I lifted my head to look at him, he slipped it beneath me. It was marginally better because it kept the pins in my hair from digging into my scalp, but it was also so much worse. It made it so I would be able to view all the men surrounding me more clearly.

Especially Macalister Hale, who stared at me shamelessly with lust burning in his eyes. I flinched from the heat of it, and my mouth went bone dry. I ripped my gaze away from him and refocused on Royce. I didn't know what the rules were. I wasn't sure if it was allowed, but I did it anyway. He was within striking distance, so I reached up and threaded a hand through the back of his soft hair.

This was a merger, but it didn't have to lack emotion or passion. I was supposed to be in control, and I decided to flex my power.

He didn't resist as I pulled up to meet his mouth with mine. His lips parted and welcomed my tongue when it slid inside, seeking out his. But he leashed his kiss. Everything was guarded about it, yet I still tasted the molten desire beneath. Or at least I wanted to badly enough, I convinced myself I did.

It was just us for a moment.

Hurried breaths, lips moving against lips, and my soft sigh.

And then Macalister cleared his throat, making Royce slip from my grasp.

A chill rippled over me as his heat evaporated, and when he moved back from the table, he knocked over something on the floor.

Mr. Shaunessy caught his elbow to prevent him from falling. "Careful."

Royce nodded. He bent and picked the item up, holding it where I could see. An hourglass. The two kissing bulbs of glass were encased in four bars of dark wood, and it was hard to tell the exact shade in the dim lighting, but the sand inside was a deep red.

Without explanation, fear gripped me just as Royce gripped the bars to hold the hourglass in front of him. Perhaps it was because the timing sand was the same color as blood and I hated the sight of it, but I knew better. It was deeper than that. I sensed this had been brought out for dark, ritualistic purpose.

"I'm reminding you again," Macalister's voice slashed deeper into my anxiety, "you are here because you've chosen to be. If you want to stop, you only have to say so. Agreed?"

My teeth were chattering, but not from the cold. "Yes, sir."

Only a hint of a smile ghosted across his lips, but it felt more real than any other smile he'd given me. He looked at his men who surrounded the table and nodded. It was a clear signal. *Let's begin.*

Hands reached out to hold me, and I gasped. Shock flooded every muscle in me, and as I instinctively tried to pull away, it drove me toward the hands on the other side of the table. My wrists were circled, and my arms gently pulled away from my body. Palms closed around my shoulders, my waist, my thighs.

None of it was rough or forceful or aggressive, but regardless, I was pinned naked to the table by seven sets of hands, and they all belonged to strangers. My eyes went enormously wide and breath seized in my lungs.

I was trapped, but I'd also been handed the key. I could set myself free at any time; all I had to do was utter a single word. I quit fighting against my restraints and tried awkwardly to adjust to my new captivity.

Was this how it was going to happen? The board would hold me down as Royce took my virginity? Was this some *Handmaid's Tale* shit? It was fucked up, but even worse . . . a tiny thrill sliced through me. It cracked open just enough room for unwanted pleasure to have me squeezing my knees tight together.

This sordid rite was like something straight out of the mythology books I found so compelling. I was a virgin sacrifice on Mount Olympus, and the men surrounding me believed they were gods.

I stared at Royce over my heaving chest. He wasn't looking at me, although I didn't get the sense it was out of shame for himself or respect for me. His attention was set on Zeus, waiting impatiently for his next command from the chairman. Or perhaps the moment his father's power would be handed to him.

The chair that had been moved out of the way was dragged back into place at the head of the table, and Macalister gestured toward it. "This is my seat," he said to Royce, his tone full of resentment. "But tonight, it will be yours."

Royce passed the hourglass to his father. When he unbuttoned his coat and lowered to sit on the throne, my heart beat so violently I grew lightheaded. He was *right there* in front of me. My feet dangled between his spread knees.

"You're committing yourself to this board," Macalister said. "By putting the company before yourself, you're giving us a tremendous gift, Marist." I shuddered when he said my name. "One which we have immense gratitude for."

Mr. Lynch and Mr. Scoffield each had a palm on the top of my thighs, but when Royce's hands closed on my knees and urged them apart, those palms slid inward.

Nervous excitement made me tremble.

I lifted my head, staring down as the men spread me open and bared my nakedness to Royce, and a horrific thought flooded my mind. This was supposed to be Macalister's seat. If I hadn't negotiated, he would be the man before me.

My feet were guided and set on the armrests of the chair, and then the two men flanking it locked both of my knees under their arms.

"What are . . ." I gasped, swallowing a gulp of air and choking on it.

The low light in the room heightened the shadows, and as they flickered over Macalister's face, he looked wicked. "Each board member will have one minute to show you his appreciation and prepare you for your partnership with Royce."

I couldn't hold onto my thoughts enough to process what he was saying. I ran after them, but they slipped through my fingers, nothing more than wisps of air. It left me disoriented and confused. Prepare me?

"As chairman, I would go first." Envy coated Macalister's voice.

Royce's warm hands skated along the insides of my thighs, creeping upward. Goosebumps lifted on my skin in the aftermath of his touch. He leaned forward, closing in as his hands glided all the way to the most feminine part of me.

"And the chairman also goes last," he whispered.

When his thumbs peeled me open, I gasped at his touch. I stopped breathing altogether when his head dipped down, and he delivered his shockingly intimate kiss.

# SIXTEEN

My heart ground to a halt. A cry erupted from my chest, and I lurched against the hands holding me still. Beyond Royce's shoulder, Macalister turned over the hourglass in his hands, and the sand began to fall.

Royce's lips were all I could feel at first, but then something soft and wet brushed over me, and it could only be his tongue.

*Fucking Mother of God.*

My head thudded back against the pillow and I slammed my eyes shut, too stunned to do anything other than endure. His palms were on the insides of my legs, and as his tongue glided over my bare skin, he pressed me further open.

A year ago, I'd stood in the upstairs hallway and wondered what it would feel like to have a man's mouth on me. Well, now I knew. It was a strange, wonderful sensation. I ordered myself not to like it, but no amount of convincing would make my body believe. The tongue on my center probed and fluttered, and heat washed along my legs. It traveled through me, tightened my nipples, and set my face on fire.

Royce Hale was going down on me while all the gods watched.

Was this really happening? My head snapped up and I opened my eyes, staring in disbelief. There he was in his black tuxedo jacket and white shirt sleeves peeking out at his wrists, adorned with silver cufflinks. His blue eyes trapped mine as his lips parted. The tip of his tongue stroked slowly over my sensitive clit in one long . . .

Indecent . . .

*Lick.*

A moan swelled out of me.

Thankfully, Macalister's gaze wasn't on us. It was focused on the top half of the hourglass, and it allowed my attention to swing back to the man pleasuring me with his mouth.

And there was pleasure, no doubt about it. Royce's tongue whipped at me and made me squirm. I wanted to split down the middle. Give the sensible part of myself an escape, and the wrong, depraved part a safe place to stay and enjoy. Not just what he was doing, but the way the men watched.

He fucked me with his mouth while the board held on to me, and I heaved air into my body, fighting the swell of satisfaction that was brewing in my center. The hands gripping me were a lie for my benefit. It made me feel like I had no choice.

Yet I made the decision repeatedly to stay with each flick of Royce's tongue.

"Time," Macalister announced.

Royce sat back in his chair and used a hand to wipe his

mouth. The action was almost as sexual as what he'd just done and caused a shiver to glance through my shoulders. His expression was corrupt, as was the thought his devilish eyes hinted at.

*I'll be back.*

When he stood, the hands on me moved, along with the grip on my legs. As if I were lying on top of a giant clock, the men rotated clockwise, each moving into the next man's spot. It meant Royce was now holding my right leg . . .

And Mr. Lynch was seated in the chair.

Panic locked me in place far more than the hands on me, but then—the hands weren't confining me. They moved, gently stroking against my skin. I reeled around, gazing from one man to another, stunned at the expressions I found. It wasn't lust, but reverence. Adoration. Like these men truly believed I was giving them a gift, and they were grateful.

Macalister flipped the hourglass, and the bottom bulb rapidly filled with a pile of red.

Mr. Lynch set his hands on my thighs and leaned in. His hot breath rolled over my damp skin just before his mouth replaced it. I jerked at the sudden contact, and all thought emptied from my brain.

I stared at Royce, and he gazed back with his unflinching eyes, the ones that saw all the way through me. I didn't want him to watch as another man went down on me, and he didn't seem to want that either. So, we held each other's gazes and pretended it was just us.

But after the blinding shock faded enough that I could think again, it was much easier to convince my body I didn't like what Mr. Lynch was doing. The man's lips sealed around me and sucked so hard his cheeks hollowed out. I clenched my teeth and tried to shift away from the uncomfortable suction.

"Stop."

It wasn't clear who Macalister's order was for, but he'd twisted the hourglass onto its side, cutting off the flow of sand and stopping the timer. Mr. Lynch paused.

"Do you not like what he's doing?" Macalister asked me.

"Uh . . ." I blinked. Once again, inappropriate laughter threatened. Was I supposed to like any of this? An evil voice whispered in my head that I already did.

"Who is in control?" he demanded.

I didn't believe the answer until I gave it. "I am."

"You're an equal. Your opinion matters, but only if you express it."

I licked my dry lips and struggled to catch my breath. If I was an equal, why were my wrists pinned to the tabletop? I wanted to ask the question but thought better of it. If the men let go of me, I'd have no excuse about why I stayed and let this happen, except that I wanted Royce.

Also, I didn't *feel* restrained. The board members' hands rested on me, but it was more about connection versus dominance. This tradition was supposed to bind us all together. I wondered though . . . was this initiation for Royce, or for me? Both of us?

Macalister was waiting for me to prove I would speak up.

"It's just, um," I stammered, "a little rough."

"Oh." Mr. Lynch straightened, and embarrassment darted in his eyes. "I'm sorry."

When he nodded, the hourglass was righted, and Mr. Lynch's mouth returned to me. I bit my bottom lip as his tongue spun circles. It caressed and massaged, and all the heat that had dissipated when he'd sat down began anew.

"Time," Macalister said.

I exhaled a long breath. I'd only endured two of the nine minutes and I was already fracturing. How was I going to last until the end?

Mr. Scoffield didn't take a seat. He stood at the edge of the table, and when his time started, he placed his hands on my hips and dragged them upward. His thumbs splayed out while he caressed me. His touch was sensual . . . until his palms inched to my breasts and his gold wedding band caught the light.

I forced myself not to think about it. I had enough shit to deal with right now. I wasn't going to feel guilty about his decision to cheat on his wife. Those were his actions, which he could stop at any time. Plus, how likely was it any of these men were faithful to their wives? Money and power could corrupt anyone.

I was fucking proof of that, wasn't I?

My eyes drifted closed as he trailed fingertips over the curves of my breasts. I pictured Royce touching me this way. It was his fingers circling my nipple. It was his greedy mouth sucking at me and creating a knot of need deep between my legs.

"Time."

It became a chant that I both dreaded and looked forward to. Each utterance of the word brought a new man before me, but one step closer to being done and Royce's return.

As Macalister had said, they used their hands and mouths. I'd just been too naïve to understand at the time. Tongues teased. Fingers touched and stroked and squeezed. Their kisses never reached my mouth, but their lips and caresses always had the goal of pleasing me.

I knew their names and faces. Alice had given me backstories and details on each member, but sex hazed the room now. It descended on the table like a fog, making it impossible to distinguish one male from another. I hid behind closed eyelids most of the time anyway.

*Close your eyes and it will be just us.*

It became dangerous as the process wore on. My body could only be primed and left hanging so many times before it threatened revolt. The pleasure had left me trembling and breathless more than once, but I clamped down. Soon after this had started, I'd come to a decision. Seven other men could fuck me with their mouths and their hands, but Royce would be the only man who'd bring me to orgasm. So much of me was being shared, I'd do my best to keep that intimate experience between us.

He hadn't asked me to wait for him specifically on this, but I would.

Mr. Shaunessy was the last board member to go before the cycle of men was over. He sat in the chair and brushed the pad of his thumb over my swollen clit before sliding it all the way inside me. I arched up at the intrusion, and when the other men gently nudged me back onto the table, Mr. Shaunessy set his lips where his thumb had just been.

His tongue flickered while his thumb thrust. Slow at first, then speeding along and the two working together felt . . .

Good.

Really, really good.

"Oh, fuck," I whispered. I'd tried to hold it back, but I was breaking down.

There were appreciative, encouraging chuckles from the board. "I think she likes that," one of them said.

Shit, I did.

Instead of imagining Royce, now I pictured Mr. Shaunessy's son, Richard. I used the humiliating memory to combat what was happening and control myself. The mental cold shower seemed to work, because—

"Time." There was relief in Royce's voice. Instead of watching me, he'd been fixated on the hourglass, beating his father to the announcement. Perhaps he'd silently pleaded for the sand to fall faster.

I sighed with contentment as Royce settled into the chair and surveyed the scene. He marveled at me, the sweaty, panting, and naked girl on the table in front of him. I was all for him now. Even without looking behind him, he sensed the turn of the hourglass. His gaze caressed across my body until it focused where he was most interested, and one of his long fingers pushed inside.

He pumped it leisurely, once . . . twice. The chair creaked as he shifted forward, and his mouth sought the bundle of nerves at the top of my slit that throbbed and ached. He found me hot and wet, and as his tongue cartwheeled across my sensitive skin, I groaned my approval through clenched teeth.

The candles in the candelabra in the alcove had become dripping, melting messes, and I could relate. Fire seared across my nerves from the insistent mouth lapping at me, and the finger that slid along, growing slicker with each pass. I was a melting, dripping mess too.

His tempo built, as did the urgency inside me.

I felt the sand cascade through the hourglass and pool at the bottom. Every single grain was one less fraction of a second that I'd have like this. As the pressure rose, so did the satisfaction Royce created.

Fuck, it felt good. His finger plunged deep and the tip of his tongue teased endlessly. My heart's frantic rhythm matched his pace. I squirmed against the table, wanting to move, needing him just a fraction of an inch higher.

I moaned loudly.

The sound was drenched with desire, and some of the men shifted. A few were aroused, their tuxedo pants bulging. It was fucked up and yet flattering. I, a nobody, was suddenly powerful enough to have this effect on them. Everyone was looking at me, not just Royce. I'd never liked it before, but this wasn't me. Right now, I was the rebranded Marist Northcott, soon to be the Hale edition.

I shuddered as his tongue massaged my clit, working to coax the orgasm from me, and the pleasure in my center ramped up. Tingling crept over my legs, signaling my climax. It bared down on me, faster and faster—

"Time," Macalister said.

The hand moving inside me froze.

"No," I gasped. "I'm so close." The words stumbled from

my lips. "Please, Royce."

That was all he needed to hear. A second finger pushed in to join the first, and it was a lot, but my body was ready for it. His urgent thrusts made me shake. I was vibrating against the table, writhing against his mouth, struggling in the hands holding onto me.

But he took it a step further. The hand he wasn't using to fuck me crawled the length of my body. The wool of his coat sleeve grazed over my stomach as his fingers closed, grabbing a handful of my breast. He thumbed my nipple, brushing back and forth.

"That's it, Marist. *Yes*." He paused his tongue just long enough to issue the order. "Give it to me."

The prince had wanted me all to himself, and I gave it willingly.

Bliss exploded in my core, firing outward and racing across my body. My cry pealed in the candlelight, announcing what was happening, and the contractions that wracked me from head to toe showed them.

There was no mistaking the pleasure gripping me more intensely than Royce's hold on my breast. The board members murmured encouragement and praise, but I couldn't discern it over the buzzing in my ears.

The orgasm lasted longer than any I'd ever had. It seemed to go on forever.

As the satisfaction crested and began to fade, I collapsed back onto the table, my shoulders slapping against the wood. I drew huge swallows in while Royce rose deliberately from his throne and cast his gaze down on me.

My stomach clenched as he slipped the fingers he'd used to fuck me with into his mouth, closed his lips, and sucked my taste from them. He watched me the whole time he did it, his eyes flaring with unsated desire.

*Jesus.*

It looked like he'd wasn't quite done enjoying me and his carnal eyes made promises. Next time, he'd have me exactly the way he wanted, and without a time limit. He'd warned me in the back seat of my Porsche that once he got inside me, he might never leave, and I knew we were about to find out if it was true.

# SEVENTEEN

Royce's hurried fingers went to the black silk tied at his neck. He stared at me with the same hungry desire he shown in the department store mirror, only this was magnified a thousand percent.

I wanted him to hurry but didn't need to say it out loud. He could tell. He practically ripped the silk tie off, jerking it through his collar before hurling it at the chair. Next came the jacket. He shrugged out of it, revealing black braces beneath, and tossed it in the general direction of his discarded bowtie. When it missed, one of the board members released me, moved to pick it up, and hung it neatly on the chair back.

Royce peeled off one suspender and then the other, and all his urgency fed into his stare. His deadly serious gaze pressed down on me, ensnaring me far more than the men surrounding me.

He moved with methodical precision to undo the line of black buttons down the front of his pleated white tuxedo shirt, untucking it from his pants as he went. I got flashes of his strong chest and trim waist as it opened, but then his fingers were at the button at his waistband, working to undo it, and my nerves took over.

It was almost laughable I was still nervous, given what I'd just been through, but I couldn't control it. My heart beat out a skittering song as he tore down his zipper.

He abandoned his undone pants for a moment and scooped his hands under my thighs, dragging my body right to the edge of the table and forcing the men around us to adjust their grip.

There was electricity between us, strong and powerful. Did he feel it too? His crystal-clear eyes trapped mine, and my heart swelled. Oh, yes. He was right there with me.

He hooked his thumbs into the band of his underwear and bent slightly, dragging them and his pants down until they were stretched across his thighs, halfway down his legs. His dick was hard and ready, and now that it was in view, the realness of what was about to happen seized me.

If I could have picked any other way for my first time, I would have. But as I stared at his handsome face, his eyes struggling between guilt and lust, I felt confident I wouldn't have picked anyone else to be with.

All the men seemed to be holding their breath. The room had gone so quiet and still, it felt like Royce and I were alone.

He leaned over and put a hand flat on the table beside my head, bringing him so he was only inches from my lips. Our warm, bare stomachs pressed together and—shit—that felt nice. His questioning gaze explored my face. It searched my eyes, caressed forehead, and landed on my lips. He studied them like he expected secrets to spill from them at any moment.

"Are you sure?" he whispered.

I inhaled a deep, preparing breath.

And nodded.

He kept his hand beside my head but straightened, rising up on it. The guilt that had colored his expression was pushed out of the way and determination took over. His other hand slipped between our bodies, and the naked tip of his cock brushed over me.

It was a velvety stroke through my wetness, but it had me clenching so tight, my fingernails dug into my palms. If I opened my hands right now, there'd be little half-moon indentations there.

"Relax," Macalister urged.

I jerked at the intrusion of his voice. He'd moved to stand at the side of the table, probably so he could have a better view.

I focused on the only man I wanted to be with. Royce's chest lifted and fell with his uneven breaths, and it was so sexy. He looked classically beautiful, the way Hermes was often depicted in marble statues.

The second time he teased himself over me, I didn't flinch. I held perfectly still as the head of his dick found my entrance and began to push inside.

My eyes widened, and I sucked in a breath through tight teeth. I was soaking wet, but no amount of preparation could truly make me ready. The stretch grew more uncomfortable the further he went. Deeper he invaded, not stopping, and my body did not want to surrender to him.

His steady, slow press into me was too much. I was too full.

It ached between my legs. It wasn't a sharp pain, but a throb of discomfort. My back bowed off of the wood, and I groaned. My face contorted with displeasure. I wanted to flee, but the men were there, and the words wouldn't come from my tongue. My mind held them back, forcing me to just wait.

*Wait for me.*

Royce's lips parted on a soft, pleasure filled sigh. His head dropped for a moment, as if regrouping, and his gaze found mine again. His intense stare centered me so the cautious withdraw of his body from mine was . . . different. Not unpleasant. I softened back into the table.

When he finished his retreat, he started his next advance. Still gentle, but this time, quicker. The stretch of him sliding into me was less uncomfortable.

"Okay?" he asked, hushed.

"Yeah," I whispered back.

Tension had made his shoulders tight, but they relaxed a degree on my answer. The fullness of him moving inside me remained, but as he eased his hips into me, the ache dulled. It faded enough until it was merely noticeable.

As I became more pliable beneath him, Royce hesitantly loosened the restraint he'd put on himself. His movements became thrusts. They turned harder and went deeper.

The arm he'd been supporting himself with moved. His hand cupped my shoulder and slid up the curve of my neck, drawing goosebumps. I stretched as best I could into his touch, even as he continued to carve a path. His palm cradled the side of my face, tilting my head back and his thumb swept over my lips, where I pulled in ragged breaths.

As his thrusts increased, the atmosphere in the room rapidly degraded from composed and collected to frenzied and desperate.

He bent down, looming over me so his lips hovered just over my uplifted chin, teasing a kiss with his hot breath. His restless hand kept moving. He dragged it down until it rested on my throat, holding me back from receiving the kiss I wanted.

Maybe it wasn't allowed.

Or perhaps he didn't want anyone else to witness it.

Our choked breaths and the sound of skin slapping against skin filled the room. He fucked me hard enough the table creaked and groaned in protest.

"You feel so . . . fucking . . . *good.*"

Royce's comment set my face on fire and satisfaction clenched deep inside me. I moaned, long and loud, and something inside him seemed to break. He snapped upright, his palm sliding to the center of my chest, his fingers splayed between my breasts.

He'd told me he would make it quick, and I sensed that was now his goal. This version of him was raw and basic. He became a man fucking for his pleasure, a slave to satisfying his own instinctive, primal urge.

His furious tempo gave me a hint of what was in store for me later, and I liked it. I wasn't going to follow him over the edge, but this? Watching and listening to him? It was deeply satisfying.

I'd never seen him come before, and he did not disappoint.

As his eyes slammed shut and his face contorted with pleasure, his movements went jerky and erratic. A great, satisfied groan burst from him. His fingers on my chest curled in, raking across my skin. And inside my body, there were rhythmic pulses, filling me with heat.

He gasped for air and stilled, letting the orgasm pass on long, labored breaths.

The board members' hands released me and drew away, leaving only Royce touching me. His palm was on my chest and there was still the connection of our bodies, and I sighed in contentment, happy for it to be just us.

He lingered longer than he probably should have because Macalister strolled to the chair and plucked the coat off of it. The heat of Royce was gone as he retreated and hurried to pull up his pants. He took the offered coat from his father, opened it, and laid it over my body. He covered me, and his action was almost tender.

The silk lining felt decadent against my sensitized skin.

"Congratulations." It wasn't clear for whom Macalister meant it. He adjusted the way his tuxedo sat on his shoulders, tugging at the cuffs of his sleeves. "We'll leave you two to get sorted. Don't keep your guests waiting too long. I'm sure most have already arrived, and I'd like to make our entrance soon."

Dismissed, the board shuffled toward the door, some of them adjusting their dicks in their pants as they filed past the table. Macalister was the last to go, waiting for something.

It was privacy. He cast a harsh look at his son. "Jesus, Royce." His tone was scathing. "Next time try to last longer than a minute. She's supposed to enjoy it, but not if you don't give her a chance."

A muscle flexed along Royce's jaw and he bit the word out. "Noted."

Macalister released a frustrated sigh, and although I kept my focus squarely on Royce, I felt his father's gaze stroke over me before he turned and went.

The click of the door closing flipped the switch on Royce, activating the other side of him. He launched over me, his hands cradling my head. "Are you all right?"

I opened my mouth, but the words lodged in my throat. His semen was dripping out of me between my legs, and the sensation was weird.

"Marist." Worry turned his eyes a stormy blue. "Fuck, please say something."

My voice was almost silent. "I don't want to live here."

He sighed with relief and dropped his head into the crook of my neck. "You are amazing. You know that? Ever since you made the deal, I've fucking tried to get us out of this. Every day, I tried. I even went to the board, but they wouldn't vote against my father."

I was verging on overload and tears stung my eyes.

"I'm so sorry," he murmured. "I should have said no. At the very least, I should have told you."

That was true. However, Macalister had said I was an equal and my opinion mattered, but only if I expressed it. And I couldn't deal with anything right now. The shock was still in my system, numbing me from processing it. I only knew what I needed right this second.

"Would you just shut up?" I pleaded. "And fucking kiss me?"

Surprise rippled through him and was gone in a flash. He crushed his lips to mine, and his kiss was all-consuming. I was grateful not to be standing when he gave it to me because I went softer than the melted wax puddling on the drip catchers of the candelabras.

He pulled his coat away, not wanting anything between us. His bare chest was tacky with sweat like mine, and I enjoyed how our skin clung to each other. Like every part of me wanted to be connected to him. He planted kisses against my lips and dipped his tongue into my mouth, coaxing me to slide mine against his. It was exactly the kind of kiss I'd craved when he'd first pushed inside my body.

Better late than never.

The kiss ended slowly and reluctantly. We both wanted more, but knew time was running out.

"You didn't answer me," he said softly, pulling me up in his arms until I was sitting. "Are you okay?"

I honestly didn't know. My emotions were on lockdown, so nothing was getting in or out. "I think so." I climbed to stand on my unsteady legs. "What about you?"

"Me?" He considered it with a dubious expression. "I'm sure it's nothing a few decades of very expensive therapy can't fix."

I wanted to laugh, except I didn't find it particularly funny.

He grabbed his coat and dug around in the interior pocket, producing a stack of tissues. My breath clung, sticky in my throat, as he gently wiped one between my legs, cleaning up the mess. It was oddly caring, yet sexual at the same time.

He disposed of the tissues as I stood naked next to the table, one hand on it to support myself. When he came back to me, he picked up my underwear and attempted to help me put it on, but I shooed his hands away. It'd be faster if I did it. We dressed ourselves quickly and quietly, him buttoning and redoing his bowtie and me pulling the heavy dress back on.

"I need your help," I said softly, turning to show him the unlaced dress.

"Of course."

The act of him lacing the corset? It was infinitely more sensual and intimate than when he'd helped me take it off. His knuckles brushed over my back, and I suspected most of the time it was intentional. Which was silly.

"I'm yours, Royce," I whispered. "You can touch me whenever you'd like."

He set his hands on me, halfway between my shoulders and my neck, and eased me back against him. His solid chest at my back was comforting, and he used his hands to angle my head to the side. It made room for him to drop his head and nuzzle a kiss into the side of my neck.

It must have given him a reminder. He stepped away and went to the black box on the buffet table, retrieving my great-grandmother's necklace. Or, *my* necklace now.

I shook my head. "Your father said it was too much."

"I say it's not." He gave me a knowing look. "Which one

of us would you like to disappoint?"

*Oh.* I smiled in understanding. Like the cat his father hated, this necklace was a small act of defiance, and I wholeheartedly approved.

Rather than go out into the entryway like the board had done, Royce unlocked the door leading to the enormous kitchen and ushered me through. It was bustling with the catering crew who ignored us. Alice had been lying in wait. She ambushed us, grabbed my wrist, and tugged me toward her while firing a glare at Royce.

"Leave us," she said to him without a hint of warmth.

Her curt tone surprised us both, but he nodded. "I'll be in the hall when you're ready," he said.

We watched him go, and then she focused in on me. "I needed to see if you're all right," she said softly. "I mean, to make sure everything is okay," she drew the words out, "with your hair and makeup."

My gaze dropped down to her hand still clinging to my wrist, and I understood the subtext. She was concerned about me. Her clipped tone to Royce was her being protective.

I gave her the best smile I could manage. "Yes. I think I'm okay."

"Good." She looked relieved, but her grip on my wrist tightened. "It's over now. You don't talk about what happened, not with me or anyone else. It stays in that room. You understand. Some people might find it . . . upsetting."

I would think so. Like, maybe the board member's wives. How was she okay with this? I wanted to ask her a million questions. And I wanted to tell her how her husband hadn't participated in the initiation, but I couldn't.

"I understand," I said.

"Good." She released me and scrutinized my face. It was impossible to tell if she was checking my mental state, or if my makeup needed a touch-up. Her voice went low. "The last thing I'll say is no one was waiting for me in the kitchen afterward, and I did not handle it as well as you seem to be."

"Oh." My heart ached for her.

"When the time comes, I hope you'll be there for whichever girl Vance chooses."

I went still. Several thoughts ran through my head, and the selfish one was the loudest. Royce was a board member now. Would he be one of the men to 'show his gratitude' to the next woman the board wanted to approve?

I couldn't think about it. One ordeal at a time, and right now I was facing down a party with a guest list of five hundred people, most of whom I'd have to talk to. The next five hours or so I'd have to pretend to be someone I wasn't, and that was going to take all my remaining energy.

Alice seemed satisfied when I nodded, but then she gave me a final discerning look, her gaze trailing over my necklace. "Luc is in the hall. Go see him about fixing your lipstick."

Royce clasped my hand in his as we assembled with the

rest of the Hales in the sun room at the back of the house, waiting to make our announced entrance. Macalister's gaze landed on the diamonds draped around my neck and his lips went thin, but he said nothing. I squeezed tighter beside Royce, our joined hands buried in the folds of my skirt.

Vance didn't have a date. When he got the nod from the event coordinator perched at the door, he flashed a carefree smile and went out. We heard the announcement and the smattering of applause, like he'd done something worthy of it rather than simply being born.

Alice took Macalister's arm and lined up in front of us, but not before glancing over her shoulder at me. "Remember to smile with your eyes, Marist."

I let out a tight breath when they stepped out onto the stone balcony and headed for the party, which was already fifteen minutes into the cocktail hour.

Royce squeezed my hand. "When we get out there, we'll do a round and then you can go find your family." His smile was sort of sweet. "Don't run off on me or anything, but if you need some time to get away, I get it. I have to mingle with some old board members, and you probably don't want to be around for that."

"No," I said.

"Have you been in the maze?"

I stumbled at his question. "The hedge maze? Not in years."

"It's closed tonight because alcohol and disorienting mazes aren't a great combination. But," his tone turned smooth, "since I have special privileges tonight, you'll meet me at the fountain in the center in forty-five minutes."

My chest tightened, and a flush raced through my body. He'd acted like he was issuing an order, but it was absolutely a request, and one he was hoping I'd agree to.

"All right."

His smile was devious and sexy as hell.

But the excitement in me died as the event coordinator waved us through the door.

"Ready?" Royce asked.

"Nope." But out we went.

Attached to the back of the Hale house was an enormous stone balcony, and steps led down to the gardens where tables had been set up on the grass lawn. Strings of globe lights hung overhead, an artificial glowing spider's web.

We strolled across the balcony, moving as quickly as my dress and heels would allow, and when we reached the top of the stairs, Royce pulled me to a stop. I looked down at the kingdom before us while my heart raced in my chest. There were a million faces staring up at us, all dressed to the nines and glasses of champagne in their hands. It wasn't just the cream of the crop of Cape Hill, it was celebrities and socialites from across the globe.

"The man of the hour, and the newest addition to the Hale Banking and Holding Company's board of directors." The voice boomed from speakers discreetly hidden behind potted plants that had been brought in. "Mr. Royce Hale, accompanied by Miss Marist Northcott."

The applause was loud, filled with cheers and whistles.

Royce let go of my hand, only so he could slip it around

my waist and hold me close. I stared up at him as cameras flashed, reminding me of all the press who'd begged me for an invite.

The prince at my side waved to the crowd. He *legit* waved to his adoring subjects, like it was an everyday occurrence. It looked like they were all eating it up too.

How many of them knew the version of Royce I did? Probably none of them.

"Chin up," he said under his smile, his lips barely moving.

My chin lifted, I pulled on my smile, and swung my attention toward the audience at the base of the steps. A few of the people from my high school years were dispersed in the crowd. Sycophants to the Hales who'd looked down on me. Yet I was the one looking down now, wasn't I? Did Royce's arm around my waist puzzle them? Did it make the girls who'd been merciless bitches to me green with envy?

My smile grew wider.

Done posing at the top of the steps, he offered his arm to escort me, and I took it, grasping my skirt with my free hand. It was a regal march down the stone staircase that had been temporarily covered in red carpet as Alice had insisted the party be themed 'Old Hollywood.'

We'd barely finished our descent before people rushed at us, congratulating him on his promotion and gushing about my dress.

It turned out to be easy to mingle when I was attached to Royce. No one wanted to talk to me. Hell, they didn't really want to talk to Royce either—they wanted to talk *at* him. Because the party was so huge, they knew their face time with him was limited and they needed to make an impression.

He played his role flawlessly. He stayed engaged in the conversations and was witty, while I just smiled and nodded, offering nothing but my ability to turn oxygen into carbon dioxide.

"You better go while there's a break," Royce said when the couple he'd been talking with left to get another drink. "I see more people incoming, and I don't have an exit strategy."

I didn't want to abandon him, but I was eager to escape. "Are you sure?"

"Go." He brushed a kiss at my hairline in a gesture that seemed like we'd been doing it for years. "I'll see you in a few."

I'd spotted my family standing near the rose garden, and in my haste, I wasn't paying attention to the faces around me.

"Marist." A male hand grasped my elbow, pulling me to a stop. "Hey."

The first thought I had when I saw him was that I couldn't run in my dress, no matter how badly I wanted to. "Richard." It came out forced and too-bright. "How are you?"

"I'm great. I was just accepted into the Leadership Fellows program at Randhurst, actually."

"Oh," I said. My gaze flicked to my parents, who seemed miles away. "Congrats. That's awesome."

"Thanks. I'm excited." Richard's curious gaze swept over me. "How about you? You look so different than the last time we saw each other."

Was that supposed to be a compliment? "I'm starting my final year in economics at Etonsons."

"Wow, cool." He didn't bother to make it sound believable.

"Hey, so you and Royce?" He leaned in as if we were going to share a secret. "How'd that happen?"

I didn't have time for this. "I seduced him."

Richard laughed like it was the most ridiculous thing he'd heard, but when I didn't crack a smile, he sobered. "No shit. Really?"

I sighed. "If you'll excuse—"

A man stepped in and joined our two-person circle, making my exit impossible.

Richard brightened. "Dad. This is Marist Northcott. I don't know if you remember her. We went to homecoming together one year."

Liam Shaunessy extended a hand and a smile to me as if all the shit he'd done in the darkened dining room an hour ago had never happened. "Hello. Liam Shaunessy."

It would be rude not to shake his hand, so I had no choice. "Prom," I said.

"I'm sorry?"

"It was the prom," I repeated. "Richard and I . . . Not homecoming."

Richard clapped his hands together, suddenly remembering. "Oh, yeah."

"I have to go. I'm sorry," I blurted out.

Mr. Shaunessy's smile was normal, but I felt his words were loaded with double meaning. "It was nice seeing you, Marist."

I wove my way through the crowd, and when I finally made my way to my family, I began to regret my decision. My father was deep in conversation with one of his co-workers, my sister stared at me like I'd been diagnosed with cancer, and my mother's eyes brimmed with tears.

"You look gorgeous," she said. She reached out, her fingers tracing the diamonds at my throat. Her voice fell to a hush. "Is that my necklace?"

Technically, no, but I was happy she was happy. I nodded.

"But Mr. Costolli said he'd sold it."

"He did. He sold it to Royce."

Her fingers paused. "Oh." Her face fell. "Royce owns it now?"

"He, uh, gave it to me."

She drew back like the icy diamonds had suddenly scorched her fingers. "What?" Disapproval splashed on her face. "No, Marist. It's too much money." She tipped her head down and looked at me with seriousness. "A man who gives you something like that is going to expect a great deal in return."

Emily looked like she was going to be ill.

"Yeah," I muttered. "We're way past that point."

My mother froze. "What?"

I shouldn't have said anything. "I'm kidding." I tried to deflect. "Have you had any of the food yet? I'm starving."

I still had no appetite, but perhaps Royce's ability to lie was rubbing off on me.

My mother looked at me dubiously, but then gave up. "I liked the spring rolls better than the caviar."

I wanted to talk to Emily alone, but as our mother prattled on about her friends and their dresses, my window closed. I only had a few minutes left before I needed to meet

Royce at the fountain. Who knew who might stop me along the way? Hopefully no more board members.

"Find me later," she whispered and clutched me tightly when I said my goodbyes.

Tables covered in white linens were dotted with black cloth napkins and surrounded the temporary dancefloor. Since it was not yet in use, I cut through it and made my way toward the entrance to the hedge maze. I was nearly there when Sophia Alby stepped in front of me, blocking my way with a smile that was as plastic as her nose.

"Marist, hey! Can we take a selfie together real quick?" She scrambled to pull her phone from her clutch which perfectly matched her gold sequined dress.

Of all the mean girls at Cape Hill Prep, Sophia had been the queen. When Royce said I was a 'nobody' all those years ago, he'd been talking to her. He'd created the virus of my social disease, and she'd been the one to disperse it far and wide.

"You want a selfie?" I wrinkled my nose. "With me?"

"Um, yeah." Her silly laugh was tinny and grating. "You look amazing, and we're friends."

Wait, what? Was she on drugs?

Sophia must have assumed I was okay with it when I hadn't moved. She cast an arm around my shoulder and held up her phone at the same high position Alice had done earlier. I bet if I had measured the angle, it would have matched perfectly.

"Smile!" she said in a sing-song voice.

My cheeks were already worn out and I was only an hour into the party, but I did the best I could. She snapped a few pictures, examined the results on her screen, and looked satisfied.

"Want me to send them to you?" she asked.

My filter temporarily shorted out from overuse. "What for?" When Sophia's face twisted, I went into damage control. I plastered on a bright smile. "Just tag me in them and I'll repost."

She liked that idea a lot. "Oh, perfect!"

"I have to run. I think Royce is waiting on me."

She nodded like she was an understanding friend, and I began to wonder if she was delusional or suffered revisionist history from our time in high school. "Of course," she said. "Tell him I said hi."

"Right," I ground out through my toothy grin.

There was a velvet rope drawn across the entrance and a sign hanging from it that announced no guests were permitted in the hedge maze, but no one stopped me when I slipped behind it and disappeared between the walls of dense evergreen.

Pebbles crunched underfoot as I wound deeper into the maze, and I was sure the underside of the train of my dress was going to look awful, but I kept going. The sun was low in the evening sky and the high walls of the hedges cast shadows, but the landscape lighting was already on. Warm, diffused light glowed along the narrow corridors and illuminated the statues standing guard at the dead ends.

The buzz from the party dimmed, and I let out a tight breath. It was lovely being here alone in the maze. A few fireflies floated in the air, their yellow flash so quick it was over by the time I focused in on it.

I didn't remember the correct route to the center, but I also may have forgotten it on purpose. It was fun to wander and guess, and more times than not, I'd found myself facing a stone cast Aphrodite or reproduction of the Venus de Milo.

Just when I started to worry about the man waiting for me, I turned a corner and the hedges parted. They bowed into a circle, and the tiered, bubbling fountain lay in the center. Glass votive candles flickered along the wide rim of its pool, which doubled as a bench.

The space was gorgeous and romantic.

Royce was a vision as he sat there beneath the fountain in his tuxedo, his elbows resting on his knees and his head hung. It stole my breath.

"The man of the hour," I said softly.

He lifted his head and his intense, hungry eyes focused in on me. As he rose deliberately to his feet, his expression was ravenous, and excitement surged inside my chest. We were alone, and there was magic all around us. It hummed in every drop of water that rained down in the fountain. It sang in each flame burning in the ring of candles surrounding it.

And it lived in every shallow breath Royce and I took together.

"Come here." He spoke quietly, as not to break the spell. "I want to ask you something."

There was rustling as my dress train dragged over the pebbled path. I was nearly to him when his hand slipped into his pocket. This time, the black box he held was much smaller and the world slowed to a stop.

# EIGHTEEN

Royce was nervous as he propped open the box and knelt by the edge of my skirt.

"Oh, my God," I cried. My hand flew to the center of my chest, perhaps to stop my heart from getting ahead of the rest of me.

I hadn't expected anything like this. There'd been no stipulation laid out for Royce to get down on one knee and propose. I'd half expected Alice to present me with a ring this afternoon, let me know when the engagement was going to be official, and when I was supposed to slip it on.

Mostly, I hadn't expected to feel this way. As if this proposal were real.

Like *we* were real.

As fucked up as today had been, the initiation had accomplished at least one of its goals—I felt bound to Royce. We'd survived and gotten each other through it.

The ring was beautiful. The center was a huge, cushion-cut solitaire, bordered all around by smaller diamonds, and a fading beam of sunlight made it glitter wildly against the black velvet box. The Costolli logo was imprinted on the inside of the lid, and I pictured Mr. Costolli sweet-talking Royce into buying the engagement ring when he'd come in for the necklace.

"I know," Royce started, "this looks like I'm asking you to marry me, and I am." His heart seemed to be racing as fast as mine was, given how quickly his chest moved.

Didn't he know I was going to say yes?

His eyes were as clear as the diamond he was presenting to me. "I'm not stupid, Marist. We both came into this arrangement with goals that have nothing to do with each other, or love, but I'm an ambitious man. Eventually," his words had gravity, pulling me under, "I will want it all."

The only thing moving in this world were the glowing fireflies around us, sparks and flashes of brilliance in the summer night.

"This ring is yours no matter what. You can take it and the necklace and the check for five million and run. I'll understand if that's the choice you need to make." He took a deep breath. "Or you can stay, and every day you wear this ring I'll know you're still with me."

"Royce," I breathed, reaching for him.

But he drew back, and his expression shuttered. "Wait. You need to understand what you're agreeing to. I'm playing the long game here, Marist. Today was probably only the beginning."

That gave me pause. "What?"

"My father's like me—he's a different person behind

closed doors. He'll use us against each other. He'll do it if it helps him get what he wants, or even if he just thinks it'll be fun." He drew the ring from its perch in the box and held it up. "So, I'm asking you to marry me. But also to trust me, and when it's all over, to give us a chance to have . . . more."

He was Hades, wanting to take me to the underworld and be his bride, and this ring was the pomegranate seed that would make me stay. I chose to go with the version of the myth where Persephone took it willingly.

"Yes," I murmured.

Both our hands were trembling as he slipped the ring onto my finger, and then he was on his feet, his arms wrapped around me, and his mouth covered mine. The kiss had barely begun before the disembodied voice of the announcer asked people to find their seats. Dinner would be served shortly.

Royce laced our fingers together and led us back to the start of the maze, knowing exactly which turn to take, and I wondered if he could run the whole thing in his sleep. We tried to sneak out without anyone noticing, but Alice once again was waiting to ambush us. Only this time, it was with her phone. She snapped pictures of us and my new ring, promising to post our "fairy tale engagement" as soon as Macalister's toast was over.

I sat at the head table with the rest of the Hales, sandwiched between Royce and Vance. My hand was in my lap, hidden beneath the tablecloth, and I fidgeted nervously with the ring as Macalister walked toward the microphone stand.

"Before I forget," Royce said, his expression alight with amusement, "I hope I haven't set a dangerous precedent. No more black boxes. That ring is the last piece of jewelry you're getting from me for a while."

I faked horror. "What? No earrings?"

Royce smirked. "Mr. Costolli tried."

When it was clear Macalister was ready, a hush descended on the lawn.

His toast was brief. He talked about Royce's tenacious work ethic and how proud he was as a father. He acknowledged the rest of the board for welcoming his son and said great things were in store at HBHC. It was a speech that hit all the right notes but lacked any real emotion. It left me just as cold as every conversation I'd had with Macalister.

I'd decided to take Alice's advice and not think about my time in the dining room. Those memories would stay there until I was ready to deal with them.

"Lastly, it gives me great pleasure," Macalister said, "to announce we have something additional to celebrate this evening." His smile was flawless. If I didn't know better, I'd think he looked genuinely happy. "Royce asked Marist Northcott to be his wife just a few minutes ago . . . and she's accepted."

The stunned silence only lasted a single second, but it felt like it dragged on forever. Then, the gasps and smattering of applause rang out, followed by every head turning to look at us. The expressions in the sea of faces ranged from confused to suspicious. All of Cape Hill put me under a microscope and began looking for flaws.

It was my nightmare come to life.

But Royce had his arm around the back of my chair, and

when the crowd swung their judgmental scrutiny our way, his hand was on my shoulder. He leaned into me, nuzzling a kiss in the side of my neck and whispered in my ear, "Pretend you like me."

It worked because his ridiculous statement made my tired smile muscles fire and a shy grin slid across my face. Liking him wasn't something I had to pretend to do.

After dinner was over, the dancefloor opened up, and Royce and I took center stage, swaying to the music and playing our roles as newly engaged lovebirds. It wasn't that difficult. Was I getting better at pretending, or was it not much of a lie?

Later, when Royce was occupied with a business discussion, I slipped out in search of Emily. Once I texted her, I discovered she was all the way over at the Hale stables with her friends. I followed the path past the hedge maze and to the narrow private road that led down the hill, and the small barn with the center pitched roof came into view.

It hadn't been a working stable in years. After Royce's mother died, the horses were sold, and the barn became a storage space. The collection of people in formal dresses and tuxedos were gathered nearby at a patio table under a tree, having their own mini-party away from the critical eyes of their parents.

As I walked up, there were cheers and smiles from the group. Most of them seemed to be drunk or high, or both.

"Emily, when'd your sister get so hot?" one of the guys asked in a too-loud whisper. A few of the girls snickered at him.

My sister was the only sober one among the group. She was stunning in her violet dress and the mermaid style hugged her curves, but her expression was like it had been earlier. Pained. I nodded my head to the side, gesturing I wanted to get away from the group and talk privately.

When we were on the far side of the house and out of earshot, she grabbed my left hand and jerked it up to stare at the ring. Her voice was filled with dread. "You did it."

"Yes."

"Oh, my God." Her face cracked. It split between anguish and fear. "Are you okay? Was it awful?"

"I'm fine," I said quietly. "I don't want to talk about it."

"Jesus, Marist." Her eyes filled with tears and her gaze ran from me. "It's all my fault."

"What are you talking about?"

Her focus snapped back to mine. "It was supposed to be me."

I bit down on my bottom lip to prevent it from trembling. "Stop it. You can't—"

"I got pregnant on purpose." She said it in such a rush it was a blur of words, and by the time her admission soaked in, she'd begun to cry. "I didn't want anything to do with the Hales. You know how Macalister is. He thinks he's entitled to whatever he wants, and that includes people. He owns everything, but he wasn't going to own me."

I took in a sharp, painful breath. I'd given Macalister so much power over me, he'd become my master.

She wiped at a tear. "Royce told me at the end of our date that it didn't matter what either of us wanted. Macalister wasn't going to give up unless I married someone else or got pregnant by the time I graduated." A wrinkle creased her forehead. "I thought it was my only way out. I'm so sorry. I didn't think you'd have to take my place."

When more tears welled up in her eyes, I went on autopilot. My sister was hurting, and I needed to comfort her.

"It's okay," I soothed. She shook as I hugged her. Or maybe I was the one shaking.

Not with anger, but with fear. Her words rang terribly true. I'd negotiated myself away from Macalister tonight, denying him what he clearly thought was his right. Was he eventually going to want to claim it anyway?

"It's going to be all right," I said, trying to convince us both.

When the worst of her tears seemed to subside, she pulled back and gave me a firm look. "Promise me."

How could I? I opened my mouth, but she cut me off.

"Just be careful. I don't trust any of them. This town is full of liars, and I think the Hales might be the worst of all. And the Marist I know would hate this life you're signing up for."

My phone chimed with a text. I ignored all the social media notifications on my screen and went to my messages. It was Royce, wondering where I was. I put on the bravest face I could muster. "I'll be careful."

She looked resigned. "Good. You might be marrying into that family," her tone was grim, "but please don't become one of them."

The conversation with Emily churned in my head as I made my way back toward the party. I took off my torturous shoes and clutched them by the heels in one hand, and since I was walking barefoot, I took the longer, grassy route to head back.

Beyond the backside of the maze, the grass stopped and gave way to the woods. The sun had just set, and under the cover of the trees, it was dark. But a stick snapped underfoot and alerted me that something was moving in there.

No, not something. *Someone.*

A pleasured sigh—distinctly male—echoed amongst the trees.

"What's got you so worked up?" I could hear the smile in his rich, vaguely familiar voice. "Thinking about Marist?"

At the sound of my name, I went stock still. I couldn't see much of him, only a sliver of his outline between two tree trunks, which meant it was unlikely he could see me.

"Okay, okay. I'm sorry." He gave a short laugh, and there was rustling as he moved. "Please don't stop."

I moved as stealthily as possible, careful not to trip over the roots as I ducked behind one of the bigger oak trees.

"I'm just saying, usually you want to go straight to fucking." He let out a staggered breath. "Fuck, yes. Suck it."

"Hmm," a woman purred. Her voice was too low to distinguish. "Like this?"

"Yeah, just like that."

I put a hand on the rough, furrowed bark and peered

around the side of the tree. My eyes hadn't adjusted to the darkness, but I saw outlines. Wicked shapes hidden among the trees. He was slumped back against one, and she was kneeling, her bulbous dress around her as she bobbed at him.

When his arms moved, she slowed. "What are you doing?"

Her voice was much clearer and terribly familiar.

"I want video of you taking me deep," he said.

She hesitated but didn't object. When her figure resumed moving, he unleashed a long moan. The phone in his hand lit up, shining down its overly bright light, and Alice blinked rapidly up against it. I could see the shaft of the thick dick in her mouth, wet with her saliva.

She slid all the way until her petal pink lips were flush around his base.

And because he was videoing, the lit screen cast enough light upward so I could make out his handsome face.

*Holy shit.*

I backed away, stumbling over the uneven ground, and almost dropped the shoes in my hand, but thankfully my hasty retreat had been silent.

"I'm going to put it on Instagram and show them how talented you are," Vance teased in a seductive voice.

I hurried away before they saw me, trying to wipe the image from my mind. Did Royce know? Did Macalister?

When I returned to the party, I found my fiancé chatting with Noemi and her husband Joseph about the perks of eloping. I slipped in beside Royce, struggling to catch my breath.

There was pride in Noemi's voice. "The press didn't find out we'd gotten married for weeks."

Royce laughed. "Yeah, that wouldn't fly in my family. Alice says the only way to control what the press says is to feed it to them." He glanced at me and did a double-take. Whatever expression I was making caused concern. "Hey. Everything okay?"

My heart was still thumping rapidly in my chest. "Yeah." I tried to act natural, and not like I'd just seen his brother's dick halfway down his stepmother's throat. "My dress is heavy, and the hill was steep."

Worry lined his eyes. He saw right through me, but hopefully he also saw it wasn't the right time to talk about it.

"Congratulations," Noemi said, derailing us.

"Thank you," we answered at the same time.

"I love the pictures Alice posted."

"Pictures?" I asked.

Noemi showed me her phone, scrolling through the feed, and Royce and I leaned in to get a better look. There were three pictures on the post. The first was us trying to sneak out of the hedge maze right after his proposal, where Royce and I were holding hands and my gaze was locked onto him.

Anxiety crawled up my back.

Maybe Alice had gotten lucky and captured the photo at the perfect second, but I doubted it. It was nearly impossible not to think the girl pictured there was in love with the man she was gazing at.

Was that how I usually looked at him?

The second picture was the engagement ring.

My anxiety shifted, leaning toward excitement when she swiped to the final photo. It was right after his father's announcement. Royce's hand cupped the spot where my neck met my body, his gaze was on me, and I was grinning. He'd whispered for me to pretend I liked him just a second before it had been taken.

In this picture it looked very much like he was in love with me.

Noemi glanced up from her phone and straightened abruptly. "Mr. Hale, it's nice to see you again. Thank you for inviting us."

I should have sensed the cold breeze, but Macalister had appeared from nowhere. He gave a polite smile. "Please, it's Macalister. Thank you for coming." He motioned toward her pregnant belly. "I hope traveling wasn't too difficult."

She shot a wary smile to her husband. "Some of us wanted to have a doctor onboard the jet, but," she emphasized her words, "we were *fine*."

A muscle along Joseph's jawline ticked. He didn't seem to like her teasing, but then again, the guy seemed rather serious.

She leaned into him as she turned toward Macalister. "Oh, I'm sorry. This is my husband, Joseph Monsato."

Joseph extended a hand. "We've met before, a few years back. Nice to see you again, sir."

Noemi's smile froze, and as the men shook hands, her expression was oddly empty. "Of course, you have."

"I didn't mean to interrupt," Macalister's attention drifted to me, "but I came to borrow my future daughter-in-law."

"For what?" Royce sounded as if he didn't like that any more than I did.

His father's chilly gaze made me shiver. "For a dance."

I stiffened and floundered to come up with an excuse, but my mind went blank as Macalister extended a hand to me. Even though I was dressed now, I felt just as naked as the last time he'd done it.

I couldn't decline or negotiate my way out of this, and I'd rather deal with it now than delay the inevitable.

His icy hand clasped around mine, and I exchanged a look with Royce as I was led away, one that asked him to rescue me as soon as possible. He stood utterly still, an elegant sculpture, powerless as his father took me away.

Under the crisscrossing strings of lights, the dancefloor was mostly empty. A few couples swayed to the fading slow song, and as Macalister brought us onto the hardwood, the next song began. Nora Jones pleaded in her smoky voice to come away with her into the night.

"Do you waltz?" he asked.

I needed to start a list of things I never thought I'd hear him say to me, and add that one. "Uh, I know how, but my dress—"

He adjusted his hold on my hand and lifted it as he stepped into my space. His other hand slid behind my back, pulling me up against him and into the dance frame. "You'll do fine. I'll keep my pattern tight."

Apprehension corded my muscles like rope twisted to the breakpoint.

Macalister was an imposing man in every aspect. Not just his dominating personality or his striking eyes, but with his physical size. He was broad and tall, and kept himself in excellent shape. He demanded perfection in everything, including himself.

His dancing was no exception. He was confident at leading, making his steps easy to follow, which I needed. I hadn't danced the waltz since I'd learned to years ago. On one hand, it was surprising he knew how, because this dance was soft and artistic. But on the other, it was elegant and refined, and a precise partnership. I knew how much he liked those things, didn't I?

I stared up at him as we moved in the boxed pattern, rising and falling with our steps. I could feel his wedding ring on his finger. Did he know where Alice was? That his partner was betraying him right now with his own son? There was a microscopic tug in my chest. I felt bad for him, just a little.

But I had to fill the small space between us with something other than tension and Nora Jones' sultry song. "Where did you learn to dance?"

"Julia taught me for our wedding."

"Oh." It was all I could find to say. The mention of Royce's mother pulled another string around my heart.

There was no emotion in his eyes, or it was hidden too far back to be seen. His expression gave nothing away. "I'd like to think she would have been very happy tonight. She wanted nothing more than to bring our families together. It may not have happened the way anyone expected it to, but I'm pleased to welcome a Northcott girl into my home."

I stumbled my steps, and he tightened his grip, preventing me from falling.

"Smile," he ordered. "People are watching us."

I did as he asked but couldn't keep the plea from my voice. "I need a little more time. I'm working to fix my family's finances." I didn't like throwing them under the bus, but could my parents' reputation really get any worse in Macalister's eyes? "I need to be home, because my parents have been hiding statements, and they still spend like they're not . . ."

I wouldn't say the word 'broke' since there were other people around, but I didn't need to. He obviously understood.

I firmed up my tone. "I'm the only one there willing to deal with reality."

"I see." His smile seemed abruptly real. "I understand needing to have control over other people to save them from themselves." The grip on my hand relaxed and softened. "Especially when you know what's best for them. You remind me a bit of myself."

I sucked in a deep breath to keep from ordering him to take it back.

"The financial advisor will take care of all of that, but I'd like you to be comfortable. I'll have him update you on his progress, and you can discuss your concerns with him at any time. All right?"

He wasn't about to let me renegotiate. I deflated and my voice lost its power. "All right."

"Good." He lifted our clasped hands and pressed his palm on my back, urging me under his arm. As I rounded the turn and came back to him, his expression changed. "I also wanted to take a moment to apologize."

Apologies typically followed mistakes . . . but surely Macalister didn't make those.

"For what?"

"I have underestimated you repeatedly." His hand on my back was higher this time, and his thumb was above the top of the dress, resting against my bare skin. "You've proven yourself to be a smart, capable young woman. One who doesn't buckle under pressure. I respect that."

Before I could respond, he dropped another bomb.

"And you're very beautiful, Marist."

His thumb edged the top of the dress, sliding subtly against my skin. No one would notice it except for me.

"Thank you," I choked out, making it seem like I was thanking him for his secret touch and not the compliment that made panic pour into my stomach.

"My son is also smart, and capable, and attractive. I would think for most girls, he'd be easy to fall in love with." Danger lurked in Macalister's eyes. It simmered in his words. "It's unlikely a smart girl like you needs a warning, but I will give it anyway, because you already seem quite enamored with each other. Falling for Royce will only end badly."

Macalister and I moved together, neither needing to pay attention to the steps any longer. We were both locked in each other's gaze.

"Is that so?" I asked.

"He's capable of many things, but loving someone else is not one of them." I must have made a face, because he looked determined to convince me. "Are you already in love? You poor thing. You fought for him today, and yet he'll sell you out the first chance he gets."

I knew what this was. Royce had warned me his father

was going to screw with us, but I wouldn't let him.

"I don't love him, and he doesn't love me. We're just play-ing the roles you gave us. I doubt he even cares about me."

"I'm glad you can see through to what he's doing. He's exceptional at manipulating people and telling them exact-ly what they need to hear. He'll lie shamelessly to get what he wants."

It sounded exactly like something Royce would say about his father.

Macalister's fingertip brushed once more on the bare skin of my back, and this time his thumb circled one of my vertebrae. "Forgive me." His voice dipped low. "This happens to be my favorite place on a woman's body."

I jolted. Royce had said the same thing a year ago. Was it just coincidence?

Macalister ignored my discomfort, and heat ignited in his eyes, melting the ice and revealing something far more disturbing.

"I should probably get back, Mr. Hale."

"It's Macalister," he said. "You didn't seem to have an issue saying my name earlier."

Royce appeared at the edge of the dancefloor, but Macalister shot him a look that dictated he needed an-other minute.

His tone lowered like it was wrapped in velvet. "You should know I'm quite impressed with you. That's twice now you've forced me into negotiations. However, I always get my way in the end." A dark look smeared across his face. "You may have spared yourself two minutes with me, but now I want more."

His words dripped with desire.

"I own you, Marist. And eventually I will have you."

I gasped and jerked free from his arms but couldn't escape the horror he'd caused.

He smiled like this was all fine and what he'd just said was perfectly acceptable. "Thank you for the dance." He nodded, a gentleman biding adieu. "We'll see each other again soon."

# NINETEEN

I DIDN'T TELL ROYCE WHAT HIS FATHER HAD SAID THAT NIGHT.

In fact, we had been engaged for three days before we saw each other again. He'd been on the board less than twenty-four hours when a software update broke the HBHC site, preventing US users from doing any online banking. It was an 'all hands on deck' crisis. My father slept in his office every night until it was resolved.

While Royce was focused on the company, it seemed like the rest of the world was focused on us. My feed was full of pictures from the party. It was beyond bizarre to see Royce and me lumped in with the real celebrities who had been there.

On Wednesday morning, my family met with the man who would handle the Northcott estate, and we signed the releases to give him access to everything. My mother had struggled with it. When she tried to back out and claim they could do it without help, I had to go the tough love route.

The harsh reality I painted for her made her cry.

But the advisor could negotiate rates and payment plans and dig us out of the hole in a third of the time it'd take us to do it on our own.

She glared at me as she signed one document after another. I'd been cold and direct because my frustration with them was reaching critical mass. After everything I'd done for my family's sake, they weren't just ungrateful—they had the nerve to act like *I* was the bad guy.

Sadly, I gained new understanding into Macalister's desire to control others. If left on their own, it was likely my family would destroy themselves.

Dread pooled in my center as I drove up to the Hale estate and parked beside the garage. Royce had told me his father and Alice were still at the office, which helped with some of my anxiety, but I wasn't looking forward to the conversation I needed to have about what I'd seen in the woods.

Or what his father had said to me.

I climbed the steps outside, and by the time I'd reached the front door, it swung open, revealing Royce in jeans and a t-shirt. He was so dressed down from the last time I'd seen him, but he still looked great. Less polished, but confident and in command.

Summer was in full effect outside, but as I came into the house, I understood why he was wearing jeans. It was freezing. "The air conditioning must be working overtime."

He quirked his lips into a tight smile. "My father says he thinks better when it's cold." He shut the door behind me, cupped a hand on my cheek, and dropped a quick kiss on my lips. "Hi."

It was crazy how powerful his effect over me was. One chaste kiss and I was suddenly warm, even as goosebumps pebbled on my legs beneath my shorts. "Hi," I answered back.

"So, this is the foyer."

*What?* I peered at him with confusion. "I can see that."

His eyes were playful. "It's where we're starting our tour."

"Oh. I see." I'd grumbled to him earlier how I hadn't seen half of the house I was going to be living in. I glanced around and pretended to evaluate the space as if seeing it for the first time. "Yes, very nice."

Royce headed to the left and showed me the formal sitting room. We saw the casual living space, a guest suite, and the all-seasons room at the back of the house where we'd waited with his family for announcements. He took me into the sprawling kitchen and showed me where the important things were. Silverware. Glasses. Everyday plates.

He avoided the dining room, pretending it didn't exist, which I appreciated.

The steps to the basement were narrow. The room to the right was the home movie theater. Leather recliners were placed in two tiered rows in front of a large screen, and a projector hung overhead.

The room on the left was the wine cellar. It was all maple-colored racks lining the walls and warm brick. A wrought iron chandelier dangled from the arched ceiling. Royce barely gave it a passing comment, but the cozy room was inviting.

"Wow, this is nice," I said as I stepped inside.

There was a dining table in the center of the room, and four wine glasses rested upside down on a silver platter in the middle. There was also a brown love seat and a wet bar against the far wall.

"Does your family do many tastings in here?" I fingered the neck of one of the bottles in the rack beside me. The label was pretty.

"No. We hardly ever use it."

The room wasn't really a cellar, it was a lounge meant for entertaining. "That's a shame. This room is amazing."

"No one comes down here, but you can whenever you want. It's quiet."

It *was* quiet. It felt like Royce and I were all alone, hidden underground. My tone was grave. "I have to tell you something."

He stiffened, bracing for whatever was coming. "What is it?"

"It's about Alice and Vance. When I was coming back up the hill, I . . . saw them together."

Royce blinked slowly. "Together," he repeated flatly. "Were they fucking?"

"Uh, she was going down on him."

His expression didn't change. "Sorry you had to see that."

"You knew?" I gasped.

"Yeah, they've gotten sloppy recently about hiding it. As you can attest."

I turned my gaze away, staring at the rack and the bottles that lay on their sides. "I don't understand. Alice cares so much about image, and if they were caught—"

"Yeah." His firm word drew my attention. "It'd be a big scandal. One that'd be much too big for my father to ignore."

How did he mean that? Was Alice doing it to get her husband's attention?

"He doesn't know?"

"I don't think so, but hardly anything happens here he doesn't know about." He took a step in my direction, closing most of the space between us. "Whatever she had with my dad, it's gone now. It ran its course. She still loves him, and she can't leave him—although I don't think she wants to, anyway."

Nervousness sapped all the strength from me. "Is that going to happen to us?"

God, his eyes were intense, and it was so beautiful, it was hard to look at. He said it quietly but with conviction. "I hope not."

Why was it painful to admit? "I like you."

"I kind of figured that out already." His half-smile was irritating.

"Royce." I didn't appreciate him being cocky when I'd made myself vulnerable.

But he slipped his arms around me and tilted his forehead until it was pressed against mine. "If you haven't figured out yet just how much I like you, then you're not as smart as I thought you were."

He delivered his first kiss slow and sweet. But the second one? It smoldered. It hinted there was fire waiting for me on the other side. All I had to do was stoke it and we'd both burst into flames.

I skimmed my hand down the front of his shirt, not stopping until I hit the bulge growing behind his zipper. In retaliation, he grasped a handful of my ass through my shorts and squeezed.

Everything went hard. His grip on me. His dick under the stroke of my hand. His mouth moving against mine.

And the sudden need to have it finally be our moment.

Whatever he was thinking about, the decision had been made. He turned us, and I stumbled back into the corner between the brick wall and the side of a wine cabinet, making the bottles rattle quietly on their perches.

Royce's hands weren't gentle or cautious. He clasped a palm over my breast and, dissatisfied it was covered, he jammed that hand up under my t-shirt. It took him no time to find my nipple through the cup of my bra, and his pinch left me hot and achy in more than one place.

It distracted me from my task, but not for long. I raked my fingernails over the denim shielding his erection and enjoyed how his eyes clouded with lust.

"We're doing this now, huh?" His whispered question was full of seduction.

"You said no one comes down here."

He stepped away, leaving me panting against the corner, but it was only so he could close the door. As he stalked back to me, his determined focus made heat pool in my body and flow to my center.

His kiss was aggressive. Brutally passionate. Tension built in me, in both of us.

He jerked the hem of my shirt up, and I raised my arms, helping him strip it off. As soon as it was done, I returned the favor, stretching his cotton shirt up over his head and hurling it to the floor.

I traced the lines of his bare chest, marveling at how good he felt in my hands. There was a ring on my finger saying I was his, and tonight he was absolutely mine.

"I want you naked," I pleaded.

He grinned a smile full of sex and sin, and it announced he had every intention of giving me what I wanted. As he reached around my body and undid the hook of my bra, he murmured it in my ear. "Same, Marist."

It was a frenzy after that, both of us fumbling with the other's pants, a race to see who could undress the other first. Except my hands were clumsy. I wasn't a virgin anymore, but this was still brand new. I'd never even seen him fully naked.

When our clothes were discarded piles around us, he yanked me away from the wall. I was walked backward, his kisses hot and greedy and distracting, and it was the bump of the hard edge of wood on the back of my thighs that announced we'd reached the table.

My heart was beating so fast but the rest of me was slow. Desire was heavy, filling me up and weighing me down, and it was what kept me from stopping Royce as he pushed me to sit on the table.

Anxiety turned tighter, screwing my throat closed and preventing words from coming out as his hands urged me down onto my back. He hitched one of my trembling legs over his shoulder, unaware of the panic that clawed in my chest, desperate to break free.

The table was hard and cold, and a man hovered between my legs, preparing to put his mouth on me, and it was too much like last time. *It was way too much.*

Somehow, I found my voice, and it sprang from me in a single, furious word. *"No."*

I slapped a hand on his head and shoved him away, then reared back on the table. He pulled back, stunned and confused while watching me scramble to my feet.

He put a low hand out, in a gesture that said '*steady.*' "What's wrong?"

My gaze darted from him, to the table, and back again. I crossed my arms over my stomach. "Not like that. Not on the table."

I'd never seen his eyes go that wide before as he realized what had caused the panic. "Oh, shit. I'm sorry. I—" He stared at the ground for a moment, lost in thought. "I wasn't thinking."

He moved toward me cautiously, like I was a wounded and unpredictable animal. Slowly, he reached for me, gauging my reaction. I allowed him to ease a hand onto my hip. To hesitantly invade my space.

"Tell me what you'd like. What you need." He sounded and looked utterly serious. "Because I just want to make you feel good."

I eyed the loveseat before turning my full stare back on him. "I want it gone. I need the memory wiped clean."

His face twisted. He wanted to give it to me, but I'd asked for the impossible.

I set my palms flat against the plane of his chest and lowered my voice to a hush. "Give me something to replace it with."

His expression was devastatingly determined. "I can do that."

Gone was the urgent, frantic dash. Now, his movements were deliberate and purposeful. The heat between us didn't flame out, it shifted and went underground, which was the most dangerous kind. We'd burn from the inside out, the foundation up, and there was no way to put it out.

While he kissed me, Royce's steady hands smoothed over the lines of my body. He touched me with awe. His un-hurried fingers skated sensually along my skin, lighting up nerves and setting off a cascade of sensations.

His methodical work made me quiver.

When he lowered himself onto the center of the loveseat, he gently grasped me by the elbows and encouraged me to climb into his lap. I put a knee on either side of his hips as he sat back with his shoulders against the cushions. We were caught in each other's gaze when my damp center brushed against him. Just the tiniest contact, but my breath cut off. It felt exciting. And good.

His palm was still on my elbow, but it coasted up my arm. It traveled over my shoulder, slid up my neck, and con-tinued until his fingers wove into my hair. His head rested on the back of the couch as he stared up at me, his eyes filled with hunger.

"I've never wanted anyone," his voice was uneven, "the way I want you."

*Oh, my God.* My heart faltered then picked up again, beating at twice the speed.

His other hand was on my waist, guiding me to move.

To rock my hips against him and rub myself along the length of him. It elicited a sigh from us both, and I shuddered with pleasure. My movement adjusted my body on him, and as I went to settle back into his lap, the head of his cock was positioned right at my entrance.

He didn't ask my consent, but he didn't have to. He held statue still and left the choice to me. If I didn't want to go further, all I had to do was lift off of him. Instead, I lowered myself on him, taking him inside me at measured pace. His lips parted so he could drag in ragged breaths as I crept down, and his head tipped further back, his eyes drifting closed.

It was still a lot, and he made me uncomfortably full, but my body seemed to adjust quicker this time. Once he was seated fully inside, I let out a tight breath. He lifted his head, opened his eyes, and simply stared at me like I was a wonderous creature.

His hand on my waist urged me once again to rock on him. The gentle, slow stroke wrung a whimper from my lips but set him on alert.

"How does it feel?" he asked.

"It feels . . . good."

A smile hinted his expression, but I moved my hips, and he went serious again.

As I hesitantly found my rhythm, his sensual hands resumed their work. They caressed my breasts, notching over my hardened nipples. They smoothed along my thighs. Slid up my back, tracing my spine with his fingertips.

Royce sat there, and his heavy eyes watched me as I rode him, my body undulating, letting me find my way. But the tightness inside me kept building. The feeling of urgency twisted harder, squeezing the air from my lungs.

I had my hands on his chest for leverage, but I lifted them and laced my fingers together behind his neck, pulling him to me. When our mouths locked together, time suspended. Nothing existed outside of this room. Nothing lived beyond the two of us, our bodies connected as one.

I writhed on him until sweat dampened our temples and moans drifted from our lips. I held his head in my arms, crushing him to my breasts, relishing the way he teased me with his mouth and teeth. His hands on my ass pushed and pulled, lifting me to keep up the urgent tempo we were both desperate for.

When my leg muscles began to fatigue, he must have sensed it.

"Lean back," he encouraged. His arm looped behind me. "I've got you."

I did as he asked, arching my back and setting my hands behind me on his knees. It made enough space so he could push a hand between our bodies and touch my clit.

"Oh, my God," I groaned, pleasure nearly overwhelming me.

I threw my head back, and beneath me, he took over. His deep thrusts shook my body all the way down to my foundation. And that fucking hand of his. It just kept stirring and moving and pleasing. I was a quivering mess as my orgasm approached.

He grunted and strained as he chased his breath, but he didn't stop driving. Not even when a loud gasp burst from my mouth and I came. Heat, coupled with deep satisfaction, poured down through me, wave after wave, seemingly endless. I'd only started to come down from my orgasm when his started.

He clamped his strong arms around my shuddering body and buried his face in my chest while a series of pleasure-soaked moans fell from his lips. He gasped one after another against my naked flesh.

Like a coin in a spiral funnel, time restarted slowly. It looped one tediously long second and sped gradually with each pass, spinning faster as it closed in on the center. Round and round it went until it was a flashing blur of movement, and then . . . time snapped back to normal as it dropped into the well below.

Royce softened his hold on me, just enough to peer up into my eyes. "That should have been our first time."

I dropped a kiss on his lips. "It was."

# TWENTY

Royce and I spent awhile kissing on the loveseat, but eventually my legs protested how I was straddling him, and I climbed off. We dressed, and when he fished his shirt off the floor, I took it and tossed it across the room.

"You look good naked," I said. "I think I like you better that way."

He chuckled as he went after it. "I also prefer you naked. Maybe don't bring any clothes when you move in."

My smile drained. "I have to tell you something else."

He had his head halfway through the neck hole of his t-shirt, and his movements slowed as he pulled it on.

"When I danced with your father, he said some stuff."

"About me." It was a statement, not a question from Royce. "Yeah."

A tight smile pinched on his face. "Don't trust anything that comes out of his mouth, but just for fun, what'd he say?"

"He basically told me not to trust anything that comes out of your mouth."

This time his smile was more of a smirk. As I looked down at my engagement ring, my shoulders slumped.

He picked up on my unease. "What is it?"

My stomach was full of acid and a sour taste filled my mouth as I worked up the courage. "He said he owns me, and eventually he'll have me."

Royce solidified. He locked down his doors and shuttered the windows, going immobile.

Had I just flipped some sort of fail-safe switch and deactivated him?

Finally, he blinked. He put his hands in his pockets and stared vacantly at the glasses on the table. "He's fucking with you. Or maybe he was just testing to see how you'd react."

I frowned.

It was hard to believe that was all it was. The look in Macalister's eyes that night had been incredibly real. But perhaps he was a fantastic actor like his son. Plus, Royce knew his father better than I did. Shouldn't I trust him?

"Okay." I still wasn't convinced but wasn't sure what else to say. "I thought you should know."

"I appreciate it." He glanced at the door and put a hand on the back of his neck, massaging it. "Do you want to finish the tour? We got kind of . . . sidetracked."

His easy smile chased away the unpleasant memory.

We were almost at the top of the stairs when Royce hooked a finger in the belt loop of my shorts and jerked me to a sudden stop.

"Hey," he said. As he moved in to join me on the same step, the banister was at my back and his expression was hard to read. "I didn't mean to make light of what he said. It's fucked up, I know. You have to remember everyone in this house has an agenda. We're all positioning to get what we want, and no one says what they mean."

I lifted my chin to meet his gaze. "Including you?"

He placed one hand on the wall beside my head, then the other, trapping me beneath his hungry stare. His gaze roved over my face and settled on my lips. "Yeah, Marist. Including me."

Royce leaned in and captured my mouth. He kissed me like a conqueror, and I was happy to be claimed as his.

Just outside of the doorway, someone cleared their throat, loud and excessive. We both froze.

I didn't have to hear anything else or see him—I already knew. I could blame the cold draft on the air conditioning, but it was really Macalister's frosty presence. Who knew how long he'd been standing there?

Royce straightened away from me the moment his father stepped into our view.

Macalister had on a full suit. Clearly, he'd come straight from the office, but it was a long ride from Boston, and he hadn't so much as loosened his tie. He stared at us with his piercing eyes and drained all the heat from the moment.

"Marist." He said my name like I'd done something wrong. "While you're here, I wanted to let you know our lawyers are drafting the prenup. They should have it to me by the time you move in."

Seeing him again was like walking into a spider's web. Hundreds of invisible threads pulled at my skin. I wanted to sound confident but failed. "All right."

His gaze flicked to his son and narrowed. "Royce and I will go over it together with you."

The subtext was clear. This wasn't a request, it was a decree.

Neither of us had a response, and Macalister must have taken our silence as acceptance because he nodded. "Well, then. Enjoy your evening."

Friday afternoon, I finished packing. I'd put it off as long as I could, but I had to move in and be at the Hale estate this evening. Macalister wanted his meeting to discuss the pre-nup after he and Royce had come home from the office.

Ever since my contentious afternoon with my parents and the financial advisor, things hadn't been great at home. My mother had been treating me to more and more pas-sive-aggressive statements as the rest of the week played out, and although I was terrified of moving into the Hale estate, a small part of me was relieved to be leaving.

She was angry. A spoiled child throwing a tantrum.

As I zipped up my toiletries bag and put it in the suitcase, she was upset I'd told her to cancel the annual ski trip to Aspen the week of Thanksgiving. My family had been going for years, but the situation now was too dire.

"It's not that much money," she whined.

Her comment grated. If I'd learned anything from this ordeal, it was that she had no concept of money. It hurt me how her youngest daughter was moving out, and yet all she cared about was some lousy trip.

"You don't even ski. You sit in the lodge with the other women and play cards."

She scowled. "I enjoy spending time with my friends."

I'd swear half of Cape Hill made the trip. It was almost more about social status than having an actual vacation.

But where were my mother's friends now? She'd given up her luncheons with them at fancy downtown restaurants and stopped donating to their fundraisers. Her friends miraculously dried up with our family's cash flow.

"Now that you're engaged to Royce, our family should be there. You know how that trip is."

"I do. I'm sure he'll take me, even though I couldn't care—" *Fuck.* Why had I said that?

"I see." She went stiff. "Well, I'd love to go, but we can't all find a Hale to take us."

I slammed shut my suitcase, wishing I could stuff myself inside and get away from her.

But she couldn't leave it be. "Think about how it's going to look if people find out we're in a tough spot, and you're suddenly getting fancy jewelry and expensive trips from Royce."

*Tough spot?* We weren't just broke, we were in serious debt. I tried to stay calm. "Expensive trips?" I said flatly. "You just said it wasn't that much."

"They'll think you're only after his money."

I zipped the suitcase closed, set it on its wheels, and gave her a cold look. "I *am* only after his money."

It had been true once.

Now it tasted like a lie.

Royce said everyone in his house had an agenda, and I was bringing my own, but as I pushed past my mother and headed for the stairs, I wondered when mine had shifted. Because saving my family was no longer my primary objective.

Getting a chance to have more with him was.

I was given the guest bedroom sandwiched between Royce's room and the library. It was decorated in white and slate blue with mirrored furniture, and like his, there was a small sitting area opposite the king-sized bed.

Unpacking didn't take long, and once I'd finished, I curled up on one of the chairs with a book, trying to pretend this was all normal and my home now.

It didn't work.

A little after six o'clock, Royce knocked on my door. He'd loosened his tie and undone the top button of his dress shirt, and although he had relaxed his clothes, he looked anything but comfortable as he stood in my doorway.

I felt it too. Awareness that there'd be something buried in this prenuptial agreement that neither of us were going to like.

He surveyed the room, noting the large stack of books I'd put on the dresser, held up by my Pegasus bookends.

"Hey." He delivered the news in a solemn tone. "He's waiting for us in the library."

I hated the tension hanging in the air. I closed my book,

climbed to my feet, and marched toward Royce. His lips pressed to mine, and for once, our kiss had nothing to do with desire. It was about connection. Partnership. Like the ring on my finger, it was a wordless promise we were together.

Lucifer was a black shadow in the hallway, and when he saw Royce, he issued a soft *meow* and brushed against his master's legs. But as we approached the library, the cat stopped and sat on the carpet. His wary green eyes regarded Macalister, who sat behind the desk and glared back at the cat with a similar sentiment.

It was overcast this evening and the curtains overwhelmed the window, so only a slice of light penetrated the library.

"Shut the door," Macalister said, presumably to keep the cat out, although Lucifer looked like he'd abstain anyway. Cats liked warm things, and the man behind the desk wasn't.

Once the door was closed, he didn't tell us to sit. Royce took a chair, so I followed suit and sat on the edge of the other. Once again, Alice's reminder about my posture flitted through my head, and I pulled my shoulders back.

Everything was so different than the last time Royce and I had been in this room. It still smelled like books, but the magic was gone. Nothing was cozy or inviting, and all the power radiated from the man in the suit who'd ordered this meeting.

"This is the first draft of the prenuptial agreement." Macalister rested his spread fingertips on a pale blue folder in front of him. "However, after our discussion, we'll need to make a few addendums."

My stomach clenched. There was a gleam in his eyes that didn't bode well.

Royce didn't notice, or he was playing his role. He settled into his chair with an air of indifference. "What kind of addendums?"

"I am concerned about the relationship forming between the two of you." Macalister's hand on the folder curled into a loose fist. "When you fall in love so quickly, it's guaranteed to end just as fast, and it will destroy the partnership we've been working toward."

Royce scoffed and sounded disgusted. "Nobody's falling in love."

I tried to mimic the same confidence when Macalister's gaze slithered over to me, but I must have failed, because the side of his mouth quirked.

"What is it, then?" he asked his son. "Lust?"

"Yeah. I'm only interested in fucking her."

The cruel, easy way it rolled off his tongue filled my stomach with stones. I reminded myself this was a lie. Not just because his father was sitting across from us, either. Royce wanted more with me. The way we'd been together in the wine cellar showed that.

"And you?" Macalister's look bore into me. "You have no feelings for Royce in anything other than a sexual capacity?"

*Jesus.* I licked my dry lips but surprised myself with how detached it came from me. "Yes, sir."

Did Macalister believe me? His head tilted as he evaluated both of us. "All right." He brought his hands together and leaned forward to rest his forearms on the desk, his attention directed at his son. "Then I don't see any reason for you to object to me pursuing a sexual relationship with Marist."

My heart stopped. "What?"

"Excuse me?" Royce said at the same time.

The library became a vacuum. Icy fingers plunged inside my chest, wringing the air from my lungs.

Was this another one of Macalister's tests? His half-smile was pure evil as he turned it on me. "As I mentioned, you're a beautiful young woman. While I'm glad you are here, I find myself wishing I hadn't traded away my time to Royce. If there are no emotions for either of you, I don't see the issue."

"No," I snarled.

He wasn't fazed, but his son?

Royce struggled. His expression was devoid of any emotion, but his hand on the armrest was clenched in a fist, so hard it was white, and I could see the tendons straining.

Macalister focused on his son, his gaze moving from the tense fist up to meet his eyes. "You'll continue your engagement and see it through the marriage. Everyone will believe she's your wife, and she will be, but in name only. When we're here, she'll be mine." His eyes were terrifying as he flexed his power. "Not yours."

*Holy. Fucking. Shit.*

An earthquake of panic overtook me. Royce had warned me this could happen. He'd said his father might take me away from him. How he felt he truly owned everything Royce had.

"I imagine this isn't appealing to you," Macalister said.

"In exchange for Marist, I would be willing to offer you stock."

It bubbled up, escaping from me in a raging blur. "I'm not a piece of property that can be bought and sold."

Macalister looked down his long nose at me. "Is that so? There's a ring on your finger and a five-million-dollar deposit in your family's bank account that says otherwise."

*Oh, my God.* I doubled over, and the bile in my stomach threatened to erupt. His harsh truth cut me into a thousand pieces.

But I inhaled a shallow breath, forcing myself to stay calm. Royce would put a stop to this madness. Right now, that idea was the only thing holding me together. And as he sat there, staring at his father in disbelief, the wheels were turning in his head. I could see him considering and plotting. He was weighing different scenarios and working up solutions.

I just needed to give him more time.

"You're married," I spat at Macalister.

He waved the comment off. "Alice and I have an understanding. Neither of us wants to limit the other."

"That doesn't change the fact that I'm not, and never will be, interested."

Why the hell did he look pleased? Perhaps he thrilled at the chase.

"I admitted I underestimated you, but now," a pompous, sexual look spread across his face, "I believe you are doing the same." The frightening desire in his gaze faded as it shifted back to his son. "How does twenty thousand shares sound?"

I didn't know exactly what HBHC was trading at, but

it was usually around a hundred dollars a share. Macalister hadn't just offered his son two million dollars, he'd offered so much more. There was considerable power connected to the shares.

"No," Royce said.

I let out a heavy, grateful breath.

Macalister's jaw ticked with displeasure. "What would it take? Fifty?"

Royce's chest moved with his rapid, uneven breath, but that was the only indication he wasn't fine. He was calm and business-like when he spoke. "I want the house."

*No.*

My heart careened through my body to my toes, hitting every painful spot on the way down. How *could* he? How could he sell me out, and how the fuck could he do it so easily?

"Which house?" His father's expression was dubious. "This house?" When it was clear the answer was *yes*, he scowled. "Don't be ridiculous."

Royce's clenched fist relaxed, just enough that the blood started to flow again, and hope sparked in me as I realized what this was.

*A bluff.*

"It's worth about the same," Royce offered.

That confirmed what he was doing, and more relief snaked through me. He'd picked one of the few things his father wouldn't trade away. While the house might have similar monetary value, it had greater value elsewhere. Maybe sentimental, but I doubted it. Perhaps it was the power. If the house was put in Royce's name, Macalister would be living under his son's roof.

And he couldn't abide that.

The thought must have hit Macalister at the same moment, because he turned so frigid, I expected to see his frosty breath on the air.

Royce had his father on the ropes and wasn't going to let up until he could claim victory. "It'll be mine eventually. Signing the house over to me is really just a formality."

"I was too generous." A humorless smile twisted on Macalister's handsome face. "I didn't have to offer you anything. It was my money that brought her here. You didn't make the deal and you don't have any leverage."

"I don't?" Royce's smug smile was almost as evil as his father's had been. "Maybe things aren't working out, and I break off the engagement. Doesn't make much sense for her to keep living here, does it?"

If I wasn't here, Macalister couldn't control. He wouldn't be able to get at me.

"One hundred thousand shares."

Royce turned to stone, but I flinched for him. That had to be more than ten million dollars, and at that volume, it'd increase his stake in the company considerably—all while decreasing his father's.

Macalister's unexpected swing had landed and caught Royce off guard. He blinked rapidly, trying to clear the disorientation from the blow. It was so much money and power.

"One hundred thousand." He repeated his father's words because there was no way he'd heard them correctly.

Realizing his opponent was stumbling backward,

Macalister went on the attack. "You'd have the second highest controlling stake in the company after me."

Outwardly, there wasn't a change in Royce, but still—it was unmistakable. I was on the edge of a collapsing cliff, and rather than help me, he took a step back. Brutal, unforgiving awareness washed through me.

He was going to save himself.

I'd been warned by both of them. Royce had told me the only thing he cared about was taking over at the company, and Macalister had said his son would sell me out the first chance he got. But no amount of warning could prepare me for the cold, distant look in Royce's eyes. It was like he was already counting his stacks of money.

He was already planning how he'd use this new influence to his advantage.

Whatever deal they'd strike, they'd both lose. I'd never let Macalister get what he wanted, and Royce's betrayal would be too much. But this wasn't about winning me. It was a power struggle between father and son, and I was merely a pawn to battle over.

I had to do something, stop this from happening. He'd tell me the truth if it was only us. It burst from me. "I'd like to speak to Royce alone."

"No."

The word came instantly, but not from Macalister, and my insides broke like glass. Shock turned my head toward Royce. *No?* How could he deny me after everything I'd done for him? I'd waited. I'd let him keep me in the dark. I'd saved him from the worst of it in the dining room downstairs.

My voice shook just as I did. "You owe me at least a conversation."

The man who I believed lived inside him, the one who'd been so caring in the wine cellar, was nowhere to be found. A terrified voice in my mind cried out that maybe he never existed at all. I'd been manipulated. I'd always known he was a spectacular liar. Perhaps the Hale who'd been telling me the truth was the one seated behind the desk and not the boy currently obliterating my heart.

Royce's tone was impersonal. "I don't owe you anything."

The engagement ring on my hand was suddenly so tight and heavy, I wanted it gone. Hot tears stung my eyes.

"Don't do this," I whispered, but hearing my plea did nothing to break through his façade. I fractured, and hopelessness seeped through each crack, forcing them wider.

"Tell me again," Macalister's tone was condescending, "how it's just about sex."

His father's challenge was the final blow.

"One hundred thousand shares," Royce demanded, "and I want that in writing." He said it fast, like a bandage being yanked off a wound, but it didn't make the pain any easier.

I went numb as Macalister stood and held out his hand.

*No*, I wanted to scream, but horror held my tongue captive. He was going to destroy everything.

They say when someone shows you who they really are, you should believe them. Now I'd have no choice.

It all moved so slowly and too fast at the same time. Royce rose from his seat and clasped his father's hand. Whatever was the truth between us, it died in that moment. It hurt to breathe, but then I didn't have to because my body refused to work. Every system ground to a halt and shut down.

Like I wasn't even in the room, Macalister gestured to the prenup on the desk. "I'll have this revised to reflect your new assets."

Royce nodded. He turned and started for the door, refusing to look at me. Maybe he couldn't, or maybe he didn't fucking care.

"*Royce*," I hissed.

He paused.

I stared at his back, waiting for him to face me. I should have known he wouldn't. It was win at all costs, and the cost had been me.

For the third time in my life, he walked out the door without glancing back, leaving me gutted.

With his exit, the atmosphere in the room changed and became more dangerous.

I was on my own. But it also made it easier to focus and respond to the threat when I didn't have anyone else to rely on. I glared at Macalister, who looked at me with desire and victory, like I was a million-dollar bonus he'd earned.

My chest heaved in labored breaths, and with it, I found strength in my anger. Maybe I'd grow hard and truly become Medusa. I'd find the power to become a monster and turn my enemies to stone.

I'd never spoken truer words. "You'll *never* own me."

Macalister took a moment to consider my statement before he pushed back from his desk and stood. He sauntered toward me, his piercing eyes teeming with domination, and by the time I realized I should run, it was already too late.

"Everyone has a price, Marist. Tonight, we found Royce's." He leaned over and placed his hands on the armrests of my chair, imprisoning me beneath him. "Now I start looking for yours."

TO BE CONTINUED IN

# O*The*BSESSION

FILTYH RICH AMERICANS | BOOK TWO

# OTHER BOOKS BY NIKKI SLOANE

## THE BLINDFOLD CLUB SERIES
It Takes Two
Three Simple Rules
Three Hard Lessons
Three Little Mistakes
Three Dirty Secrets
Three Sweet Nothings
Three Guilty Pleasures
One More Rule

## THE SORDID SERIES
Sordid

Torrid

Destroy

## SPORTS ROMANCE
The Rivalry

## THE NASHVILLE NEIGHBORHOOD
The Doctor

# ACKNOWLEDGMENTS

First and foremost, I need to thank the incomparable Sierra Simone for her advice, her support, and her brilliance. After she'd agreed to beta read, I immediately texted my husband, "She said yes!" like I'd asked her to prom—that's how excited I was. I don't know how she found time in her crazy writing schedule to provide such a thoughtful critique of THE INITIATION, but I'm beyond grateful. I also want to thank her for being an inspiration. Her writing is on a whole other level, and it's one I hope to reach someday.

There are several authors and book friends I want to thank. Strong, wickedly smart women who never hesitate to lend advice, lift others up, or be generally awesome. I am so privileged to call you my friends.

Thank you, Skye Warren, for guiding me to make it a trilogy and not put Medusa on the cover. (LOL) Thanks to Kyla Linde for being so great with my blurb when I sent her a hot mess. Thanks to Veronica Larsen for listening to endless, rambling voicemails. And a big thank you to Sarah MacLean, Becca "Can't wait to read your sex bank book" Mysoor, Laurelin Paige, Kennedy Ryan, Aubrey Bondurant, Len Webster, Marni Mann, and Elle Kennedy.

I owe an enormous amount of gratitude to my publicist Nina Grinstead. Her advice at every stage of the process was spot-on, and this book would be nothing without her.

To my beta readers Andrea Leftkowitz and Nikki Terrill, thank you. The draft I submitted to them wasn't easy, but they dialed me in to where I needed to be. I can't tell you how much I appreciated it. A huge thank you to them for being brave and delivering news they didn't want to, but needed to.

As always, thank you to my editor Lori Whitwam for cleaning up my dirty and grammatically incorrect words.

I owe a big thanks to my father for answering all my questions about corporate structure, board meetings, and stocks. I promise him I'll read BARBARIANS AT THE GATE as long as he never reads this book.

Thank you to my cousin's husband Wes for giving me a sexy, beautiful Medusa illustration.

And I have to say thank you to my amazing husband, who I love more than anything. He put up with a solid week of me telling him, "I've only got one more scene left to write, so I'm finishing tonight!" Thankfully, he's used to my bullshit lies by now.

# ABOUT THE AUTHOR

Nikki Sloane fell into graphic design after her careers as a waitress, a screenwriter, and a ballroom dance instructor fell through. For eight years she worked for a design firm in that extremely tall, black, and tiered building in Chicago that went through an unfortunate name change during her time there.

Now she lives in Kentucky, is married and has two sons. She is a three-time Romance Writers of America RITA© Finalist, also writes romantic suspense under the name Karyn Lawrence, and couldn't be any happier that people enjoy reading her sexy words.


Website: www.NikkiSloane.com

CPSIA information can be obtained
at www.ICGtesting.com
Printed in the USA
FSHW010136050819